DEAR ROSIE,

LOVE LETTERS BOOK TWO

S. J. TILLY

Dear Rosie,

Love Letters Book Two

Cover: Lori Jackson Design

Model Image: Wander Aguiar Photography

Editors: Jeanine Harrell, Indie Edits with Jeanine

& Beth Lawton, VB Edits

This book is dedicated to the hard days.
And to the people who drag us through them and out the other side.
Because there is another side.

PROLOGUE – ROSIE

(AGE EIGHT)

The surface is warm under my palm as I press the back door closed.

It clicks. And I wait. But there's no shouting from the other side.

I exhale.

Then I turn and run.

My stained sneakers are quiet on the grass. The overgrown lawn silencing my escape.

I'm sure mowing will become a chore of mine, but I'm not big enough yet.

Maybe next year.

But that's a next-year problem. And I have enough problems already, so there's no point in wasting time thinking about a future one.

I slow as I reach the chain-link fence.

The little can of grease I stole from the gas station keeps the gate from creaking as I carefully push it open.

My shirt already has one tear, so I'm careful not to catch it on the broken piece of wire as I shimmy through.

Once the gate swings closed, I let my cheeks puff out on my exhale, the final obstacle done.

It's a little later than I usually meet Nathan, but he'll wait.

He always does.

A stick crunches under my foot, and I hurry through a few more steps until the forest surrounds me.

I breathe in the air.

It's dirt and grass and that freshness you can only get outside.

Once I'm about twenty feet in, I turn right.

My house is the second to last one on my end of the street, two stories of... bad.

Nathan's house is all the way on the other end of the street. It's on a big corner lot, and it's really nice.

I've never been inside, but I've studied it from the back, wishing my bus route went past it so I could look at the front unnoticed. But someday I'll see the inside.

When our friendship isn't a secret anymore.

I smile at the thought.

I bet it smells like flowers inside.

I bet his mom is nice. She probably puts snacks out.

Lost in my daydream, I don't realize I've reached the meeting spot until I see Nathan's bright white shirt.

He's sitting on the thick log—where we've scraped the bark off to make the sitting part smoother—with his head lowered.

I bite down on my smile when I see the bag of marshmallows beside him.

It's become a tradition, him bringing the fluffy snack.

He's shown up with them every couple of weeks, ever since he found out they were my favorite.

"Hey." I keep my voice quiet, like I always do, as I step into the little clearing we made around the log.

"Hey." Nathan digs the toe of his shoe into the dirt, still keeping his gaze down.

He's gotten taller in the last year.

When I boost myself up onto the log, my sneakers dangle several inches above the ground.

I start to reach for the open bag between us, but I pause, noticing the flattened marshmallow in Nathan's hand.

"You okay?" I ask. Nathan never wastes food.

He shrugs.

And my stomach starts to twist.

Nathan has been my best friend for two years. And I've never felt this weird sort of feeling from him before.

"What's wrong?" I start to shift toward him, but then he stands.

"I gotta tell you something."

That twisting inside me starts to hurt.

He still won't look at me, his face aimed toward the ground.

I swallow, my throat suddenly dry, and I watch the way the tree-filtered light hits his hair.

I stare at the shades of brown, feeling the sudden need to memorize them.

As the silence stretches, I slide off the log.

I want to stand if he's standing.

"What do you need to tell me?" I whisper.

Nathan's shoulders lift as he takes a deep breath.

But he still doesn't speak.

My nerves are on fire.

Whatever this is, it isn't going to be good.

"Please tell me," I say so quietly that I'm not sure he hears me.

Then he lifts his head, and I finally get to see his face.

He looks... sad. Like the kind of sad you feel at a funeral.

Oh god, I hope his mom didn't die too.

I take a step toward him.

But then he speaks. "We're moving."

My feet stop.

I shake my head. I didn't hear him right. "What?"

"I wanted to tell you." Nathan's brows push together like he's in pain. "I just didn't know how."

Panic starts to well up inside me.

Move?

Nathan's going to move?

"Off our street?" I ask.

Nathan keeps his lips pressed together as he nods.

We won't be able to meet in the woods anymore.

My heart beats faster. "Out... out of town?"

Nathan nods again.

My knees tremble.

Out of town means I won't even see him on the bus.

I clench my hands into fists. "Are you still going to be in Wisconsin?"

Maybe if he's still in the state, I could see him at football games or something. He'll be in high school soon. And I know he'll play varsity.

But then Nathan makes it worse. "We're going to Ohio."

The backs of my legs bump into the log.

I hadn't even realized I was backing away from him.

Ohio.

I don't know how far away Ohio is from Wisconsin. But I know it's far. Far enough that if he goes... I'll never see him again.

A weight presses down on my chest.

"When?" I choke out.

Maybe... maybe if I have enough time, I can convince his mom to bring me with them.

If I can just meet her, let her get to know me, she might like me.

And then his mom will want me to come.

Even if it's just for a little bit.

"Tomorrow."

Nathan's reply pierces straight into my heart.

Tomorrow.

That panic inside me flares into an inferno.

There's no time to make his mom like me.

There's no time.

Tears rush down my cheeks.

"P-please don't leave me." I clutch my hands in front of my chest, begging him to stay.

Nathan's expression crumples. "I'm sorry. I don't want to go."

My lungs struggle to fill.

This is... this is the worst thing that could happen to me.

"You can't go," I choke out. "My dad—"

My words cut off, my voice failing me.

Like it does every time.

Nathan steps toward me. "What about your dad?"

I shake my head, pinching my eyes shut.

I shouldn't have said that.

The time I actually open my mouth... the one time I dare to say something... is when Nathan is leaving.

Nathan is leaving me.

My only friend.

That funeral sadness drapes across me. And it makes me feel hot all over.

"Nathan!" His mom's voice filters through the woods, and I blink in that direction.

It's time for him to go have dinner with his family.

The night before they leave.

I press my hands against my shirt, over my heart. Pushing to keep it in.

I was late getting here, and now he has to leave.

Forever.

"Rosie." Nathan steps so he's right in front of me.

So close.

And so close to becoming out of reach.

He puts his hand on my shoulder. "Does... does your dad hurt you?"

Why now?

Inside, I scream at myself.

Why does this have to happen now?

Why now, when he's so close to disappearing from my life, why does Nathan have to ask this question now?

More tears stream from my eyes.

Why has no one else ever asked me this before now?

I shake my head.

There's no point in telling him.

His mom shouts again.

Nathan looks over his shoulder, then back at me. "Rosie, does he hurt you?"

I shake my head, slower this time, and answer with the best truth I have. "Not like that."

I can hear the defeat in my tone.

"What does that mean?" He tightens his grip on my shoulder.

But then his mom yells again.

He has to go.

Nathan has to go.

We both know it.

Nathan clenches his teeth.

I'm still crying.

I can't stop crying.

But they're silent tears now.

The kind you can't control.

The kind you can barely feel.

The ones that just come and come and don't stop.

"You have to go." My words come out scratchy.

"I don't want to." Nathan's tone is so sincere that it makes everything worse.

I try to shrug. Because he might not want to. But he will.

Everyone leaves.

Nathan steps back, his hand slipping free from my shoulder.

The place where his palm was feels cold.

"I'm sorry, Rosie."

His mom shouts his name, sharper this time.

Nathan's mouth twists, his hazel eyes full of words, but he doesn't say any of them.

He turns. And walks away.

And I stand there. Watching him leave me.

He looks back over his shoulder, his eyes meeting mine one last time, then he disappears into the trees.

When he's out of sight, I lean against the log and lower myself until my butt hits the ground.

The damp earth soaks into my jeans. But I don't care. Because my favorite person in the whole world is moving. And I know what that means.

I'll never see Nathan Waller again.

NATHAN

(AGE 12)

Not like that.

What did she mean?

How could she say that so... normal? Like hurting her in any sort of way was okay.

The pizza I forced myself to eat for dinner churns in my stomach.

Mom knows I like to play in the woods, but she doesn't know I've been spending all my time with a girl. I don't know if she'd freak out, but there's no point in telling her now.

She was mad that I took so long to come back to eat, but then she just gave me a hug. I guess she could tell I was sad about moving.

I look out my bedroom window to the woods behind my house.

It was almost two years ago that I stumbled across Rosie in that forest.

I was just walking around, bored, and she was sitting on the ground, building a little house out of broken sticks. I was impressed and wanted to try building one myself, so I asked if I could sit down with her, and that was that. Almost every day since, even in the winter, we'd meet in the woods.

None of my friends at school know about her. She's younger, so they wouldn't know her.

I frown at the woods.

It's like *no one* knows about Rosie. I never hear anyone say her name. And she never talks about anyone else. And that makes my stupid heart ache.

Because Rosie is amazing. She's funny and smart and easy to talk to.

She's my best friend.

And I'm never going to see her again.

I stand.

No.

I can't just give in like that.

I can't never see Rosie again.

I need to at least say goodbye.

I never said goodbye.

Moving around the boxes piled in my room, I rush out into the hall.

My feet fly down the stairs, and I grip the banister at the bottom to spin me toward the front door.

"Where're you going?" Dad hollers.

"Just gotta run down the street." I shove my shoes on. "I'll be right back."

Before Dad can tell me not to, I open the front door and run out.

I'm on the sidewalk before I realize what I'm doing.

I should go to the woods. It's the only place we've ever met.

But the sun is setting, and there's no way she'll still be out there.

I've never heard her dad calling for her, but she has to go in for dinner sometime.

Her dad.

My hands ball into fists at my side.

I've never met him, and she doesn't talk about him, so I don't even know what he looks like.

Rosie doesn't talk about her mom either. I just know she died the year before I met Rosie.

I remember my mom going to the funeral. She said people from the neighborhood should show their sympathy. But she didn't make me or my brother go.

I was glad at the time. I hate funerals. Especially for people I don't know.

It's so weird to be sitting there, feeling no certain way about the dead person when people around you are crying.

I was glad I didn't have to go. But now I wish I did.

Even if I didn't know her then, I could've been there for Rosie.

Like you were there for her today?

The last image I have of Rosie is burned into my memory.

Her light blue eyes on me, watching. The color looking even brighter with the constant shimmer of tears.

I wanted to hug her.

Wanted to tuck her dark red hair behind her ears.

I wanted to get that look off her face.

That look of a broken heart.

The one I put there.

I start jogging.

I'm going to hug her.

I'm going to tell her goodbye, and I'm going to hug her and tell her I'll never forget her.

When I reach the walkway that goes from the sidewalk to the front of Rosie's house, I slow.

I know which house is hers because I've seen her get off the bus and walk there, but I've never been inside.

The concrete under my shoes is cracked, and dandelions stick up in the grass.

The front of the house is normal. Plain. With paint peeling in places.

But I don't care what her house looks like.

One step leads up to her front door, so I step up onto it and ring the doorbell.

This close to the house, I can hear the TV playing inside.

It's so loud I don't know if they'll hear the bell.

I press the doorbell again.

A second later, the door swings open.

The movement is so sudden that I stumble back off the step.

"What do you want?" the man filling the doorway snaps.

He's standing on the high ground, two steps between me and him, so I know he looks bigger from this angle. But from here, he looks huge.

And angry.

There's none of Rosie in his features.

She's girly and soft and all pretty eyes and thick hair.

This man is square jawed and narrowed eyes and a greasy comb-over.

And I know—I just *know*—it would be a bad idea to ask for Rosie.

Does he hurt you?

Not like that.

I force my mouth into a big smile. "Hi. I'm fundraising for—"

I don't even have to finish the lie.

The door slams in my face.

Unease crawls over my skin, thinking about Rosie being stuck in a house with that man.

Backing away, I look up at the windows on the second story, but I don't see any movement behind the curtains.

No sign of Rosie.

The woods are empty and dark enough now that I'd need a flashlight if I hadn't walked this path a hundred times before.

But as I reach our spot, it's easy to tell it's empty.

Something in my chest pleads with me to go back to Rosie's house, hoping she'll be the one to answer the door.

But I don't do that.

I lift the bag of marshmallows that's still sitting on the log from before.

Rosie rolled it shut, but she didn't take it.

I slip my handwritten letter underneath the bag, then set it back down.

Hopefully she'll come back for it tomorrow.

ROSIE

I shove the branch out of my way, my stumbling steps taking me off my usual path.

The deep, hiccuping sobs make it hard to walk straight.

I was planning to come out here today.

Planning to see Nathan one more time.

Hoping he'd come out here too.

But when I looked out our front window, after eating the cheese sandwich I made for lunch, I saw it.

The moving truck.

Leaving.

It almost made me throw up.

I had to slap my hands over my mouth to keep my sounds in.

I was planning to see him.

But last night I cried myself to sleep. And then I slept in late.

Too late.

Because Nathan is gone.

My foot catches on a root, and I fall forward, my palms meeting dirt and pine needles.

Wincing, I get back on my feet and brush my hands on my pants.

"Stupid," I hiss at myself.

Using the back of my hands, I wipe the tears from my eyes.

A spot of white catches my attention, and for one tiny second, I think it's Nathan.

It's not him.

It's the marshmallow bag.

More tears fall.

I wanted to take it last night. He usually lets me keep them. But it didn't feel right. Even when my grumbling stomach sent me back home.

After I got home, I ate ramen in my bedroom, then I took a shower. And I swear I heard the doorbell while I was in the bathroom, but when I got out, everything was still the same.

My hands are too sore to boost myself up onto the log, so I just grab the bag with plans to sit on the ground.

But a piece of paper slides off the log and floats through the air.

I catch it.

And with shaking hands, I unfold the paper and flatten it on the log.

DEAR ROSIE,

I'M SORRY I WAITED SO LONG TO TELL YOU. I KNEW IT WOULD SUCK, AND I DIDN'T WANT TO MAKE YOU SAD.

BUT NOW WE'RE BOTH SAD, AND I DIDN'T GET TO TELL
YOU GOODBYE.
I DON'T WANT TO LEAVE YOU.
~~IF YOUR DAD~~
IF YOU EVER DON'T FEEL SAFE, CALL SOMEONE.
I DON'T KNOW WHAT OUR PHONE NUMBER WILL BE
YET, BUT MAYBE YOU CAN WRITE TO ME?
OUR NEW ADDRESS IS:
323 KENDEL WAY
CLEVELAND, OH 44111
YOUR FRIEND,
NATHAN

I crouch at the top of the stairs, waiting for Dad to leave.

He doesn't leave the house much, just to go get food and beer.

He left once last week, but it was the day after Nathan moved, and I didn't know how long it would take them to get to Ohio. So I decided to wait.

But it's been two weeks since he left, and I think that's enough time for Nathan to get to his new house.

The front door slams, and I wait a handful of long seconds before I scurry down the staircase.

The sound of an engine starting signals the next step, and I hook just one finger around the edge of the living room curtains to peek out.

Dad's pickup is backing down the driveway.

That foreign sense of safety fills the house with his absence.

If you don't feel safe, call someone.

I reread that sentence so many times.

Call who?

His truck disappears out of view, and I turn to look at the clock on the wall in the kitchen.

Once two minutes go by, I open the door.

If Dad caught me doing this... I don't know what would happen.

The letter itself is bad enough, but using Mom's envelopes and stamps, even though they've just been sitting in her night-stand since she died? He might actually kill me for touching them.

But staying in contact with Nathan is worth the risk.

With my pulse beating wildly, I run across the yard and sidewalk to our mailbox.

I open the door and slip the envelope inside, then lift the little metal flag on the side of the box.

It should be fully dark by the time Dad gets back, and all I can do is hope he won't notice there's outgoing mail.

Holding my breath, I close the mailbox and wonder how long until Nathan gets it and writes back.

Dear Nathan,

I'm sorry too. I never even asked you how you felt about moving.

And I'm sorry for crying so much. And for not saying goodbye.

I wish I would have asked you for a hug before you left.

A hug would be really nice.

I hope your new house is nice.
If you send me your new phone number, I can call
you. But don't call me. My dad won't like that.
I miss you.
Your best friend,
Rosie

My fingers tremble as I reach into the mailbox.

I've checked it every single day since I mailed my letter to Nathan, getting more and more defeated as each day passes without a response.

But this time, an envelope sticks out from the rest.

It's the same size as the one I sent him.

It must be...

I drag the rectangle out of the stack of mail.

It's upside down.

Holding it on either side, I twist it in my fingers until the top side is up.

But it's not addressed *to* me. It's addressed *by* me.

UNDELIVERABLE

I blink at the bold red letters stamped across the front of the envelope.

Undeliverable.

No.

Something inside me breaks.

Please no.

I slam the mailbox shut, leaving the other mail there, and sprint back to my house.

It can't be.

I rush through the front door and up the stairs.

Dad shouts something at me, but he doesn't get up from his chair.

I'm gasping for breath when I get to my room, but I still manage to shut my door quietly before leaning against it.

My eyes jump over the envelope.

Nathan Waller
323 Kendel Way
Cleveland, OH 44111

I checked it so many times when I wrote it, but I must've messed it up.

I press my ear to the door, making sure Dad didn't decide to come upstairs to yell at me for running in the house, but I don't hear anything.

I move to my bed and drop to my knees, digging the notebook out from between my mattress and box spring.

Setting it on the bed, I open the notebook and take out Nathan's letter, then spread it open next to the envelope I just took out of the mailbox.

Word by word, I check that I copied it right.

I check it again.

And again.

I keep checking it, and my heart sinks deeper each time. Because I copied it right.

I copied it right, but it's wrong.

That's what undeliverable means. It means I don't have Nathan's real address.

I don't have any way to contact him.

Struggling to breathe, I rip another page out of my note-book, carry it over to my small desk, and pick up my pen.

My hand is shaking so badly that it's hard to read the words I write.

ROSIE

(AGE 19)

"And we're here now with tonight's fan favorite, wide receiver Nate Waller."

I lift my gaze to the TV on the opposite wall.

The volume isn't loud, but the hospital waiting room is quiet at this time of night.

I shove my hands under my thighs and watch as a man—I used to know as a boy—steps into frame.

His hair is darker now.

Darker yet with sweat. And it's matted to his head, but he still looks incredibly handsome.

"I can only catch it if my quarterback throws it." Nathan grins at the reporter, and I close my eyes.

I feel a smile try to tug at my mouth, but it doesn't quite form.

How different our lives became.

How far apart we floated.

I inhale deeply and try to ignore the antiseptic tinge in the air.

Closing my eyes, I listen to Nathan's voice as he talks about his game tonight.

It's not the first time I've heard it since he moved away all those years ago.

The first time I heard it... I cried.

It had been a bad day—bad in every sense of the word—so I was already in a sad mood.

I was in a gas station, setting my candy bar down on the counter, and the guy working the register had a small TV playing behind the displays of energy shots.

I wasn't paying attention to the TV. Didn't care what was on, letting the audio float over me. But then the guy on the TV said Nathan's name. Upbeat. Casual. Just like the guy on the TV now.

But that day, standing in the gas station, when I heard it, I froze.

I hadn't known.

Hadn't realized Nathan had made it to the professional league.

I had no idea.

So I looked at the TV. And I watched him walk into view on camera, a decade after I'd last seen him, and I hardly recognized him.

Then he started speaking, and his voice was different too.

And it was all too much.

I left my candy on the counter and ran out the doors.

I was crying before I even got into my car.

Crying for myself.

Crying over the fact that I didn't recognize the man on the screen.

And even crying a few happy tears for Nathan. Because he'd achieved his dreams.

A nurse clears her throat, and I open my eyes.

She explains the next steps and hands me the paperwork I'll need when it's time to claim my dad's body.

I thank her and then slowly weave my way back through the hospital toward the front doors, where I entered after following the ambulance in.

And as I drive home, I think of the two men who have consumed my life.

My tormentor and my savior.

Only one knowing their role.

It's a short ride home, and when I get there, I walk past the living room, keeping my eyes averted from my dad's favorite chair, and head upstairs to my room.

I shut the door behind me, even though no one else is in the house, and I walk over to my desk.

It's sized for a child. A little wobbly. But it fits perfectly under the window, looking out into the woods.

I sit in my chair.

My dad died tonight.

And that means I'm free.

But I need to be free of Nathan too.

Reaching into the top drawer, I pull out a notebook and tear out a sheet of paper.

My hand shakes a little, and before I reach for my pen, I reach for my bag of marshmallows.

They're minis—easier for me to savor than the big ones. But I still only put one in my mouth.

I let it dissolve on my tongue as I stare down at the blank page.

When the marshmallow is gone, I grab my pen and start writing my second letter of the night.

Dear Nathan,

It's time to let you go...

Once I've signed the letter, I fold the paper into thirds, but I don't put it in an envelope.

I stand and go to my closet, where I crouch down.

When I find the right shoebox, I open it up.

Papers folded just like this one fill the box. Only the first one is in an envelope.

The first letter I ever wrote him. The one that got returned.

I press the letter currently in my hand against my chest and breathe.

I have no idea what I'm going to do now.

No idea where I'll go.

There's no one left to tell me what to do.

No one to care.

I lift the letter to my lips and place a soft kiss on the paper. Then I slip it into the box at the end of the row.

The last of dozens of letters I've written to Nathan.

Letters I've written but never mailed.

ONE
ROSALYN
(AGE THIRTY-THREE)

Hissing, I jerk my hand away from the sizzling bacon. "Fuck me."

My coworker snickers. "You okay, Boss?"

I shake my hand out and smile at Presley. "Totally fine."

She grins. "Well, we're ahead of schedule, so you can probably chill a bit."

I look at the clock on the oven in my client's kitchen. We're twenty minutes ahead. Meaning we have just enough extra time to allow for one mess up.

Not that we'll mess up.

Presley has been working for me for about six months now, and I wish I'd found her sooner.

For the past ten years, I've been the sole chef at Rosalyn's Restaurant.

The name is a misnomer—I own a catering business, not a restaurant. And cooking on-site in my clients' kitchens, instead of my own, is as close as I'll ever get to a brick-and-mortar location.

But that's okay, though. I make enough to survive. And to pay Presley—hopefully enough for her to stay.

I look around and let my shoulders relax.

The desserts are done. The appetizers are started. And we have all the ingredients we need prepped for the mains.

"You two doing okay? Need anything?" Hannah, our client and owner of this beautiful mansion, steps into the kitchen.

I try to keep my cheeks from turning red as I face her, hoping she didn't hear me curse over burning myself. "We're looking good, thanks."

Hannah smiles as she takes in the chaos of food covering her kitchen island and counters. "It's impressive how you keep this all straight."

My own smile feels a little more normal now. "I wonder at it sometimes too."

"Well, if you think of anything you need, just let me know. I'm gonna run up and shower now." Her eyes move to the clock I just glanced at. "Shit, I'm more behind than I thought." She starts to back away. "I have someone coming over in a bit to do my hair. If they show up before I'm back down, will you let them in and send them to the living room?" Hannah presses her hands together, grimacing like she hates to ask for help. "My husband should be home soon, but I don't know who will get here first."

I nod. "Not a problem," I tell her, meaning it. If this lady only knew the sort of shit I've been asked to do before, she wouldn't blink an eye at this.

"You're the best, Rosalyn!" She grins and rushes out of the kitchen.

"She's really nice," Presley comments after Hannah disappears.

"Has been so far."

Presley snorts. "You're such a pessimist."

I shrug. She's not wrong. I've dealt with too many shitty people not to be.

My employee moves closer to my side and lowers her voice. "I heard her husband is a pro-football player."

"Yeah, I heard that too. But I haven't met him yet."

This job was a last-minute booking. Apparently, their previous caterer fell through a few days ago, so their event planner from Meghan's Moments, who I've worked with before, called and asked if I could fill in. And since I could, I said yes before asking who the clients were.

As soon as Meghan said the husband was a retired football player, my insides started to twist.

Which was stupid because Nathan doesn't play for Minnesota, so there's literally no reason for me to have thought he might be the client.

But twenty-five years or not, there's no way I could cater Nathan's wedding reception.

That would be... crushing.

Which is ridiculous because we don't have that sort of history. We were just kids. And we were just friends. And since then... Well, it's not like I know him anymore.

I don't even remember the last time I thought about Nathan Waller.

Okay, that's not true. I thought about him two nights ago.

I was lonely.

And horny.

And I'd seen his stupidly handsome face on a magazine in the checkout lane at the grocery store.

And sue me. He's fucking hot. So... I thought about him.

"And..." Presley leans closer. "Do you know who it is?"

Her question reminds me that we're talking about a different athlete.

"Maddox Lovelace," I tell her—the name that doesn't mean anything to me.

Her mouth drops. "This is Mad Dog Maddox's house?"

"Mad Dog?" I scrunch up my nose at the silly nickname.

I didn't look him up. All I needed to know was that his last name wasn't Waller.

"I thought he got married like last year or something." Presley tilts her head. "I forgot you said this was some sort of belated wedding reception."

"How do you know this stuff?" I hate to stereotype, but Presley, with her French-braided hair and full-sleeve tattoos, doesn't strike me as a football fan.

She rolls her eyes. "Because he's a hot-as-fuck professional athlete, and I'm not dead."

I can't help but laugh.

"I take it you don't watch?" she asks.

"Never had time." I tell her the truth.

There were times I was tempted.

Times I wanted to look up my old friend, find out when his games were... But I always stopped myself. I had to stay focused.

Had to work two jobs to support my third one.

Had to spend every spare moment cooking and baking once I quit those other two jobs.

Had to put my all into this company. Because I had to make it work.

Because I didn't want to spend my life working for someone else. And I couldn't spend another second working for another man. They'd controlled my life long enough.

Presley sighs. "You gotta get a life, Boss. And trust me." She fans herself with her hand. "After you see this man, you'll understand my obsession." Her eyes widen. "Do you think he'll have his teammates here? Oh, or his brother?"

Presley sounds so excited, but I have no idea who she's talking about.

The doorbell rings, saving me from a reply.

I step back from the island. "I'll go let the hair person in if you want to get started on the meatballs."

"Hair person." Presley snorts, then moves to the sink to wash her hands.

As I walk through the large home, I glance down at myself, hoping I'm not covered in bacon splatter.

We'll change into all black for the event, but for prep, I wore my usual comfy jeans and a forest-green T-shirt under my canvas apron, which seems to be free of major stains.

The doorbell rings again.

Rude.

I hurry the last few yards, not wanting Hannah to hear this person's constant ringing.

I close my fingers around the door handle and pull it open before the person can press the bell again.

And then everything stops.

Because standing before me, taller than I realized he'd become and close enough to touch, is the only best friend I've ever had.

It's my Nathan.

He's here.

Really here.

Standing before me.

Oxygen dances just out of reach, and spots start to dot my vision as I try to make sense of what I'm seeing.

Nathan is here.

At the same house I'm at.

This should be a beautiful moment.

One where we embrace and cry.

When we say how much we missed each other.

But I can't do that.

Not with him.

Not after... everything.

Panic wells up inside me.

I can't pretend everything's been okay since he left.

And I can't tell him the truth. Can't put my burden on his shoulders.

And... God dammit, I can't breathe.

Even if I could, I don't know what to say.

"Hey there." Nathan grins. "I'm Nate, best friend of the groom."

His grin is perfect. Happy.

Nathan holds his hand out.

He's holding his hand out because he just introduced himself. To me.

Like we're strangers.

Because we are.

My fingers feel like ice as I reach out and place my hand in his.

His palm is warm and so much larger than mine. And I want to melt into the feeling.

I want to ask him to hug me.

I want to tell him how much I missed him.

But I won't.

Because he doesn't remember me.

And he's not my Nathan anymore.

TWO
NATE

Fucking hell, this woman is a damn knockout.

Her hand trembles in mine, and I have to stop myself from reaching out and placing my other hand on the back of hers.

I've seen it before, the starstruck behavior. And I've learned to ignore it, because by not addressing it, no one ends up embarrassed.

So when her wide blue eyes blink up at me, I pretend not to see the sheen of tears.

She must be a superfan.

I give her hand another shake before I let go.

Her hair is a deep shade of red, pulled back into a high ponytail, and I want to wrap my hand around it.

I clear my throat.

I'm a thirty-seven-year-old man. Not a creeper.

I will not pop a boner standing in my friend's doorway.

Maddox's doorway.

If this woman in front of me is one of Hannah's friends, Maddox will kill me if I try to fuck her.

The woman steps back, pulling the door open wider.

She doesn't say anything, but I take the silent invitation and follow her inside.

When she moves behind me to shut the door, I glance over my shoulder, wanting to get a look at her body without her noticing.

My glance turns into a stare.

I have to resist lifting my fist to my mouth, wanting to bite my knuckle to stifle a groan, because good lord below, I'm going to hell for the things I'm willing to do to get my hands on that fucking ass.

I bite the inside of my cheek.

Is she the type of woman who's into butt stuff?

With a body like that, she fucking should be.

Her ass is thick. And grabbable. And I bet it would jiggle if I smacked it.

The woman turns around, and before I can notice anything else, I notice the apron.

My grin grows.

"You catering?" I ask, hardly hiding my excitement.

If she's with the caterer, then she's not Hannah's friend.

And she's fair game.

The woman nods, also looking down at herself, like she forgot what she was wearing.

Her apron is tied tightly around her waist, causing it to pull snugly across her tits. And her tits match her ass. I want to take a fucking nap on them.

Maybe she'd be willing to take off everything... but the apron.

Her cheeks are pink when she looks back up at me, and I work to school my features.

"So..." I lift my brows. "Need help in the kitchen, or should I go find Maddox?"

She swallows, and I find myself leaning toward her, anxious to hear her speak.

"He's not home yet." Her voice is quiet, a little soft, and I need to find a way to make her say my name. "You can—"

The doorbell rings, and my little redhead startles so badly that she lets out a squeak of surprise.

I bite down on a laugh as I reach out and lightly grip her upper arm. "My apologies for ringing the doorbell twice. That's loud as hell."

She looks up at me, and I wish I could read her expression.

It's alarm and something that looks like... sadness—but probably isn't.

Poor girl is overwhelmed.

"I need to get that," she whispers, keeping her gaze averted from mine.

My hold on her arm is loose, so when she steps away, my hand falls back to my side.

She moves to open the door for the newcomer.

She's not exactly short, maybe five foot five, but she's short compared to me.

I'm not the tallest dude I know, but at six foot three, I'm taller than most wide receivers. And even though my playing days are over, and I can't run like I used to, and I don't work out as much as I used to, I still stand up straighter and pull my shoulders back before the girl without a name turns back around.

A stranger follows her into the house, and I step to the side to make room for them.

"Hannah asked me to have you wait in the living room, if that's okay." The caterer tells the other woman. She starts to walk past me before she pauses. "You can, uh, come with."

Nate.

Just say my name, Beautiful. Let me hear it on your lips.

I dip my chin and hold my arm out, gesturing for them to go ahead.

The stranger gives me a smile, a nod, and a once-over before she follows the caterer down the hall.

Following, I run a hand through my hair. I could probably use a haircut, but I've kind of enjoyed the shaggy look. And, based on the perusal I just got, the style is working for me.

I slow my steps, and when the women turn toward the living room, I veer off toward the kitchen.

"Smells good," I state as I stop in front of the island currently covered in food.

The girl on the other side of the counter snaps her head up at the sound of my voice.

"Thanks..." Her eyes narrow, then widen. "Holy fucking shit. You're Nate Waller."

Two fans in a row.

I smile. "Last I checked."

She slaps her hand down on the counter.

We both look down at the wet slapping sound, and she lifts her hand, revealing a squashed meatball.

She shakes her head—at me or the meatball, I'm not sure. "Craziest day ever."

"And the party hasn't even started."

The girl wiggles her brows. "Are there more of you coming?"

I spread my arms out. "I'm a one and only."

She snorts. "Football players, I mean."

I give her a slow nod. "A handful."

She bounces on her toes. "Like who?"

I tilt my head. "I feel like it'll be more fun if you just wait and see."

She purses her lips, then nods once. "That's fair. But blink once if Max Lovelace will be here."

I hold my eyes open for a long moment, then blink.

The girl fist pumps the air, but my eyes are locked on the light blue ones of the woman who just stepped up beside her.

The redhead still looks leery, so I try to break the tension. "Would you ladies like a signature?"

The chatty girl nods so fast her braids bounce around her shoulders. But the other woman just stares at me.

Close enough to a yes.

Knowing my way around Maddox's house, I stride across the kitchen to the cupboard in the far corner and pull out a notepad.

Snagging a pen too, I turn around and lean against the counter, now on the same side of the island as the ladies.

"Can you make it out to Presley?" The girl is drying her hands on a towel, having washed off the meatball remains.

"Sure thing." I write my usual *thanks for the support*, then tear off the page and hand it to her.

"Best day ever," she says as she takes it.

I move my attention back to the redhead. "And your name?"

THREE
ROSALYN

And your name?

A slender dagger slips between my ribs.

There's something so poetic about this moment.

The humor and the horror.

Nathan—Nate—thinks I'm a fan. And every time he says something nice, it wraps another cord of barbed wire around my throat.

I fight against the scraping pain and hold his gaze as I reply. "My name is Rosalyn."

I wait for it.

The recognition.

For him to put it together.

His smile softens. "Nice to meet you, Rosalyn."

That sharp bit twists, moving deeper into my chest.

He really doesn't remember.

"Hi. Can I join you?"

I look up at the unfamiliar voice and find a lanky boy standing a few feet away.

He's looking down at my mini stick house.

I nod. "Sure."

I know strangers are dangerous, but I've seen this boy riding his bike down the street before.

He sits down across from me. "I'm Nathan. What's your name?"

I roll a stick between my fingers. "Rosalyn. But... people call me Rosie."

It's only a little bit of a lie. My mom was the only one who called me Rosie, and she's gone now, but I still like it.

"Nice to meet you, Rosie."

I blink as the memory turns to ash, drifting away.

Nathan scribbles on his notebook, and I beg my eyes to stay dry.

Beg my body to behave.

I can*not* have a mental breakdown.

I cannot.

"Rosalyn's a pretty name." Nathan tears the page out of the notebook and holds it out to me. "Make sure I spelled it correctly."

Hearing him say my name out loud is another twist of that dagger. Because there's still no recognition.

I take the piece of paper from him and press my lips together, holding my breath.

Rosalyn – Always nice to meet a fan.

A fan.

And below that, underneath his famous signature, is his phone number.

I read it again.

The first letter Nathan has written me since I was eight, and I think he's flirting with me.

He's flirting. And I feel like I'm dying.

FOUR
NATE

Rosalyn looks like she's on the verge of tears again.

I open my mouth to ask if she wants a hug or something, but I'm cut off by Maddox.

"Waller." His voice is loud, and Rosalyn jumps.

This girl is really going through it tonight.

Maddox's big frame strides into the kitchen.

Presley's mouth drops open.

"Quit harassing our chefs." Maddox stops on the other side of the island from where I am next to Rosalyn.

I hold my hands up, one of them still gripping the notebook and pen. "Just chatting."

He lifts a brow. "Looked like you were being a diva, forcing your signature on people."

I roll my eyes. "The only diva here is you, Mr. Sends His Food Back."

Maddox lowers his eyelids, like he couldn't be more annoyed with me. "That was once. And it was entirely the wrong order."

I look at Redhead Rosalyn and shake my head. "He could've just eaten it."

"I'm taking away your best man status." Maddox sighs.

"Hate to remind you, but the wedding has already happened, brother from another mother. Can't take it back now." I grin.

"You're a pain. And you better not be wearing that for the party."

I brush my free hand down my chest, smoothing down the California team logo. The California team I was playing for when we beat the Biters for the game of all games.

The T-shirt is a little tighter than it used to be. But that's from doing less running and more lifting. It certainly has nothing to do with tacos.

I put him out of his misery. "Don't worry, Dad, I brought my church clothes. I just didn't want to sit around in a fucking bow tie all afternoon."

"Which begs the question, why are you here *three hours* before the party?"

"Because you're not supposed to see the bride." I walk around the island and pat him roughly on the back. "Figured you'd want company."

Maddox heaves out a breath. "Fine, come keep me company and leave these nice women alone." He turns his attention to Rosalyn and Presley. "And truly, thank you for coming today. I know it was short notice, and we appreciate you saving our asses." He eyes everything on the counters. "Looks great already."

I watch as he officially introduces himself to the two women.

Watch as they shake hands.

Watch the way Rosalyn hardly reacts at all over meeting Maddox.

Hell, she almost looks like she relaxes. Which is strange, because if you're a fan of football, you should automatically be a fan of Maddox. Especially if you live here, since he was a star player for the Minnesota team. A team his brother is the starting quarterback for now.

"Are you from here?" I blurt out the question, causing all three of them to turn toward me. But I'm only looking at Rosalyn.

Her eyes widen, and she glances away before answering. "Moved here when I was nineteen."

I lift my brows. "And that was... how long ago?"

She bites her lip. It's a wildly rude question, but she still answers. "Fourteen years ago."

I do the math. Thirty-three. Perfect for my thirty-seven.

"Where did you live before here?"

Maddox pushes a hand against my shoulder. "That's enough interrogation. Don't throw off their schedule."

I let him push me back away from the kitchen. "My apologies, Rosalyn. Please forgive me."

FIVE
ROSALYN

Where did you live before... Please forgive me... My apologies...
This day is turning into the biggest mind fuck.

As soon as Nathan steps out of view, I turn and rush into the pantry.

Presley is going to think I'm losing it, but I need a moment.

The lights above come to life as I close the door behind me. I have to assume they're based on movement, but I appreciate not having to find a light switch through my mounting panic.

Standing still, I shut my eyes and focus on breathing.

Inhale. Exhale.

I do it again.

This doesn't have to be a huge deal.

So what if Nathan doesn't recognize me?

So what if maybe he doesn't remember me at all?

Even as I try to tell myself it's okay, the thought makes me press my hands to my stomach.

Another breath.

Calming my racing heart, I remind myself that I didn't

recognize him the first time I saw him on TV either, so it shouldn't be this much of a shock.

Yes, my hair and eye color are the same. But the last time he saw me, I was eight. And I was always a *big-boned* kid—as one of my teachers had said—but I'm more than that now. I'm a grown-ass woman with a grown-ass ass. And a soft center. And tits that have needed underwire support since I was sixteen—basically when I learned how much I enjoyed cooking.

But... it's okay.

Because if he doesn't realize that I'm me, then he won't ask me what life was like after he moved.

If Nathan Waller has forgotten me... I can be Rosalyn instead of Rosie.

I take another slow breath.

I haven't talked to Nathan for two and a half decades, but in the few minutes we've interacted since he arrived, I can tell he's just as fun and easygoing as he was when we were kids.

Relaxed. Confident.

Easy to be around.

My next exhale comes out in a huff, and I square my shoulders.

I'm going to finish making tonight's food with Presley.

I'm going to make sure everything goes smoothly for Hannah and Maddox.

And I'm going to find a way to simply enjoy Nathan's nearness before I never see him again.

Because I can't see him again.

Taking a fortifying breath, I step out of the wonderfully stocked walk-in pantry. And the door—that's disguised to look like a regular section of cupboard—closes behind me.

Presley is staring right at me.

"Look," I sigh, but she bats her eyes.

"I don't know anything about football players. I don't have

any time." She mocks as she twists her fists under her eyes in a crying gesture.

It's over the top. And precisely what I need.

A laugh bursts out of me, and I shake my head. "Oh, shut up."

If everyone here wants to pretend that I'm fangirling instead of what I'm actually doing, which is riding the fine line between a nervous breakdown and a panic attack, I'll go with it.

As we get back to work, I use the fancy espresso maker that Hannah gave us free rein over. The double shot of caffeine will hopefully help focus my mind.

When Hannah hurries through the kitchen, I offer to make her a latte.

She accepts but then asks if I wouldn't mind bringing it to the living room.

When the drink is ready, I hate my past self for making the offer, because all I want to do is hide in the kitchen. But as I carry the yellow mug across the house, I don't run into any old friends.

"You're a lifesaver." Hannah takes the mug from me, smiling under a pile of curlers.

I ask the hairdresser if she'd like one, but the woman just grunts, so I take it as a no and make my way back to the kitchen.

The party is being held in the backyard, where tents, tables, and flowers are set up, and ribbons are flowing in the breeze.

Through the windows, I can see strings of lights hanging throughout the trees, and I just know it's going to be magical.

I'll miss walking through it since I volunteered to be the one who stays in the kitchen, making sure everything is heated at the right times and to the right temperatures.

Presley, along with two other women, who will show up in two hours, will act as waitstaff, carrying the trays around, swapping empty dishes for fresh ones, stocking the food tables.

It's a good system. And today it will play into my desire to stay unnoticed.

Back in the kitchen, we fall into the routine.

And I almost forget about Nathan.

Almost forget that the house of cards I've built is being tapped on by a giant football player's finger.

I almost forget. But then he saunters through the kitchen.

My jaw almost drops open because, sweet and savory Jesus, he looks like he belongs on a runway.

His six-foot-something frame is wrapped in a navy blue suit, with a crisp white shirt underneath and... hamburger help me, he's wearing a bow tie.

Nathan pauses, hand held over a tray of toast points topped with burrata, blended sweet peas, and chili oil.

His eyes are locked on mine, silently asking permission.

I dip my chin.

Nathan picks up the triangle of toast and winks.

He fucking winks at me.

Heat slithers down my spine, and I clench my thighs as I'm reminded that *this Nathan* is all man.

My body doesn't care that he can stare right at me and not know who I am.

My body doesn't care if he doesn't remember me at all.

All my body wants is his giant hands touching us.

Tasting us like he's about to taste that bite.

Nathan turns, heading farther into the house, but my eyes follow him as he shoves the whole thing into his mouth.

I hold my breath. Wanting him to love it.

Nathan's steps falter, and he tips his head back as he chews.

The profile view of him is... devastating.

His jawline. The way his throat works when he swallows. That tiny head shake he does and the way his hair moves with the motion.

He turns his head to look at me over his shoulder.

"Good?" I whisper.

"Divine," he whispers back, and I swear his eyes are on my mouth.

Then he's gone.

And my condition is bordering on cardiac arrest.

"I think I just got pregnant," Presley groans.

This time I have no argument. Because I think I might have too.

Fanning my face with my hand towel, I grab my backpack off the floor. "I'm going to go change."

Presley nods, already in her event clothes.

After locking the door to the closest powder room, I turn the tap on cold and stick my wrists under the running water.

That damn wink has me wishing I'd packed a whole handful of extra underwear in this bag.

I let my head drop forward as I continue to try to freeze the lust out of my body.

If Nathan keeps this up, I'm going to cave and start flirting back.

And I can't do that.

That would be a bad idea.

I lift my head and look at my reflection in the mirror.

But if I'm just Rosalyn tonight... would it really be that bad?

SIX

NATE

The August night air is warm, but the breeze makes it comfortable.

It's been a fun night. I've seen a lot of old football buddies. Got to harass Maddox's little brother some. Also got to introduce him to the one caterer, Presley, when she walked through the garden with a tray of food. But I've danced myself out, and no matter how many good conversations I have, my mind keeps wandering to the beautiful woman with the red hair.

When I didn't see her out here with a tray, I wandered through the house, taking the longest way possible to a bathroom, and found her elbow deep in plating.

Not wanting to be a total pain in the ass while she was working, I didn't bother her. I kept on walking.

But now that the night is winding down...

A large hand slaps down on my back. "What's that dumb look on your face for?"

I jab my elbow into Tony Stoleman's side. "Keep picking on me, and I'm gonna tell my mom."

He snorts. "Your mom won't yell at me. She loves me."

I don't argue because I can't.

He smirks, knowing it's true.

I try to backhand his stomach because he's a cocky dick. But he dodges.

"Quit being salty. My mom loves you just as much." He hooks an arm around my shoulder. "Come to the dessert table with me."

I walk with him. "Need me to make a plate for you and pretend they're for me? Is someone calling you out for eating all the pastries?"

"Not yet, but I'd rather avoid the drama."

Tony and I go back a ways. He's probably my closest friend aside from Maddox, and I trust him with my life. But I also know he's a shady bastard, and his love for baked goods is the only soft thing about him.

Tony tells me about the flight he has to catch tomorrow, back down to Arizona, but I'm only half listening as I fill up a little plate with desserts.

"What's this?" I interrupt, holding up one of the sweets.

Tony darts his hand out, taking the dessert from my grip, and shoves it into his mouth.

"Are you serious? There's a whole fucking tray of them right here," I gripe, picking up another one.

Tony grins, mouth full. "Stolen food tastes better."

I roll my eyes and take a civilized bite of what has to be some sort of homemade marshmallow.

I forgot how much I used to love eating them.

"It's like an inside-out s'more," Tony says, sticky marshmallow garbling his words.

Looking at the half-eaten thing in my hands, I have to agree. The oversized fluffy white marshmallow is stuffed with some sort of semi-firm chocolate, and the sides are coated in crushed graham crackers.

I shove the rest of it in my mouth.

Damn, that Rosalyn woman knows how to make food.

I pick up another one.

When I was hanging out with Maddox earlier, I not so subtly asked him about the caterer, which is how I found out that my curvy little Rosalyn is the owner of the catering company.

Not that it makes a difference in how attractive I find her, but being a business owner is hot. And it's a good bit of information to know.

"What's your deal?" Tony asks, eyes narrowed, bringing me back to the moment.

"No deal." I take a bite of the second inside-out s'more. "Just wondering how I'm gonna get the caterer to call me."

"You got a party coming up?"

"No..." I trail off and think about his question. "Huh. Well, that could work."

Tony lifts a brow. "Should I even ask?"

I smirk at my friend. "Probably not."

SEVEN
ROSALYN

"This is for you." Hannah holds out a bottle of champagne.

"Oh, you don't have to..." I try to refuse. She's already given us a bigger tip than the last two events combined.

"I must. We have too much left, and your team killed it tonight." She practically shoves the bottle into my hands.

Reluctantly, I accept the champagne. "Well, thank you. It was an easy event to work."

It really was. No one was rude. Even the drunk people were friendly. And everyone loved the food.

"Glad to hear." Hannah smiles. "Now excuse me while I go wrangle everyone who's still left." She shakes her head. "Swear they'll be here another two hours."

Darkness has completely fallen outside, and the inside of the house, even though everyone has mostly stayed outside, is set for the party mood—all the lights are on low, even in the kitchen.

I eye the bottle.

It's awfully tempting. Especially after the sudden *guest* appearance today.

Presley, the only one of my crew still here, takes the bottle from my hands and yanks the cork out.

The pop is loud in the quiet house.

I laugh. "Thirsty?"

"Boss." Presley lifts her brows. "If you don't drink this willingly, I'm going to waterboard you with it."

I grimace, imagining bubbles up my nose. "Fine."

She nods and pulls a coffee mug out of the cupboard.

Presley fills it, then hands it to me. "I know the boss lady gave it to us to drink, but this way, guests who leave won't think you're getting drunk on the job."

"I knew I liked you," I tell my employee before taking a sip.

Her expression turns smug. "Obviously."

I take another, larger, sip. "You having some?"

Presley shakes her head. "I gotta drive home."

"Oh, duh." I knew this.

Usually we ride together in my catering van, but with the location of this house, it made sense for Presley to pick me up on her way over and put all the food in the back of her vehicle. And since we don't both need to be here for the final cleanup, I'm just going to catch an Uber home.

"Plus," Presley starts, putting the leftover food into containers, "booze isn't my drug of choice. And I got a brownie at home calling my name."

I snort. "Maybe sneak a little to-go container of the apps into your bag. You might need it later."

Presley presses a hand to her chest. "Best boss ever."

I lift my mug of champagne in a mock toast.

We pack up the food.

I take another drink.

We load the dishwasher.

Presley refills my mug when I'm not looking.

We hand-wash the pots and saucepans.

I have some more bubbly.

We unload and reload the dishwasher.

I send Presley home. And I polish off my mug.

Leaning against the counter, waiting for the dishwasher to complete its cycle, I eye the bottle on the island next to my empty mug.

The bottle is half-gone. I'm more than half-buzzed. But...

I press my lips together and close the distance.

Knowing it's probably a bad idea, I pour some more champagne into my mug.

I'm not driving.

I shouldn't have to interact with anyone else tonight.

I can have a little more.

I stop pouring when my mug is a third full. But then a glass slides across the countertop.

It's a low-ball glass, empty except for a single ice cube, telling me it used to be filled with some sort of hard liquor.

Surrounding the glass are long, masculine fingers.

I don't have to look farther to know whose hand it is.

I don't have to, but I can't help it.

Muscular forearms.

White sleeves rolled up.

Biceps bunched under the bright material.

I drop my eyes back to the glass in front of me.

His fingers flex, twisting the glass on the counter. "Unless you prefer to drink alone."

Nathan's voice is quiet, meant just for me.

And god dammit, I shouldn't.

I really, truly shouldn't.

But I have just enough of the golden liquid flowing through my veins to not care about the consequences.

So right now, at this exact moment, I don't care if this is the worst idea I've ever had. Right now our childhood history doesn't matter.

Tonight we can be Rosalyn and Nate. Two adults, sharing a drink.

I tip the bottle.

A rumble rolls out of Nathan's chest. "There's a good girl."

I almost moan.

Why is that so hot?

And does he talk like this to everyone?

I pour the rest of the champagne into his glass.

It's too full. An absurd pour. But I can't be tempted with more than I already have. And I can't function with him saying stuff like *good girl* in this dimly lit kitchen.

Setting the bottle down, I fortify myself to look up and meet Nathan's eyes.

And I have to stop myself from throwing a fit when I finally do.

How is he hotter every time I see him?

I don't know what happened to his suit jacket, but it's gone. And along with rolling up his sleeves, he's undone his bow tie, and his shirt is unbuttoned low enough to see that ridge between his pecs.

Does he know what he looks like?

Did he leave his bow tie hanging like that just to tempt me to pull him close?

EIGHT
NATE

She can't take her eyes off me. And the attention has me more turned on than I've been in a long time.

Slowly, I lift my glass—filled to the brim with champagne—to my lips.

The movement passes through her line of vision, and her gaze catches on the glass, following it to my mouth.

I take a drink.

I've already had a few whiskeys. I don't need more. But I do need more of this tempting woman.

My swallow is deliberate.

Then I take another mouthful.

Rosalyn lifts her eyes to mine, and her blue irises appear darker in the dim light.

I swallow.

There's something about Rosalyn that feels... right.

And I don't know what exactly it is, but I want to find out.

She wraps her fingers around her mug and mirrors me, lifting it to her mouth and pressing the rim against her lips.

She takes a drink.

Then a second.

I set my glass down. "Did your team leave you?"

Are you alone?

She sets her mug down. Then nods.

I step to the side, moving toward the end of the island. "What do you have left to do?"

How long do I have to wait?

She keeps her eyes on me as I continue to move around to her side of the island.

Nothing left between us.

"Dishes." Her word comes out breathy.

"Can I help you?"

Can I help you take your clothes off and have you say my name like how you just said the word dishes?

She blinks at me. "Help me?"

"Yeah, Beautiful. Can I help you finish?"

God, I want to help her finish.

I slide the tip of my tongue against the corner of my mouth.

Is it hot in here?

I think it might be too hot in here.

We should probably get naked.

I swear she mouths the words *help you finish* while her eyes lock on the movement of my tongue.

She shakes her head just a little. "You don't need to help me."

I lean down, bringing our faces closer than we've been before.

Her breath hitches.

Her eyes jump up to meet mine, then drop back to my mouth.

I bend, bringing us even closer as I reach across the counter for my glass.

Slowly, I stand back up, bringing my drink with me. "You shared your champagne with me." I take a large swallow. "Drying some dishes is the least I owe you."

NINE
ROSALYN

No.
    I need to say no.
    But my head nods.
    And I hand Nathan Waller a dish towel.

TEN
NATE

Our fingers brush when I take the blue checkered towel from her, and even though we shook hands when she answered the door, this feels like so much more.

Rosalyn turns away, giving me her back as she moves to grab another towel off the counter.

Her work clothes are sexier than they have any right to be. The head-to-toe black. The stretchy pants that hug every inch of her ass and hips but are loose down her legs. The scoop-neck T-shirt that clings... to everything. The no-nonsense ponytail.

I shift my stance and take another drink of my champagne.

I'm not a creep.

I won't act like a creep.

I won't get a boner until the appropriate time.

"Where do we start?" I try to sound casual and not like I'm being choked with lust.

She faces me, then bends down and pulls the dishwasher open.

A plume of steam fills the space between us, and it makes Rosalyn appear like she's from a dream.

Or a long-ago memory.

ELEVEN
ROSALYN

I clear my throat. "I just need to dry these, then refill the washer."

Nathan takes a step closer. "Do you have to wait for that... load to be done?"

He paused, like he didn't want to say the word *load*. And now my mind is stuck on the dirtiest connotations of that word.

Blinking the thought away, I use my towel to grab a hot plate out of the dishwasher. "I usually stay to empty the final... round." I can't bring myself to say load. "I try to make it so I don't leave any cleanup work for the clients."

Nathan makes a humming sound, then does the same thing, grabbing a plate with his towel and drying it.

The muted music and chatter from the backyard are our soundtrack as we work in silence.

I reach for a bowl on the top rack, and Nathan's fingers bump against mine as he reaches for the same one.

I jerk my hands back and lift my eyes.

Nathan is looking right at me. "Oops."

His expression is serious and his voice is low. I don't think us touching was an accident.

The heat in his eyes is more than I've ever experienced, but I can't make myself look away.

The energy between us is causing my blood to simmer beneath my skin.

It's official. My body doesn't care at all about our history.

It doesn't care that there can be no future between me and Nathan.

It only cares that he's close.

And he's interested.

Maybe I really am his type. Or maybe a part of him recognizes our previous bond. That natural chemistry we always had.

Chemistry that's changed from something friendly into something much more adult.

Nathan keeps eye contact as he lifts the bowl and runs his towel around the outside.

He's drying a freaking bowl, and it's making my panties wet.

I'm blaming the champagne.

I drag my eyes away from his and grab another dish.

More silence stretches between us as I hand Nathan dirty plates from the sink and he places them in the newly emptied dishwasher.

Each time our hands touch, a jolt of electricity zings up my arm.

And I keep getting warmer.

The last plate slides into place, and I hand Nathan the dishwasher soap.

While he starts the appliance, I dry my hands, then toss the towel onto the counter.

When I turn back around, my chest bumps into his.

I automatically reach out to steady myself. But the only thing within reach is Nathan, so I grab his shirt, bunching the material at his sides.

He moves closer until our bodies are nearly flush.

"I normally don't do this, Beautiful." He ghosts his hands over my arms. "I usually prefer to take it slow. But tell me you feel it too?"

He doesn't specify.

He doesn't need to.

Because I can feel it. I can feel the tension crackling in the air between us.

But I lie. "Feel what?"

The side of his mouth pulls up.

He doesn't believe me.

TWELVE
NATE

She's such a pretty little liar.

I wrap my fingers around her upper arms and keep her steady as I walk into her, making her walk back.

"W-what are we doing?" There's a lace of panic in her voice, but it's muted by desire.

And I don't miss the way she said *we*. Because she already knows what *we're* about to do.

"We're going into the pantry." I reach around her side to pull the door open.

She steps back, entering the tiny room. "Why?"

"Because, Ms. Rosalyn." I move her farther into the room until the door swings shut behind me. "I need to taste you."

THIRTEEN
ROSALYN

My lips part on a gasp.

And Nathan moves. Claiming his taste.

Our lips meet.

My body leans into his.

My neck arches.

And I kiss him back.

I kiss *him*.

My Nathan.

The man who's held my broken pieces together for so long.

Who's been both my best friend and a figment of my imagination.

The man I haven't seen in twenty-five years.

The man who's lived an entire life since walking away from me that day in the woods.

My heart squeezes painfully.

I want this and hate this. Because I want him to know it's me.

I want him to desire *me*.

But maybe that's not supposed to happen.

Maybe I'm supposed to have this experience with him this way. With anonymity.

Maybe I need to experience this, with him, just this once.

Because he's here.

And he's kissing me.

I open my mouth.

FOURTEEN
NATE

She opens for me. And I push my tongue into her mouth.

I slide my hand up her neck, up the back of her head, her silky hair so soft against my palm. And I don't stop until I'm gripping the base of her ponytail.

Rosalyn moans, and I tug her hair just enough to tilt her head back.

Then I deepen the kiss, tasting the champagne on her tongue.

I push in farther.

Her fingertips claw at my sides.

I rock my hips against her.

And she presses into me just as hard.

We both moan.

Rosalyn is just as fucking primed for this as I am.

And I'm going to show her just how good we could be together.

FIFTEEN

ROSALYN

Nathan tugs my hair again, tilting my head back even farther, and the sensation on my scalp travels through my body, straight to my nipples.

Our mouths break apart. Our panting breaths loud in the small room.

I slide my eyes open, needing to remind myself this is real.

The overhead light illuminates the look on Nathan's face.

And it's the look of a man who isn't done yet.

He slides the hand not in my hair from my shoulder to the front of my throat.

Then down, until it's pressed flat against my chest. The bottom of his palm covering my cleavage.

"I'm going to touch you now." He slides his hand an inch lower. "Tell me if you don't want this." He shifts his hand again until he's palming my breast over my shirt. "You can tell me no. But you should do it now."

My heartbeat is thudding so loudly that I hardly hear my answer.

But I tell him the only thing I can.

The truth.

I drag my hands down his sides until I'm gripping his belt. "I want this."

His lids lower, and he lets out a sound deep in his throat.

Then he's backing me into the shelves.

SIXTEEN
NATE

My mouth crashes down on hers again, only this time she battles me for control.

It's frantic.

Hungry.

Passionate.

Exactly what I hoped for from this little sexpot.

Her body is warm and soft, and I want to strip her fucking naked.

I want to inspect every inch of her.

But not yet. Not in this pantry.

But later.

I need to get at least one orgasm out of her. After that, she'll be more relaxed.

Then we can go somewhere else for rounds two and three.

SEVENTEEN
ROSALYN

Nathan's large hand squeezes my breast, and I groan against his lips.

My head is spinning in the best way, and I let my newfound boldness take over.

I trace my fingers along the top of his pants until my hands are over his belt buckle.

I felt it earlier. The hardness pressing into me as he backed me in here.

And I want to feel more.

I curl my fingers into the top of his pants.

His hips jump.

And I scrape my teeth over his tongue.

He groans.

I reach in farther, my fingers between the fabric of his pants and his tucked-in shirt.

And then I feel it.

The base of his cock.

A very thick cock.

My pointer and middle finger spread, trying to get a feel for his size.

We both moan at the contact. And we both break away at the same time, looking down between us.

My hand shoved down Nathan's pants.

His hand covering half my chest.

I've only ever been with men smaller than me.

My height or shorter. Men who weighed less than me. Slender limbs.

Men I felt safer around simply based on size.

But Nathan... He's the biggest man I've ever been this close to.

Biggest... everywhere.

And yet, even as he tightens his hand in my hair, even as he holds me captive, I've never felt safer.

A new warmth—one that feels a lot like gratitude—fills my body.

The hand on my chest slips away, and Nathan uses it to grip my wrist.

He keeps his hand there a moment, and his cock twitches between my fingers, but then he pulls my hand free of his pants. "Me first."

I'm not sure what he means, but he lifts my hand to his chest, and I instinctively cling to him.

"Now be my good girl and stay quiet." He uses my ponytail to pull my face closer to his. "Can you do that?"

I flex my fingers against his chest muscles. "I'll try."

His lips brush against mine. "If you're only going to try, then we should probably hurry."

The comment reminds me that we're in my client's pantry, behind a door that doesn't lock.

But then Nathan slides his hand down the front of my pants, and I can't think anymore.

EIGHTEEN
NATE

Her pants are just loose enough around the waist for my hand to fit, and the pretty redhead clings to me as I wiggle my fingers past the band of her underwear.

She's so fucking responsive.

I moan into Rosalyn's mouth when my fingers reach her core.

She's so fucking soaked.

My fingers slip through her folds, and I wish I could hump her leg while I touch her, needing the contact.

But I want to stretch this out. I want this to be the first of many orgasms for her. And I don't want to come in my pants.

Rosalyn's inhales are choppy against my mouth.

Her body arches into my touch.

I push my hand lower, my palm facing her body, and I push my fingers into her entrance.

"Is all of this for me?" I growl against her lips. "You this wet just for me?"

She whimpers in response, and my cock jumps.

NINETEEN
ROSALYN

I grip his shirt, keeping him as close to me as possible.

The feeling of his hand... Of his fingers... It's overwhelming.

Nathan rocks his palm against my clit.

He slides his fingers in and out of me.

He lets out low groans each time my core clenches around him.

And I'm barely able to stand.

I drop my forehead to his chest, and he lets go of my ponytail to palm the back of my neck.

His grip is possessive.

It's everything.

It's all I've ever wanted.

I clench my eyes shut.

I focus on staying up.

I focus on enjoying the moment.

He keeps his focus between us.

His fingers don't stop.

He doesn't slow down.

And as soon as he shifts his hand and his thumb rubs across my clit, I know I'm nearly there.

His thumb swipes again.

My body starts to tense. Bracing for what's next.

"You close, Beautiful?" Nathan presses his mouth against the top of my head.

I nod, my forehead bumping against his chest.

"You gonna make that pussy come all over my fingers?"

I nod again.

He moves his thumb with greater purpose.

"Tell me," he demands.

"I'm close," I pant.

The first shimmer of an orgasm dances up my spine, and a tear trails down my cheek.

He shoves his fingers impossibly deeper. "Tell me how close you are."

"I'm there." My voice breaks. "Don't stop. Please, Nathan. Don't stop."

Then his thumb hits me just right, and I convulse around his fingers.

TWENTY

NATE

I breathe her in, holding her body against mine as she trembles through her orgasm.

She's so perfect.

So reactive.

So...

She called me Nathan.

I blink.

No one calls me that.

Not anymore.

Not since I was a kid.

Something prods at the back of my mind.

Something I've missed.

With my mouth still pressed against Rosalyn's hair, I study the color.

The deep red. The way it almost looks black under my shadow, and how it glowed under the sunlight when she opened the front door.

The body against mine starts to relax, and I carefully slide my hand out of her pants.

She called me Nathan.

The woman, Rosalyn, lifts her head from against my chest and looks up at me.

She looks up at me with bright blue eyes and tears on her lashes.

And the world shifts around me.

Because *she* called me Nathan.

The girl from the woods.

The girl who was my best friend.

The girl who looked at me, with those same blue eyes, filled with the same sparkling tears... the last time I saw her.

A lifetime ago.

A moment ago.

And just like that, I remember.

"Rosie?"

TWENTY-ONE
ROSALYN

My bliss vanishes.

My body tenses.

He called me Rosie.

He knows.

And before I can have a conversation with my champagne brain about how to handle this, my flight response decides for me.

I rush past Nathan.

He fucking knows.

My hands slap against the pantry door, and I shove it open.

"Wait," Nathan calls, but I don't stop.

The door clicks shut behind me, silencing whatever he might have said next.

I have to go.

I have to go right now.

Along with my personal reasons for needing to run, I just let a party guest finger me in a client's pantry.

If I had time to berate myself, I would.

I cannot let the Lovelaces find out. If this got out, it could ruin my business.

I snag my backpack off the kitchen floor and glance at the still-running dishwasher as I hurry past, knowing I can't stay to empty it.

Great, add an incomplete cleanup job to my list of failures tonight.

At least everything else that we brought went home with Presley in her vehicle, so it's just me and my bag that need to disappear.

Not pausing to check if the coast is clear, I jog straight to the front door and pull it open.

Thankfully there's no one to see me rush down the front steps.

As I hurry down the driveway, I pull my phone out and order a ride home. But I make the pickup address a house farther down the street.

I'm not sure if Nathan would actually pursue me out of the house, but I prefer not to stick around and find out.

Pursue me.

Because he remembers who I am.

TWENTY-TWO
NATE

I stare at the back of the closed pantry door.

It can't be...

My eyes drop to my hand, still half raised in the air.

But it was.

That *was* her.

I know it was.

I remember...

I swallow against the growing tightness in my throat.

I remember her.

I remember her now.

But... I'd forgotten.

I lift my hand higher.

I'd forgotten about Rosie.

How could I have forgotten about Rosie?

My heart thumps inside my chest.

I remember now.

And she remembers me too.

My heart thuds loudly behind my ribs.

I know she knows.

Even if she hadn't recognized me when she first saw me, I introduced myself...

She did too.

But she called herself Rosalyn.

I called myself Nate.

But I can feel it. That knowledge. That awareness.

I can see it now.

She knew it was me all night.

And she didn't say anything.

My Rosie didn't say anything. And when I figured it out, she ran.

And I don't understand why.

We were friends.

It's been... twenty-five years, but we'd been friends.

I think about the last time I saw her.

How I'd told her we were moving the next day.

How she cried.

I haven't thought about Rosie in so long.

That tightness moves down my throat into my chest.

She was my best friend for those few years we knew each other.

And then I had to move.

And...

I remember leaving her that letter in the woods.

Remember tucking it under the bag of marshmallows.

Fucking marshmallows.

I'd forgotten about those too.

I haven't had a marshmallow in so long.

Until tonight.

I think about that. About the dessert Rosie made.

Did she make them because she still loves them?

Did she think about me while she made them?

Something twists inside me at the thought that maybe she's

thought about me all these years, when I forgot.

I look back at my fingers, still shiny with her slick.

What a turn the night has taken.

I fingered Rosie Edwards without even knowing it.

I glance at the closed door, then, remembering how her body reacted to my touch, I shove my two fingers into my mouth.

The taste of her settles on my tongue.

My pretty Little Rose, tasting like home.

Maybe I didn't know who she was this time, but the next time I have my hand down Rosie's pants, I'll have her screaming my name.

Using my free hand, I adjust myself, then follow Rosie's route out of the pantry.

Hands washed and clothes straightened, I rest my hip against the counter across from the dishwasher.

I already planned to spend the night on the couch in Maddox's library, so with nothing else to do, I pull the business card out of my pocket and wait for the dishwasher to finish.

Hannah gave me this card.

I run my thumb over the raised letters.

Letters spelling out *Rosalyn's Restaurant.*

TWENTY-THREE
ROSALYN

"Oh shit!" I rush the rest of the way down the short hallway from my bedroom to the kitchen.

The oven timer is beeping, and I'm sure it's been going off for several minutes.

The towel around my hair tips to the side as I bend down, and I have to hold it back with one hand while I open the oven door with the other.

Smoke billows out, stinging my eyes.

"Fuck me." I slam the oven door shut, hurry across to the opposite wall of my apartment, and open my sliding patio door.

The tiny balcony is literally only good for fresh air. And even though I'm sacrificing my air-conditioned air, I leave the door wide open.

Giving up on my hair towel, I yank it from the top of my head and toss it toward the hallway.

My wet hair slaps against my shoulders, soaking through my robe, but I ignore it and go back to the oven.

Sighing, I turn off the oven and grab my hot mitts. Then I

yank open the door and use the mitts to fan away the remaining smoke.

I try not to pout as I pull out the pan of burnt tarts. But since they're still trailing smoke, I carry the pan out to the balcony and set the whole smoking mess on the small iron side table.

I originally bought this table so I could have a plant. Maybe two. But I've killed everything green I've ever put out here, so now it's become my *Fuck, I burned it* table.

Standing on my balcony in my robe, I drop my head forward in defeat.

Then my smoke alarm goes off.

"Of course."

Hands still inside the mitts, I grip the pan, tip the burnt tarts onto the table, then hurry back inside.

Guess I won't be tasting this test recipe.

Using the pan as a giant fan, I wave it back and forth under the smoke detector, sending crumbs everywhere, but I'm beyond giving a fuck.

Finally, after a long minute, the shrill beeping stops.

I'm not sure I should be thankful the smoke detector doesn't call the fire station, but in this case, I am.

Though a hot, muscled firefighter might just be the thing I need to stop thinking about Nathan.

Not Nathan. Nate. Calling him Nathan is exactly what got you caught.

I drop the pan in the sink and shuffle back down the hall to my bedroom.

It's been almost a week since that night in the pantry. Since I ran away from my childhood friend like the giant chicken I am. And no matter what I do, I can't get him off my mind.

Every night, late at night, when I can't stop myself from thinking about our encounter, I question myself.

Should I have stayed?

Should I have told him who I was before he put his hands down my pants?

Should I have laughed it off, dropped to my knees, and sucked his cock?

Should I just tell him everything?

But then, in the light of day, I remember all the reasons why it's a bad idea.

There's too much history.

Too many bad days in the last twenty-five years to even try to answer when he undoubtedly asks how I've been.

Too much at stake.

I can't risk all that heartache over a fling.

And a fling is all it would be because we don't even know each other anymore.

It's been too long.

And Nathan didn't just move away to have a normal life. He went on to become a famous football player. He's retired now, sure, but he's famous, nonetheless.

Hell, the man has been on the cover of magazines. In his underwear.

I eye my nightstand, then shake my head.

My apartment still reeks of smoke from my failed tarts. I do not have time to play with my silicone boyfriend.

Grumbling over the way I have the worst luck, I shrug off my robe and toss it onto my bed.

Then I just stand there, naked, with my feet planted wide and my arms straight out at my sides while my hair drips down my back.

My shower was supposed to be a quick rinse off, but then I decided to wash my hair, and I lost track of time.

Now I'm sweaty again, and I want to get back in the shower, but I have a new batch of tarts to make.

Thankfully my ceiling fan is spinning at its max, and the breeze is helping to cool me down.

Just another glorious day in my life.

And it's then, as I stand there, like a chubby, naked starfish, that my phone starts to ring.

In the kitchen.

I grind my teeth.

I'd love to ignore it, but as a business owner, I can't do that. It's always easier to answer the phone than to try to call back and catch someone.

So, in nothing but my skin, I hurry back to my kitchen.

My phone is on the small island, and I lunge for it.

As I lift it to my face, I remember my patio is wide open and the apartment building across the street is occupied.

Hitting answer, I crouch behind the island.

The movement parts my parts, and my vagina is blasted with cold air from the floor vent below me.

I force a smile into my voice. "This is Rosalyn."

"Uh, hi," an unfamiliar male replies. "You're the caterer, right?"

"Yes." I shift so my knees are together, feeling weird talking to this stranger while completely nude.

"Cool." The voice is definitely young. "I'm, um, Blake, and I'm in charge of our company picnic, and I wanted to see if you could cater it."

If the kid didn't sound so awkward, I would wonder if this was a prank, but I'm not really in a position to turn down jobs. Not after putting new brakes on my van last month.

"If I can, I'd love to," I tell him. "What's the date of the event?"

"Next Thursday."

My brows go up. "Like a week from today?"

"I know it's last minute, but... I'm gonna be honest. My boss sent me an email an hour ago asking if I'd finished planning the picnic. But I didn't even know there was a picnic." Panic causes his voice to rise.

"It's alright." I try to calm him as I put my phone on speaker and look at my calendar. "Depending on how many people you're expecting, I can probably make Thursday work."

"Seriously?"

"Seriously." I smile at the sound of his relief. *Poor kid.*

I spend a few more minutes talking to Blake. Getting the location—some courtyard of an office building in St. Paul. The number of people—he thinks around thirty. And what sort of food they're looking for—classic summer fare.

I take a gamble and add a five percent upcharge to my usual rate since I'll be squeezing this between a birthday party the night before and a retirement party the next day, but Blake doesn't hesitate at the cost.

Corporations usually have money to spare, and his boss deserves a higher fee for putting Blake through all this stress.

"I'll send you an email with the contract, then we can finalize the menu."

"Perfect. Thank you so much," Blake tells me, then ends the call.

Reaching up, I slap my phone onto the island, then grip the counter and try not to groan as I pull myself back up.

Feeling suddenly more positive than I have in a while, I hurry my naked ass back down the hall to find clothes.

I have a menu to work on.

TWENTY-FOUR
NATE

Leaning against the wall next to my office door, I smirk.

I know I should feel bad for putting Blake through the stress of thinking he's late on a project, but the kid needs to learn how to relax. He was my intern for almost a year before I hired him on as my assistant, but he still walks on eggshells around me.

Maybe I've been too easy on him.

Overcoming this difficult situation will be good for him.

Really, it's a win-win all around.

Blake gains confidence.

Rosie gets a gig.

And I get to see Rosie.

And since Blake was too flustered over the whole company picnic thing, he didn't question the fact that Rosie's business card was stapled to the paper with all the details about time and place.

I push off the wall and head back to my desk.

There's a chance Rosie will look up Catch Tech, the company name. And if she does that, she might click on the

Who We Are section of the website. Which could lead to her reading the name of the owner and CEO.

My name.

I drop heavily into my chair and have to grip the edge of my desk to stop myself from rolling back.

I started this company a couple of years ago after I retired my cleats and moved to Minnesota.

Tech has always been my thing.

Fucked around with it in college, got a degree in computer science while I played with Maddox at HOP University, and closely followed popular tech companies during my playing days.

Now I own Catch Tech, where my team helps other companies develop apps that mimic and interact with their websites.

Among other things.

Those other things got me into trouble a few times in my twenties, but I keep those activities to a minimum nowadays.

I grin, thinking about Tony.

It was good to see him at Maddox's party. Even if he is the one who got me into the less legal side of the World Wide Web.

But what's a little hacking between friends?

"Why are you smiling like that?" A feminine voice sounds from my doorway.

"Thinking about Tony Stoleman," I tell Hannah.

She snorts as she steps into my office.

Hannah, wife of my best friend, is the person who runs my accounting department. And her presence reminds me that I have actual work to do.

Leaning forward in my chair, I rest my elbows on the desk and focus my mind on the present.

TWENTY-FIVE
NATE

From the conference room, I look down at the courtyard below.

Where my company picnic will be held in less than an hour.

A dozen stories down, I watch the head of red hair move between tables and umbrellas, organizing the food she's worked so hard to prepare.

It's been nearly two weeks since I saw Rosie. Since I had my hands on her. But now that I know it's *her*, I can recognize her from this distance.

How I didn't recognize her...

How I forgot...

I slide my hands into my pants pockets.

I've done a lot of thinking since she ran out of that pantry.

A lot of thinking and a lot of remembering. And every unlocked memory makes me feel just a little worse.

I remember that last day in the woods.

I felt sick all morning.

I'd been dreading telling her I was moving.

We were just kids, but I knew it would hurt to tell her goodbye.

And it did. It sucked. It was hard for my twelve-year-old self to face.

But her reaction was... bad.

I'd forgotten about it. Somehow pushed it out of my brain. But I remember her crying.

Sobbing.

And I remember that she'd said something about her dad that made me believe he might be hurting her.

My stomach twists.

Please let that not be true.

He was there when I tried to see her one last time. And even in my distant memory, I remember him being scary.

I think of those *less than legal* people I know and wonder if we need to go fuck up his life. Some belated justice for scaring young Rosie.

I inhale deeply.

That same night, I wrote Rosie a letter. Left it at our spot in the woods, under that bag of marshmallows. But I never heard back from her. And I have to wonder if she even got the letter.

She might have gotten it and chosen not to write. But it's just as likely a squirrel took off with the bag of marshmallows, and the letter disappeared into the woods.

Leaning closer to the glass, I watch Rosie tip her face back, like she's soaking in the sun.

Since the pantry, I've thought about that first moment when Rosie opened the door.

Over and over, I've replayed it.

Her nervousness.

How quiet she was.

That constant shimmer of tears.

How I offered her a fucking signature because I thought she was an overwhelmed fan.

I rock back on my heels.

I'd say I owe her an apology for that. But considering Rosie let me finger her without telling me who she really was... I think we're even.

With that in mind, I step away from the windows.

Time to go check in with my caterer before the picnic starts.

TWENTY-SIX
ROSALYN

"Looks good," I tell Presley.

"Thanks." She flicks a rogue ice cube back into the cooling tray. "I think just the desserts are left to get outta the van. I'll get it if you'll organize the spring rolls."

"Deal." I nod.

After discussing the menu with Blake, we agreed cold food was the easiest for logistics and the most refreshing with the warm summer weather.

And even in the heat, hauling ice around in our wagon is still easier than setting up grills and warming pans.

So we have cold salads and pastas, mini sandwiches and chilled chicken skewers.

The courtyard thankfully has tables and chairs already in place, with bright red umbrellas sticking out of the center of each table. And Blake arranged for a row of food tables, also under umbrellas, so no one should be getting sunburned this afternoon—my pale ass included. And the shade means that the ice should last through the ninety-minute event.

Honestly, I love working corporate events. They're short and usually drama-free.

Presley takes one step away from the table to get the desserts. But before she takes a second step, she freezes.

"What?" My heart jumps. "Did we forget something?"

Presley shakes her head, but she's not looking at me. Her wide eyes are looking *past* me.

I have the irrational urge to ask her if she sees a snake. But her expression might be more shock than fear.

"Should I hold still or turn around?" I ask in my best *cautious* voice.

"Um... probably hold still," she replies quietly.

"What?" I hiss. "Is it a fucking snake?"

She blinks and moves her gaze to my face. "What?"

"Never mind." I shake my head.

Her stunned expression lifts into a smile. And I don't trust it.

"I'll go get those desserts." Presley keeps smiling as she rushes past me.

I barely stop myself from shouting after her, still not completely convinced it isn't a snake.

Slowly, to avoid any sudden movements, I turn around.

And then it's my turn to freeze.

Because striding across the lawn is a man.

A tall man with tousled brown hair, mesmerizing hazel eyes, and a body made to climb.

A body wrapped in tailored pants and a tight black T-shirt.

His perfect lips are in a flat line, and I know his trimmed beard would feel scratchy against my mouth.

I take one step back.

I don't even mean to. I just do it.

Nathan shakes his head once, and I stop.

My heart is already beating wildly, and it only gets worse as he closes the distance between us.

I remind myself to breathe.

Nathan comes to a stop before me.

"Hello, Rosie."

Rosie stares up at me with wide blue eyes.

She's so fucking pretty.

So fucking stunning.

And at seeing me, her first instinct was to back away.

Run away.

My jaw ticks.

I want to grab her shoulders and ask her why she ran from me.

And I want to shake her for trying to do it again right now.

I want to slam my mouth against hers.

I take a slow inhale through my nose.

And I keep my hands in my pockets.

"N-Nate?" she whispers, glancing around. "What are you doing here?"

I give her another small head shake. "You call me Nathan."

She digs her teeth into her lower lip.

I hadn't planned to say that, but I don't want her calling me Nate. I don't want her pretending that we have no history.

"Nathan." She whispers my name, and the gentle sound of it goes straight to my balls. "What are you doing here?"

The side of my mouth pulls up. "Thought I'd make sure things were going smoothly before my employees come down."

"Your..." Her brows furrow. "Your employees?" She glances up at the building beside us.

I nod.

"Catch Tech is your company?" She asks, like she can't believe it.

I slide my hands out of my pockets and mime catching a football. "Wide receiver, remember?"

She rolls her lips together. "I remember you foisting your signature on me."

My lips pull flat.

I want to tell her it's her fault for not telling me who she really was.

I want to say she was the one acting all nervous and weird.

I want to tell her women act like that around me all the time.

I want to make it her fault.

Because all that is true.

But it's not the whole truth.

"I'm mad you didn't tell me who you were." I take a step closer. "But I'm more mad that I didn't recognize you." I squeeze my hands into fists, the anger at myself still so fresh. "I should have recognized you. And I didn't."

TWENTY-EIGHT

ROSALYN

That spot low in my belly twists.

I should have recognized you.

It shouldn't hurt.

It's not like this is new news.

But hearing him admit it out loud...

"I'm really sorry, Rosie." Nathan's tone is nothing but sincere.

I know he means it.

And if he's going to be truthful, then so will I. "It's been a long time, Nathan."

He shakes his head. "I should've—"

"I saw you on TV," I blurt out.

His mouth snaps shut.

This is all so... complicated.

I try to slow my racing heart.

I can't believe Nathan is here. And I can't believe this is his company's picnic.

But I didn't set out to deceive him the night of that party just so he'd end up feeling guilty.

He narrows his eyes. "You watched my games?"

"No." I blush, not sure if it would be better or worse if I had. "I was always too busy."

Nathan nods toward the table of food behind me. "Building your own business."

Multiple jobs. Starting a new life. Running from my past.

"Something like that," I answer.

"But you saw me on TV?" His eyes are still narrowed, like he's trying to figure out why this is relevant.

I take a deep breath. "I was in a gas station, and there was a TV on behind the counter. Some after-game interview thing was playing, and... they said your name. That's how I found out you played. I hadn't known." I meet his serious gaze. "I didn't recognize you either. It—"

Memories of how I felt in that moment crawl up my throat, stopping me from saying more.

It was such an awful feeling. Realizing I didn't know my childhood friend anymore. Especially after all the letters...

I swallow down the lump of sadness building in my throat.

But that friend is here. Standing in front of you, after all this time.

Nathan takes another step forward, putting us closer than professionally acceptable.

I try to blink away the building tension in my eyes, but a traitorous tear slips from my lashes.

"Aw, fuck." Nathan reaches up and brushes his thumb across my cheek. "Please don't cry, Beautiful."

He shuffles a bit closer.

His scent surrounds me. The same expensive cologne that clung to me after I'd clung to him in that pantry.

"Why am I here?" I whisper. Worried this might all be some game.

Knowing I couldn't handle it if it is.

"Because I wanted to see you again," he whispers back. No mincing words. No pretense. "And because your meatballs are delicious."

A puff of humor leaves my lungs as another tear breaks free. "You should've told Blake. There are no meatballs on the menu."

Nathan swipes his thumb across my cheek again. "Next time."

I let those words sink into my chest.

Next time.

Nathan leans closer. "I have one question."

"Just one?" We're still whispering.

"For now." He's so close I can feel his exhale on my lips. "Did you think about me when you made those marsh-mallows?"

The marshmallows at the party.

The dessert I make for every event.

My mouth opens. But I don't reply.

Because I don't want to.

I don't want to tell him they remind me of him every time.

I don't want to admit that I learned how to make them when I was sixteen just so I could pretend I was making them for him. So I could feel close to him.

I can't lay that much of myself out for him.

Not like this.

Not when my heart feels like it's going to crawl out between my ribs.

He makes a humming sound as he straightens, his hand sliding off my cheek. "Interesting."

I roll my lips together.

He might not know the details, but apparently, the truth was still written across my face.

The sound of a wagon rattling has me taking a step back. "I have to finish setting up."

Nathan takes his own step back. "One more thing, Rosie."

Every time he uses my old nickname, a piece of the wall I've built around myself cracks.

I exhale. "What is it, Nathan?"

I swear his eyes darken as he swipes his tongue across his lower lip. "Tell me what's for dessert."

I know what he's really asking. And there's no point in avoiding it. He'll either know now or when he comes back to eat.

Presley pulls the wagon up next to me.

Without explaining myself, and pretending my cheeks aren't flushed, I pull out the tub I want from the stack.

Lifting the lid, I pick up one of the two-toned pink and green squares.

I should be using tongs. But it's for Nathan. And after the pantry, we're beyond being professional.

I ignore the giant grin on Presley's face as I turn back to Nathan.

"It's cherry lime." I explain the colors as I hold it out.

Nathan slides his fingers against mine as he takes the marshmallow from my hand.

He bites off half. Then, as he chews, he looks at the half-eaten treat, inspecting it before putting the rest of it into his mouth.

My eyes slip down to watch his throat as he swallows.

I can't believe he put it together just from the s'mores from the Lovelace party. But he's right. I did think about him while I made these.

I always think of him when I make marshmallows. How could I not?

And I didn't really intend for them to become my signature dish, but they have.

Nathan holds his hand out. "One for the road?"

I've also always wondered if he'd like them. Or if he would've outgrown them. And now I have my answer.

Presley thrusts the tub in front of me.

I pluck another marshmallow out and place it on Nathan's exposed palm. "Don't spoil your appetite."

His eyes drop to my mouth. "Impossible."

Heat fills my veins, and Nathan drags his eyes lower, over my chest, before he turns and strides away.

When Nathan disappears into the building, Presley pretends to collapse over the wagon. "God. Damn. How do you two make marshmallows hot?" Still draped, she lifts her head to look at me. "Tell me we're here because he wants to make sweet, sweet love to you."

I snort and roll my eyes. "You're ridiculous."

Ignoring her reply, I turn back to the food table and distract myself with work.

TWENTY-NINE
NATE

"You did good." I clap Blake on the back.

The kid—who's actually a man in his twenties—stumbles forward, dropping his brownie into the grass. "Oh, uh..."

He bends to pick it up, and I can't stop my eye roll. I hardly touched him.

I'm sighing to myself when my gaze lands across the courtyard, and I find Rosie watching me.

She glances away quickly, but I see her fighting a smile.

"Thanks, Mr. Waller. I'm glad it all came together." He brushes the brownie off, then takes a bite.

I've given up on correcting him. He's clearly never going to drop the *Mr.* bullshit.

"You can have tomorrow off. Paid," I tell him.

Blake's brows shoot up. "Serious?"

"Serious."

"Hey, Blake." One of my employees stops on the other side of me. "Great job on the caterer."

"Thanks," Blake replies cheerily.

"Where did you hear about her?" she asks my assistant.

I slowly turn my head to look at Hannah.

"Rosalyn?" Blake makes a thinking sound, but I keep my eyes on Hannah. "I think her card was just with the planning stuff."

"That's handy," Hannah replies to Blake but slowly turns her head to look at me.

It *was* handy.

Easier than framing a baby.

And after Blake booked Rosie's company, I made sure to be the last one out of the office, and on my way past his desk, I took the card back.

It's currently in my wallet.

And if I take it out to run my thumb pad over the raised letters every night, that's nobody's business but my own.

"Blake, do you mind if I talk to Waller for a moment?" Hannah leans around me to ask him.

"No problem." Blake is already backing away as he answers.

I'm a good boss.

Fair. Considerate. And yet Blake can't seem to get away from me fast enough.

"You intimidate the poor guy," Hannah says like she's reading my mind.

My face scrunches. "That's dumb."

Hannah laughs. "It's true."

"If this is gonna be a lecture, just know that the only way I could go easier on him is if I did his job myself."

She snorts. "First, this isn't a lecture. It's an investigation."

"Investigation?" I turn to face my lead accountant.

Hannah keeps her gaze forward. In Rosie's direction. "Second, Blake will settle into his role. Even if you did spring this whole picnic thing on him."

I turn so I'm back to facing forward, shoulder to shoulder

with my best friend's wife. "I have no idea what you're talking about."

Hannah hums. "It's funny"—*I know this isn't going to be funny*—"I told Maddox about the *annual* picnic, and he said it was the first time he'd heard of it." *Fucking Maddox. Doesn't he understand bro code?* "Which means it was a recent idea. Which is cool, but then I was wondering if annual would be the correct term for the event." She pauses, and I'm sure it's for dramatic effect. "Technically, it doesn't matter if it's inaccurate, but I had to itemize the expenses, so I had to look at the event name over and over." It takes all my strength to not pinch the bridge of my nose. Leave it to Maddox to marry a damn nerd. "Then I saw the caterer's name." Another pause. "And what a lucky coincidence that I gave you her card not more than two weeks ago. Good timing."

I hum.

"Except there's one other thing."

Of fucking course there is.

"And that would be?" I play into her hand.

"The way you look at her."

I sigh. "And how do I look at her?"

Hannah waits a beat. "Like you already love her."

I can't stop looking at him.

He's so... magnetic.

Handsome. Tempting. Built.

The kind of man that makes you want to break the rules. No matter how dangerous the consequences might be.

His eyes meet mine, and I look away.

I can't believe I cried when I talked to him.

Crying is literally the last thing I want anyone to see me do. But my emotions got the best of me.

That night, when I first saw him on TV, it broke a part of me.

And to talk about it, in front of the man himself...

When *he* brushed my tears away...

It was gentle. Intimate.

And it healed a part of me.

Then he asked about the marshmallow...

Nathan figuring out my obsession with the little sweets should have been mortifying.

But he made it sexy.

And he looked at me like he wanted to devour me next.

And I don't know what to do with that.

Don't know what to do about Nathan, period.

My eyes lift on their own, back to *him*. Except he isn't standing across the yard anymore.

He's walking away.

THIRTY-ONE
NATE

I don't turn around.

I want to.

I can feel Rosie's gaze on me.

Can feel her attention.

But this isn't the time—or place—to sort out what's so obviously between us.

I slide my hands into my pockets, where I have three marshmallows shoved in each, and keep walking.

THIRTY-TWO
ROSALYN

The setting sun reflects off my windshield as I park in my assigned spot in front of my apartment building.

Nathan never came back after he left, and I'm still kicking myself over how let down that made me feel.

I haul my work backpack off the passenger seat and sling it over my shoulder.

Slamming my door behind me, I look at the sliding door on the side of the van and groan.

I want to leave all the tubs and containers for tomorrow. But I also know I'll hate myself if I do that. So, with a sigh, I drag the door open and take an armful of containers.

It takes some juggling to get through the building's front door. And I break out in more than a little sweat as I carry everything up the two flights of stairs to my door. But I eventually get inside and dump the pile of tubs on my dining table.

The downside of corporate is that they don't often make a plan to keep the leftovers, but I know a gal over at Marie's House—a place that houses families and women in need—who is always happy to take any extra food for their residents. So after dropping Presley off at home, I stopped there, meaning I'm home later than normal.

I eye the clock, wanting dinner of my own, but I drop my bag on the floor and head back down to my van.

THIRTY-THREE
NATE

I hesitate, my finger hovering over the screen.

I could just call her.

I have her phone number from her card.

But I want *her* to call *me*.

I want her to be the one to reach out.

And I could lie to myself about all the reasons why.

But it's simple.

I just want it.

I want her to push through whatever resistance is holding her back.

I want her attention.

I inhale. Then I press the submit button.

THIRTY-FOUR
ROSALYN

The wine sits on my tongue, and I close my eyes as I soak in the rich flavor.

My lower back aches from maneuvering all the large tubs and lids in my cramped sink, but I got everything washed.

I could've saved some for the morning, but now I can sleep in.

It's a mild evening, and the breeze from the open balcony door feels nice after a day dodging the sun, moving from umbrella to umbrella.

I adjust my feet on my little coffee table and lift the wine-glass back to my lips.

But before I can tip my glass back, my phone vibrates with a notification.

I lift it off the couch arm.

It's a new email for my business account.

Opening it, I see it's the confirmation for the final payment for today's event.

Then I set my wine down and hold the phone closer to my face.

Is that...?

He wouldn't.

I close the email, then reopen it.

"What the fuck?" I whisper into the darkening room.

I pull up my bank account.

My pulse is skittering.

I don't know how to feel about this.

I refresh my bank app, and sure enough, the extra eight thousand dollars is still there.

An eight-thousand-dollar tip.

I plant my feet on the floor and lean forward.

What is he doing?

I've gotten some big tips before. Even a few thousand dollars once.

But nothing this big, and certainly not for this small of a job.

Eight. Thousand.

My head spins, and—probably against better judgment—I pick my wine back up and take another sip.

Then another.

I can't accept this.

I can't...

Eight.

An image of myself, sitting on the forest floor, crying my eight-year-old eyes out flashes into my mind.

Is that why he chose that number?

Because the last time we saw each other was when I was eight?

I gulp the wine this time.

The money would be nice. And if it was from anyone else—literally anyone else—I'd accept it.

I stare at my new bank balance and groan. Because I know I can't keep it.

Even if I never see Nathan again. With our history. With what happened in the pantry... I have to give it back.

Swallowing down the rest of my wine, I stand.

Leaving the glass next to the sink, I turn off the few lights that are on and head to my bedroom.

Inside my nightstand, beside the velvet bag holding my silicone friend, is a small piece of paper. With Nathan's signature.

And his phone number.

THIRTY-FIVE
NATE

It only takes a few minutes before it happens.

My phone alerts me to a text.

> Rosie: Nate, this is Rosalyn Edwards.
> Although generous, I can't accept your tip.

I smirk at the phone.

Does she realize how that sounds?

And does she really think I need her last name to know who she is?

I might've forgotten about Rosie once. But I remember her now.

> Rosie: It's too big.

This time, my smirk grows into a grin.

> Rosie: Seriously, I can't take it.

I shake my head and type out my reply.

Me: Rosie, you're killing me.

Me: And it's Nathan.

As I wait for her to realize what she said and how it sounded, I lower my left hand and stroke Charles.

He rumbles under my touch. And when I stop—hovering my hand over his ribcage—he twists his neck so he can bump his little orange head against my palm.

"Such a needy boy," I pretend to complain.

He meows in response.

I look back at the phone screen and wonder if Rosie is lying in bed like I am.

Wonder if she's stripped down to her underwear, like I am.

Wonder if she's feeling warm.

Wonder if she's read her texts and is thinking about my cock now.

Wonder if she's remembering the way she spread her fingers around the base of it when she shoved her hand down my pants in the pantry.

And I wonder if she'll touch herself tonight.

THIRTY-SIX
ROSALYN

I crawl onto my bed, face-plant onto my pillow, and groan. Loudly.

What is wrong with me?

It's too big.

I can't take it.

I groan again.

And I can't even act outraged over his response being unprofessional.

He may have been my client tonight, but he was my friend first. And somewhere between friendship and client, I managed to shove my hand down his pants and get my fingers on his oversized dick, so professionalism is out the fucking window.

I roll onto my back and stare at the phone screen, wishing I had someone to tell me how to reply.

I decide to go with avoidance.

> Me: Nathan, thank you for the $8,000 offer, but I can't allow you to do that.

> Nathan: Rosie, it wasn't an offer. It's already complete. And it's for a job very well done.

I roll my lips together.

> Nathan: And if you try to reject the payment, I will just submit it again.

I was wondering whether there was a way to return a payment. But I believe Nathan. I think he would just send it again.

I just don't understand why.

Why is he doing this?

Does he know that I'm... struggling?

And it's not like I'm struggling to buy myself groceries. I'm not there. Anymore.

But I need upgrades.

I need a bigger place. Bigger kitchen. More storage.

I need a garage to park in and an elevator instead of just stairs so I can load up for events without having to walk food down two flights of stairs and through the weather to pack my van.

I need enough *needs* that I wouldn't use this extra money for *wants*.

But none of that changes the fact that it doesn't feel right.

I sigh.

> Me: Why?

> Nathan: Because you earned it. I'm not taking it back, Rosie.

> Nathan: Moving on to more important things...

> Nathan: Will you join me for a drink tomorrow night?

I blink at my phone.
Then I blink again.
Join the famous Nate Waller for a drink? In public?
It begs the same question.

Me: Why?

THIRTY-SEVEN

NATE

"She's asking me *why*, Charles." I shake my head.

My fellow bachelor shares an incredulous look with me.

Why?

Why do I want to get a drink with a beautiful woman?

Why do I want to see Rosie again?

I type out my answer.

> Me: Because talking to you for five minutes today wasn't enough.

> Me: Because I want to know you again.

THIRTY-EIGHT
ROSALYN

I press a hand over my chest.

Because I want to know you again.

At this rate, having Nathan back in my life is going to give me heart failure.

Just like dear old Dad.

> Nathan: Say yes.

I close my eyes.

This is a bad idea.

I shouldn't.

> Me: I have to work Saturday morning.

As soon as I hit send, I realize that could be taken the wrong way.

> Me: Meaning I can't stay out late tomorrow.

"This fucking girl."

Charles purrs louder.

> Me: 8pm at the Booze Hooch

I send the St. Paul address.

> Me: Unless that's too far. I don't know how close you live.

FORTY

ROSALYN

I lift my head to look out my bedroom window, toward the St. Paul skyline.

> Me: That's not too far.

> Nathan: So you'll come.

I drop my head back down.

> Me: I'll try.

> Nathan: Promise me.

My fingers hesitate over the screen.

> Me: I have a job tomorrow. If something goes wrong, I could still be working at 8.

It's mostly true. Though I doubt anything would keep me that late.

> Nathan: I can wait all night.

He's not going to let this go.

And if I'm honest with myself, I don't want him to.

> Me: Fine. If I'm going to be late, I'll let you
> know.

I lower my phone onto my chest and roll my neck so I'm staring at my closed closet door.

My phone vibrates.

And keeps vibrating. With a call.

My poor pulse skips again.

Nathan is calling me.

Nathan. Is calling me.

I sit up.

We were texting. He doesn't need to call.

The phone continues to vibrate.

I take a deep breath. And press the button to accept.

"Hi, Rosie."

My eyes roll back.

Saying *hi* should not sound that erotic.

I hold the phone a few inches from my ear so he hopefully can't hear how out of breath I feel. "Hi, Nathan."

He lets out a short hum of appreciation that I feel in my nipples. "I just need to hear you say it."

"Your name?" I ask quietly.

Another hum, with a hint of humor. "No, though, that was a nice bonus. I need to hear you promise you'll come tomorrow night."

I swallow as his voice vibrates through the phone against my palm.

"I promise," I whisper. Meaning it.

"Good girl." His words crawl across the line. "Sweet dreams, Pretty Rosie."

Then he hangs up.
And I reach into my drawer.

FORTY-ONE
ROSALYN

I take a deep breath in an attempt to steady my nerves, then I pull the door open.

Cool air flows around me as I enter the Booze Hooch, and I force my shoulders to relax as I step through the entryway.

My Uber got me here right on time, but I have a feeling Nathan is already here.

Except the bar is so packed I have no idea how I'll find him.

Fucking Nathan.

How did I let him talk me into this?

I take a few more steps into the crowd and have to stop myself from biting my lip so I don't mess up the gloss I applied in the car.

I tried not to overdo my look, but I still did my makeup and hair as though this was a date and not just old friends catching up.

Old friends who finger each other.

I shuffle another step, then reach back and lift my hair off my neck, letting the cooled air flow over my heated skin.

The whole ride over here, I did nothing but stress.

Stress about wearing my thick, straight hair down.

Stress about the low-cut tank top I chose to wear. About the flowy pants that felt casual before but now feel a bit too dressy.

My sandals are silent amid the noise as I shuffle and glance around.

In my hand, my phone vibrates.

Nathan: Back left corner, Beautiful.

Old friends who call each other Beautiful.

I slowly lift my gaze.

The lighting is dim.

Tall tables fill the center of the room, booths border the perimeter, and people are standing everywhere. But in the back, standing tall, with a hood pulled up over his hair, is the man I'm looking for.

I slip my phone into my purse.

I have the length of the room to compose myself.

It's just drinks.

Just some catch-up.

No expectations.

FORTY-TWO
NATE

I watch her duck and swerve through the throng of bodies. And I think about what Hannah said.

I haven't stopped thinking about what Hannah said.

How do I look at her?

Like you already love her.

I rest my hands on the tabletop to keep myself from pressing my palm over my heart.

It's impossible.

Impossible to love someone I don't even know.

But... it's Rosie.

Her deep red hair flashes as she passes under an overhead light.

It's *my* Rosie.

And I probably don't love her. I don't know that I've ever really loved a woman. Not like that. But there's something there.

Something I've never felt before.

Something that feels a little like destiny.

She emerges from the crowd before me.

Destiny wrapped up in a curvy little package.

FORTY-THREE

ROSALYN

I stop across from Nathan, the tall round table between us.

His eyes are intense on mine. The irises dark in the shadows under his hood.

He's wearing a gray T-shirt under his unzipped black hoodie. And the sleeves of his hoodie are pushed up, bunching around his forearms. It's a little warm for the hoodie, but it's inconspicuous all the same.

And it might keep people from realizing who he is, but the whole getup... just makes him look hot as hell.

When I finally drag my eyes back up, I find his are taking me in, trailing down my body.

He's touched me. Kissed me. Seen me. But right now, I feel like he's stripping me naked.

And I finally accept that this was never going to just be drinks.

FORTY-FOUR
NATE

She's a goddamn goddess.

I already know this.

But seeing her tonight. In that outfit... I never had a fucking chance.

And if I get my way, this evening will end with my handprints on her ass and her coming on my cock.

Someone bumps into her, and she takes an unsteady step closer.

I narrow my eyes at the back of the man who caused her to stumble. And my weight shifts as I ready myself to go after him.

But then a hand settles atop mine on the table.

I snap my gaze back to Rosie.

She's beside me.

Touching me.

Calming me.

I turn to face her.

I'm not a violent man. Have never even thought of beating a man for such a small reason. But as I stand here, staring down into the bright blue eyes of my past, I feel an impossible urge to destroy anyone who has ever harmed Rosie.

"Nathan," she says as she starts to pull her hand away.

And there's only one thing I can do.

FORTY-FIVE
ROSALYN

Quicker than I can process, Nathan hooks his hand around the back of my neck and drags me to him.

I press my hands against his chest to brace myself, but I don't do anything to stop him.

I don't want to stop him.

I let him guide me.

Let him press his lips to mine.

A moan leaves my throat as I do more than *let him* kiss me.

Rosie's lips part, and her tongue slides against mine.

Moaning into her mouth, I tighten my hold.

Her hair is silky against my palm.

Her body is soft against mine.

Visions of stripping her bare dance behind my eyelids, and I'm forced to pull my mouth away from hers.

"Dammit, Rosie," I pant, pressing my forehead against hers. "This isn't what I had planned."

There's a puff of breath against my mouth. "That's a shame."

My lips pull up into a smile, and I open my eyes. "I'll be honest, I had hoped to do this later. But I wasn't planning to start with my mouth on yours." My voice is gruff, but I make it loud enough for Rosie to hear.

"What were you planning to start with?"

I press my thumb against the side of her neck as she speaks, absorbing her racing pulse.

"Well." I tip my head back enough so I can look into her eyes. "I was planning to order us some drinks, ask how your day of cooking was, and maybe let my knees bump against yours under the table."

A soft smile pulls at her mouth. "Sounds very respectable."

I huff. "It would've been."

"We could still give it a try." Rosie tries to step back, but I don't release my hold of her neck.

"Nah." I smirk. "I like this version better."

As I lean in, her smile grows, and I feel those damn words expand inside my ribcage.

Like you already love her.

FORTY-SEVEN
ROSALYN

The sounds of the bar feel like a barrier between us and reality. Like the noise will make it impossible for people to see us.

Like no one will notice us making out like our lives depend on it.

His hand is warm on my neck.

His lips are demanding on mine.

His other hand slides down to grip my side.

I lean in.

And I remember the pantry.

The way I melted into him there too.

The way I let him touch me.

The way I combusted around his fingers.

How he made me shatter without even knowing who I was.

This time, it's me who breaks the kiss.

Nathan's grip loosens as I step back.

"You said something about a drink?" I ask, hearing the breathiness in my voice.

He nods once. "Whatever you'd like."

My gaze drops to his mouth. Then lower.

Nathan clears his throat.

Caught, and not caring, I don't rush my gaze back to his. "Something strong."

"So... not champagne?" His expression is neutral, but I hear the teasing in his tone.

I shake my head. "Not champagne."

Nathan dips his chin and pulls out one of the chairs at the table we're standing beside. "You stay here. I'll find us something good." He starts to step back, then pauses. "Did you drive here?"

I press my lips together, then shake my head.

My eyes are drawn to his throat as he swallows.

"Good." He dips his head toward the tall chair, then he disappears into the crowd.

Good.

I force myself to take a slow breath.

Making out the second we were close enough to touch was not what I expected, but it's oddly worked to break the tension that's plagued me all day. Of course, the stress tension was just replaced with sexual tension, but that can be worked through.

Setting my purse on the table, I take this alone time to climb onto the chair. It's always awkward getting onto these, so I appreciate the fact that Nathan isn't here to watch me shimmy back and forth on the seat, adjusting my clothing.

Situated, I find the back of Nathan's head and watch as he waits for his order.

The hood up makes him stand out in the sea of T-shirts and less, but I get that he does it to hide his identity.

Because he's famous.

It's still hard to believe that the lanky kid from the woods grew up to be a well-known professional football player.

My heart swells.

For all that happened.

For all the ways our lives went in different directions.

I'm happy for him.

I'm happy he got to be happy.

He deserves it.

FORTY-EIGHT
NATE

Pitcher in one hand, two glasses in the other, I turn away from the bar and immediately catch Rosie's eyes on me.

Her expression is soft.

Warm.

And the calmest I think I've seen her.

I lengthen my stride and close the distance between us.

"What's that look for?" I ask, setting everything down on the table.

Her cheeks pinken, and she hesitates. Then she lifts a shoulder. "Just thinking how proud I am of you."

I open my mouth to reply, but no words come out.

How proud I am of you.

My throat tightens.

Fucking Rosie Edwards, walking back into my life after twenty-five years, appearing out of nowhere, saying shit like this, and flaying me open.

Sure, women have complimented me before.

Touched my arms or my stomach, telling me how good I looked. Or congratulating me on a win.

I force down a swallow.

But no one outside my family has ever told me they were proud of me.

And fuck if it doesn't feel good to hear that.

I lean toward the girl with pride in her eyes and press my lips to her temple.

It's all I can do at the moment without embarrassing myself.

Pulling back, I grip the back of the other chair at the table and drag it so it's next to Rosie's.

I keep my eyes averted as I sit.

I keep them averted as I pour us each a glass of watermelon mojitos.

I keep my gaze averted until I turn in my seat. Until my knees bump into hers.

Then I raise them.

And I feel it.

I fucking feel it.

And I don't know how it's possible.

I don't know if it will last.

But I feel it.

I feel the way I'm looking at her.

Like I already fucking love her.

FORTY-NINE
ROSALYN

Nathan locks his gaze on mine as he hands me one of the drinks.

The cold glass is heavy in my grip.

He lifts his own. "To marshmallows."

A small sound leaves my throat, and I press my lips together.

Then I tap my glass to his. "To marshmallows."

Together, we raise our glasses and drink.

The fresh taste of watermelon splashes over my tongue, followed by mint and the mellow heat of expensive alcohol.

It's dangerously good.

I take another sip.

Nathan lowers his glass to the table and turns even more toward me, placing his hand on the back of my chair.

I shift so I'm facing him too, sitting sideways on my chair, just like he is, putting my knees between his.

"So, Miss Rosie Edwards, when did you get into cooking? And when did you start going by Rosalyn?"

I take another drink, delaying my answer, wondering how much truth to give him and deciding on my own question.

"When did you start going by Nate?"

He smirks but still replies. "High school. We'd moved—just to the next town over—and I thought it sounded cooler."

My heart twinges at the thought of him having to move again.

"It does sound cool," I say seriously.

Nathan shakes his head. "It was a teenage impulse that followed me the rest of my life. But now most people just call me Waller."

"Should I—"

"You call me Nathan," he answers before I finish my question. "Just like I'm going to keep calling you Rosie. Now it's your turn."

With nowhere else to put them, I rest my hands in my lap. "When I moved to the Twin Cities, I decided to go by my full name. It sounded more grown up, and it felt like a good way to start the next chapter of my life."

"When did you say you moved here? When you were nineteen?"

"Yeah." I remember him asking this before he knew who I was. And even though I knew it would come up, I don't really want to talk about it.

I concentrate on relaxing my fisted hands and change the topic by answering his other question. "I'd been working in different restaurants since I was sixteen. And so I found a job here as a line cook and started working on my plan for my company."

Fingertips trail through the ends of my hair, and I feel myself tipping my head toward his hand, wanting more.

"Did you go to school for cooking?" He leans closer to me so I can hear him better.

"Just self-taught."

"Impressive." His eyes move to where his fingers are still playing with my hair.

"Not really." I lift a shoulder. "I just couldn't afford college."

His gaze moves back to mine. "You didn't let it stop you. And I've tasted your food, Rosie. It's fucking delicious."

"Thanks," I say quietly.

"Did you end up working in restaurants because you already liked to cook? Or was it working in them that made you like it?"

"I started cooking at home when I was younger." I reach for my glass. "I found an old cookbook in that Goodwill over by the library." I pause, taking a drink as cover. Nathan's family wasn't the type to go to Goodwill, and I feel a little weird having brought it up. "It was a thick Betty Crocker cookbook that was a little banged up and a lot old, but the previous owner had written all sorts of notes around the edges of the pages."

"What sort of notes?" Nathan sounds genuinely curious.

"Random stuff. She—I assume it was a she—would cross out cook times and write in what she thought was better. There were notes on ingredients to add if you wanted to make it sweeter or less salty. Substitutions she'd used if she was out of something. The notes weren't profound or anything like that, but it caught my interest. I'd never really thought about food that much since there wasn't much..." I catch myself. "Since we didn't have that much variety at home."

We didn't have much food in general. Or at least I didn't.

I was stuck with instant packets of soup and peanut butter sandwiches mostly. But I don't really want to talk about that.

Even though I think Nathan knew. I'm pretty sure that's why he started bringing me marshmallows.

Appreciation fills my chest.

He was such a good friend to me.

And I want to tell him.

I was never a scrawny kid. Even when I chose hunger most nights, preferring to stay in my room rather than be near my dad, my body has always just been... thicker.

But Nathan still knew I could use the treats.

Of course, once I figured out how to cook, I finally got to eat my fill, and I filled out my curves even more.

Of course, Dad, classic piece of shit that he was, never missed an opportunity to call me fat. Tell me I should go for a run or that I'd never get a boyfriend if I didn't start cutting back on the calories.

As if I'd wanted a boyfriend.

I'd wanted fewer men in my life. Not more.

A warm hand slides over my shoulder. "What was your favorite thing to make?"

"Soup," I tell him, then I take a long drink of my mojito.

Nathan's brows go up. "And yet you didn't make any for the Lovelace party or for my picnic."

Mentally, I brush away the cloying memories that threaten to pull me under and smile. "Soup doesn't exactly qualify as summer finger food."

Nathan purses his lips. "Fair enough, but I want to try some anyway. I've never met a soup I didn't like."

"I'll make you soup someday, Nathan Waller," I say, even though I'm sure it's a lie.

I doubt we'll see each other after whatever happens tonight.

He takes the glass from my right hand and puts it in my left, then holds his hand out between us.

I lift a brow. "What are you doing?"

"Shaking on it." Nathan holds his hand closer to me.

I roll my eyes, but I place my palm against his. "Is it even binding if we don't spit in our hands first?"

Nathan lifts our joined hands toward his mouth. "If you want me to spit, Rosie, just say so."

His gaze is molten, and I press my knees together tighter and whisper, "Not at the moment."

Nathan drops our joined hands onto his thigh and tips his head back with a groan. "Dammit, Rosie." His hood slides off his head as he shakes it. "You're gonna be the death of me."

A small laugh leaves me at his dramatics. "You started it."

He straightens back up so he can look at me. "And you made it worse. Better. Pick your poison."

I grimace at the word poison while I swallow down more alcohol.

I set my glass down and slide my hand out of his grip. "You've lost your disguise."

Feeling bolder now that my glass is nearly empty, I lean toward him and reach up, my fingers catching on the material of his hood.

Nathan hunches his shoulders, lowering his frame enough so I can pull the material back up over his hair.

The black hood stops at the top of his forehead, but pulling it forward causes some of his hair to hang down into his eyes.

Keeping my attention on my hands, I gently tuck his hair back under his hood, the strands soft against my fingers.

FIFTY
NATE

My eyes close.

The feeling of Rosie's fingers running through my hair is nearly too much.

I press my knees in toward each other, squeezing Rosie's knees between mine. "I'm tempted to mess up my hair just so you'll do that again."

Rosie lets out a small laugh, and it makes me smile.

"Can't have everyone here knowing your true identity."

I crack my eyes open. "Sure can't."

She sits back and lowers her hands to her lap. "What was it like?"

I open my eyes the rest of the way. "What was what like?"

We both reach for our drinks.

"Playing in front of all those people?" Rosie gestures around with her empty hand, like we're in a stadium. "Being famous. Getting recognized." Her hand drops to her lap. "You know it's crazy, right? That the boy I knew grew up to be a freaking professional football player."

I grin as I take a drink.

"I couldn't believe it," she murmurs.

I remember what she said yesterday. "The gas station TV?" She nods.

"I can see how that would be a shock." I try to picture if our roles had been reversed, but I don't know what I would've done.

"I left my stuff on the counter and ran out crying." Rosie snorts and shakes her head before taking another long drink of her mojito.

"I..."

She holds up her hand to stop me.

I quit talking, but I reach up and grip her wrist, then lower her hand to my knee.

"I was upset that I didn't recognize you. I don't want you to think that I was a stalker about it, but I thought of you often while I still lived on that street. Hard not to when I'd see your old house every day. So when I saw you on TV and realized I wouldn't have recognized you if you'd walked past me... it just made me really sad. And it made me realize how much time had passed." She flexes her fingers on my thigh. "I'm not telling you this to make you feel any sort of bad, more to explain why I can't hold it against you for not recognizing me. And when you figured it out, you handled it much better than I did."

I tighten my hold on her wrist. "How would you know how I handled it, Pretty Rosie?" I lean closer. "You bolted out of that pantry before I could react."

She bites her lip. "Sorry about that."

I lean a little closer. "Why did you run? And why didn't you tell me who you were before we..." I trail my eyes down her body.

Her chest hitches on her next inhale.

"I don't have a good answer I can give you," she nearly whispers. "It had been so long. I didn't know if you'd even remember me. And you were flirty, but I didn't think I was actually your type. I hadn't expected... what happened."

"My type?" I narrow my eyes. "Beautiful chefs?"

"Yeah, that's what I meant." Rosie rolls her eyes. "I'm talking about *curvy girls*, you dork."

My mouth gets stuck, half twisted up, half twisted down.

She says curvy girls like she means to say something else. And then, in the same breath, she calls me a dork.

I don't know if I should growl or laugh.

"First, receiver, remember?" I let go of her wrist to hold up my hand, fingers spread. "Big hands. I need big hips to fill them. Big..." I drop my gaze to her cleavage. "Hips," I repeat, not wanting to sound like a total creep. "And second." I grab Rosie's drink and set both of our glasses on the table, then pick up the pitcher and refill them. "You're the one who would do extra credit math assignments for fun. So *you're* the dork."

Rosie laughs, and I realize it's the first full-size laugh I've heard from her.

It's mesmerizing.

I want to hear it more often.

"Thank you," I say before I can overthink it. "For what you said earlier, about being proud of me."

Her smile is so soft it breaks a piece of my heart.

"You don't have to thank me for that. It's true."

"I'll thank you anyway. It means a lot." I hand Rosie her newly filled glass. "And for what it's worth, I think it's really awesome that you own your own company too."

Rosie lifts her glass for a new toast. "To a pair of proud dorks."

I tap my drink to hers.

FIFTY-ONE
ROSALYN

Nathan tells me about his first game.

He tells me what it was like to play in front of tens of thousands of people. *Unreal* was his answer.

Nathan talks about the places he lived.

We finish another round.

I ask him questions about ending up here. And he tells me that he moved here to be close to his best friend, Maddox. But that Maddox thinks he moved here just because he liked the state.

I keep asking questions, learning more about his life, and he keeps answering.

And it's easy. Because talking to him is easy.

Just like it used to be.

We start another round.

He asks me about my company.

Asks me about the name, and I tell him it's a nod to my faraway dream of owning a restaurant.

He asks me how I would decorate the restaurant. And I tell him.

About the wicker chandeliers. The pale peach walls. The comfortable chairs. The marshmallow flights.

He takes a large pull off his drink and asks, "Do you have a boyfriend?"

I slowly shake my head.

"Anyone you're seeing casually?" he asks.

I shake my head again.

"Me either." Nathan holds my gaze.

Tonight has been fun. Comfortable. Easygoing.

But we haven't stopped touching.

His knees pressing against mine.

His fingers in my hair.

My pulse constantly leaping.

I lift my drink to my lips. Not sure what else to say.

Nathan sets his empty glass down next to the empty pitcher. "Rosie."

I swallow down the rest of my courage, then set my empty glass next to his. "Yes, Nathan?"

His nostrils flare like he's holding himself back from something. "I'm going to order a ride home." His eyes drop to my mouth. "Will you come with me?"

I let my own gaze lower to his mouth. "Yes, Nathan."

His lips twist up on the side, and a low sound comes out of his throat.

I expect him to say something more, but he doesn't. Instead, he sits up straight and pulls his phone out of his pocket.

This is going to be the best worst idea of my life.

And as I slide off the chair, I promise myself I'll make the most of it.

Then I'll move on.

FIFTY-TWO
NATE

Rosie sways as she stands, and I reach out to grip her upper arm.

"Easy, Beautiful."

Her skin is so soft and warm under my touch that I can't help but rub my thumb up and down.

Pretty cheeks turn pink before me.

"You okay?" I ask.

Rosie nods and lets out one of her genuine smiles.

I catch it in my mind, tucking it into my pocket for later. For one of those times when that sadness shines from behind her eyes. I can't explain why, but every time I see that darker emotion lurking behind her gaze, I feel responsible for it. And I feel like my new obsession is going to be making Rosie smile.

She reaches out and rests her fingertips against my chest. "I'm going to run to the ladies' room. I can meet you out front."

I shake my head and slide my grip down her arm until I'm holding her hand. "I'll walk with you and meet you outside the bathroom door."

She looks like she might argue, but Rosie just dips her chin in acceptance.

Gripping her fingers in one hand, I use the other to order a ride home.

We split ways when we reach her door, and I step into the men's room.

My vision is slightly unsteady, and as I stare at the bathroom wall, I admit I got a little drunker than I intended. But Rosie seems to be in about the same position, and we've fooled around before, so I think it's okay to bring her home.

I'm bringing Rosie home.

I remember so much now.

Washing my hands, I remember feeling so fucking sad as the weeks went by and I didn't hear from her.

Remember the evenings sitting in my room, looking out the window to our new backyard that backed up to another backyard.

The lack of forest.

The lack of Rosie.

I remember missing her.

And then I grew up. And I forgot.

I forgot all about Rosie. Until she moaned my name in Maddox's pantry.

And now that I remember it all, I want to know even more.

Our conversation tonight was a good start. But it was just a start.

I exit and lean against the hallway, waiting for my girl.

And when the door opens, I hold out my hand, and she takes it.

FIFTY-THREE
ROSALYN

Nathan holds my hand tightly as he guides us through the crowd to the front door.

I feel overheated.

Overstimulated.

Someone looking down walks right toward us, and Nathan reaches out with his free hand to grip the guy by the front of his shirt.

The man looks up, his face instantly hardening at being manhandled.

"Watch it," Nathan snaps. "You almost ran over my girl."

I don't know if it's Nathan's tone or size, but the other man puts his hands up and apologizes.

Nathan lets him go and tugs me forward.

As we pass the man, I bite my lip and keep my gaze on Nathan's back. It feels very inappropriate to smile over the incident, so I do my best not to.

A few steps later, we're stepping out into the night.

The sidewalk is mostly quiet, and I take a deep breath.

Being in the bar together was safe.

We may have kissed, a few times, but it had to stop there.

Now we're heading to Nathan's house, and there will be nothing to stop us.

Which is the point.

But even though I want this, I feel like I might hyperventilate.

Nathan pulls his phone out again, only glancing at the screen before sliding it back into his pocket. "This is us," he says as a black SUV pulls to the curb right in front of us.

I follow him to the rear passenger door. "Is this your driver?"

Nathan grins down at me. "It's an Uber." Then he opens the door for me.

I mouth the word *oh* then climb in.

Last night, after the whole *eight-thousand-dollar tip* thing, I did an internet search for Nate Waller's net worth.

It's rude, I know, but I needed to make myself feel okay about keeping the tip, even though I'd already transferred half of it to Presley.

I didn't actually get an answer for his net worth. I just saw the dollar amount of his last contract. It was over thirty million. For one year.

That was all I needed to see because I can't even conceptualize that amount of money. Let alone a dozen years of playing and making money like that.

Presley has yet to see the new deposit in her account, but when she undoubtedly tries to give it back, I'll mention all those zeros to her. That should make her keep it. Along with the fact that she's more than earned it.

The opposite rear door opens, and Nathan climbs into the seat next to me.

Other than wanting to feel less guilty about the tip, I don't care how much money Nathan has. His richness doesn't affect me. But there's something about knowing he's super rich but still takes an Uber like everyone else that makes me smile. Even if it is one of the big fancy Ubers.

He catches me smiling. "What's that look for?"

I shake my head. "Nothing."

"The BCH building?" The driver looks back at us through the rearview mirror.

"That's the one," Nathan replies.

The driver nods, then pulls away from the curb.

Nathan slides closer to me on the bench seat.

He twists and reaches for me, and I close my eyes, expecting a kiss.

Then I hear the sound of nylon against plastic.

I open my eyes as Nathan pulls the seat belt across my body.

He uses one hand to hold the belt away from my body, but when metal meets metal and he clips the buckle in, he lowers the strap, and his fingers graze my chest.

"Safety first." His voice is quiet, and I have to focus on holding his gaze.

My eyes want to drop to his lap.

I want to look for the bulge of what I know is hidden beneath his pants. Because when he said safety, I thought condom.

And I'll blame my recklessness on the booze because I don't want him to wear one.

I don't want to put safety first. I'm already on the pill. And if we're going to have our night together, I don't want to have anything between us.

I lose the fight, and my gaze drops.

Nathan makes a clicking sound with his tongue. "Dirty girl." He says it like he knows exactly what I'm thinking.

Then he slides back across the seat and buckles himself in.

I reach up and aim the air vent in the ceiling toward my face.

Nathan chuckles, but then he does the same thing.

FIFTY-FOUR

NATE

I watch the screen of the driver's phone that's mounted to the dashboard.

Seven minutes.

Five minutes.

Four.

Rosie is silent next to me, watching the city pass through her window as we head into downtown St. Paul.

Three minutes until I have Rosie in my building.

Two.

The way she looked at me when I said safety...

The way her eyes dropped down to my lap...

I'm thinking the same thing you are, Rosie Baby.

I *want to take you raw.*

One minute.

And I'm a man who gets what he wants.

The vehicle slows.

And my wait is up.

FIFTY-FIVE
ROSALYN

The vehicle stops, and my breath catches.

We're here.

And I'm really doing this.

As Nathan thanks the driver, I slip out my door and gulp down air.

When I hear footsteps nearing from around the back of the SUV, I slowly exhale, trying to appear calm.

Nathan appears, and he stops before me.

He holds out his hand. "Ready?"

I slip my palm into his. "Ready."

Nathan squeezes my fingers, then starts across the sidewalk to the massive building before us.

As we step through the front doors into the moodily lit lobby, Nathan reaches up and tugs his hood off.

His hair is messy, and it makes me want to touch it. Makes me want to brush it behind his ears again.

"Evening." A man behind a desk off to the side greets us.

I smile at him as Nathan greets him back.

I take in the man's black polo shirt with *Security* embroidered across one side of his chest.

"Fancy," I whisper to Nathan as we stop at the elevator bank.

He makes a sound of amusement while he presses the Up button. "It's a bit much, but it's close to my work." The elevator doors slide open. "And I like the view."

We step inside.

Nathan selects number thirty-three. The highest floor.

Nerves dance up my spine.

That's high.

The doors slide shut, sealing us inside.

My hand is still in Nathan's, and he tightens his grip.

"Rosie," he says quietly, and I look up at him. "We don't have to do anything you don't want to."

My mouth opens, but he flexes his hand around mine again, and I realize my fingers are trembling.

"That's not—" I stop and force myself to calm down. "I want to. I'm just... heights freak me out a little." I glance away, then back up at Nathan. "And... it's been a while. Since..."

Nathan's chest expands as he turns to face me. "It's been a while since what, Rosie?"

I focus my gaze on his chest. Like a coward. "Since I've been with a man."

He steps closer, his body nearly touching mine. "How long?"

I step back on instinct, bumping into the wall. "Years," I admit quietly. "It's been years."

Six years, to be exact, but embarrassment is already lighting up my cheeks, so I don't tell him the specifics.

I flick my eyes up to meet Nathan's.

But he doesn't look amused or surprised like I expected.

No. He looks hungry.

Nathan steps into me. Pressing himself against me.

Pressing his hardness into my body.

"Fuck," he groans and releases my hand. Warm palms cup my face, and he tips my head back. "How many years, Rosie? How many years has it been since a man stuffed himself inside you?"

I open my mouth to pull in air.

No one has ever talked to me like this. And as much as I didn't want to tell him, I can't resist.

I can't say no to Nathan Waller.

"Six."

His lids slide closed, and he leans into me more. "Six years."

Lust pools low in my belly at his tone, and I arch into him.

Something grows against me.

He's getting harder.

He slides his hands down to the sides of my neck, his thumbs meeting at the front of my throat, his fingers overlapping in the back. "I'm gonna stretch you out, Little Rose. Your poor neglected pussy is gonna be so sore tomorrow."

My knees sway, and I reach up, gripping his forearms.

The elevator doors slide open.

The fingers around my neck tighten the smallest amount as Nathan rocks his hips into me.

We both groan.

I dig my nails into his forearm.

I might have been nervous when we got into the elevator, but this man's filthy words pushed all the worry aside.

Now all I feel is *need*.

FIFTY-SIX
NATE

I drag my hands down from Rosie's neck, sliding my palms over her breasts, before gripping her elbow and pulling her out of the elevator.

The two yards from here to my door feel like a mile.

I unlock it quickly and shove it open, and Rosie follows me inside.

The door slams shut behind us, and I'm tempted to tear her clothes from her body and fuck her right here.

Six years.

The caveman part of my brain shouts that it should be thirty-three years. That she should have waited for me.

But I'll take six.

I keep hold of Rosie's arm as we kick off our shoes and she drops her purse to the floor.

A loud meow breaks through the silence of the condo, and Rosie startles next to me.

"My roommate, Charles," I explain as the oversized furball stands on the kitchen island, yelling at me for being out late.

"He's so cute."

"And he knows it." I start across the large great room, bringing Rosie with me. "I'll introduce you later."

She lifts her free arm and gives my cat a wave as we pass him. And fuck if that doesn't make me like her even more.

We haven't even kissed since the bar, but all I can hear is our labored breathing as I rush us through the dining space, into the hall, past my office, past the workout room and laundry room, past the guest room, past bathrooms.

I don't stop.

I don't give her a tour or tell her where anything is.

I just bring Rosie straight to my bedroom.

FIFTY-SEVEN
ROSALYN

My head swivels as we go.

The condo, or penthouse, or whatever this massive apartment is, has a few lights on, but most of the light comes through the wall of windows that runs the entire length of Nathan's home. He was right about the view, and the ambient city light is enough to see by.

I want to explore.

I want to see how he lives.

I want to meet his cat.

But I want him more.

Want to feel his hands on me more than anything.

Nathan steps through a doorway, pulling me into his bedroom.

It's made up of neutrals. Tans and greens and real wood furniture.

It's calming and classy and so Nathan that it makes my heart ache.

The door slams behind us, followed a second later by another loud meow.

"He'll watch if I let him in."

It takes me a second to understand his meaning.

He's talking about the cat.

But I don't have time to laugh because Nathan is here.

In front of me.

Facing me.

And his eyes are filled with fire.

"I want you naked, Rosie." He reaches for the button of my pants. "I want every stitch of clothing off you."

The bedroom has the same dim light filtering through the windows as the rest of the home, so I swallow down my insecurities and grip the hem of my shirt.

I pull it up and over my head while Nathan unzips my pants.

He pushes them down over the swell of my hips, and they drop to the floor, pooling around my feet.

In my bra and thong, I reach for Nathan. "I want to see you too."

He's staring at my chest.

"Nathan—"

He grips my hips for balance, then lowers himself to his knees.

He grunts, and I don't know if it's from kneeling on the hardwood floors or from the way his jeans are bulging, which can't be comfortable.

"I don't know where to start," he murmurs.

But he lied, because a heartbeat later, he has his face pressed into my cleavage.

His lips open, and I feel his hot mouth on my skin.

The hands on my hips apply pressure as they move up my sides and around to my back.

Expert fingers undo my bra, and he yanks the material off my body.

And then warm lips close around one of my nipples.

His groan vibrates through my body, and I grip his hair to steady myself.

Then he sucks. Hard.

And wetness coats the inside of my panties.

His big hands move everywhere.

Pinching my other nipple.

Cupping my breasts.

Squeezing my ass.

It's all so much.

Those six years might as well be a lifetime, because no one has ever touched me like this.

No one has ever touched me like they might die if they don't touch all of me.

Fingers curl around the band of my thong and start to tug it down.

I shift, helping him get them off, and I know the moment he sees the evidence of my arousal.

"Jesus, you're fucking perfect," Nathan growls as he applies pressure to my ankle.

I lift my foot, letting the pant leg and thong slip free.

Then I repeat the process until I'm standing completely naked in front of a kneeling Nathan.

He leans back onto his heels with my damp panties balled in his fist. "Red fucking curls," he groans.

I squeeze my thighs together.

I hadn't thought to worry about my shaving status, but it sounds like he approves.

He moves his eyes up to meet mine. "Are you on birth control?"

I wet my lips and nod.

I can't form words. Not while Nathan brings my thong up to his face and inhales.

His eyes shut, and he moans.

"You're turning me into a fucking freak, Rosie." He shoves the garment into his pocket and opens his eyes. "And I don't even care."

My mouth is open.

He just sniffed my underwear.

And... and Christ, why was that so fucking hot?

Nathan grips my hips again, and as he leans forward to press a kiss to my stomach, he slides his hands across my ass cheeks and down around to the juncture between my thighs.

His fingers find slickness, and I jolt at the touch.

He doesn't ease up, though.

He doesn't pull his fingers back or still.

He slides them farther between my legs, teasing my entrance.

"Six fucking years," Nathan murmurs against my skin. "The first thing you're going to feel in this tight slit is my cock. Not my finger."

A tongue drags over my nipple, and I snap my eyes open, not remembering closing them.

Not my finger.

He's telling me that he's not going to prep me.

That he's going to shove that big cock of his inside me and nothing else.

Wet fingers slide back the way they came.

Nathan spreads me as he uses a fingertip to trail over my back entrance.

I grab his shoulders as a new heat zips through my body.

"Has anyone ever been here, Rosie?" Teeth trail over my breast. "Have you ever taken a dick here?"

I shake my head.

I shake it again.

"Never," I whimper.

He applies pressure with his finger. "My good girl." Moving his hands, he grips me right where my ass meets my thighs. "But not tonight."

Not tonight.

I can't keep up with him.

His words.

His hands.

His fingers and questions.

I'm spiraling.

Nathan pushes up to stand but doesn't let go of his hold on my ass. So when he straightens, he lifts me off the ground.

Then he literally tosses me onto the bed.

I land on my back, sinking into the soft mattress, my body bouncing with the motion.

Nathan stands at the foot of the bed with hooded eyes, watching.

He shrugs off his hoodie, then reaches back with one hand and pulls off the T-shirt he was wearing underneath.

"It hasn't been six years for me, but it's been a bit." He opens the button on his jeans. "And I'll use a condom if you want me to. But I want to take you bare, Rosie." He pulls down his zipper. "I'll pull out and come all over those pretty tits, just to be sure. But I want to feel you. With nothing between us." He shoves his pants down and grips his length through his boxer briefs. "Now tell me what you want."

My eyes are locked on his hands as he pulls down the band of his boxer briefs and lets his dick free.

My pussy throbs.

"I want that," I say as he strokes himself. "I want what you want."

I knew he was big.

He's a big guy.

I've felt his hardness against me.

I had my fingers touching the base of his cock in the pantry. But he's... large.

And I've never craved that pleasurable sort of pain. But I'm ready to try it.

I'm ready to try anything with this man.

Emboldened by the hard dick he's gripping in his hand, I spread my legs. "I want you to take me raw."

I grip my dick tighter.

Take me raw.

Hearing her quiet voice saying those words...

Precum drips from my tip.

After letting my dick go, I plant my hands on the mattress and crawl up the bed between Rosie's spread thighs.

She reaches for me. And the feeling of her hands on my bare chest sends a burst of electricity through my body.

"My Rosie." I brace my weight on one hand, next to her head.

She slides her hands up and over my shoulders.

Her fingernails dig into my skin, like she's bracing herself.

I use my thighs to push her legs wider.

"Tell me if it's too much." I reach between us with my free hand. "Tell me if you need me to stop." I slide my hand up my length until I'm fisting my tip against her entrance and I can reach her clit with my thumb.

I start to rub.

Rosie's eyes widen, and she digs her fingers harder into my shoulders.

She's so fucking ready for me.

So ripe for my touch.

I drag my cock up her slit and rub the head against her clit, replacing my thumb.

"Nathan," she pants.

I lean closer, putting my lips just against hers. "Let go, Beautiful. I'm not going to fuck you until you let go."

I add my thumb back, making quick circles around her bud.

It's only been a minute.

Only a fucking moment.

But she's there.

I can feel it.

I lower my mouth to her ear. "Come for me, Little Rose. Come, and I'll give you what you want."

I bite down on her earlobe and press my thumb on her clit while shifting my dick back to her entrance. And her back arches.

Rosie throws her head back into the mattress and lets out a throaty moan as her pussy starts to convulse.

That's when I shove my hips forward. Sinking every inch of my cock inside her.

And that's when she screams.

FIFTY-NINE
ROSALYN

Pressing my knees into Nathan's sides, I tighten my arms around his neck, hugging him to me.

A cry rattles around in my head, and it's not until I gasp for breath that I realize it's from me.

"Fuck," Nathan grunts against my ear as he pulls out just an inch, then thrusts back in.

Another cry leaves my mouth. But it's not from pain.

There isn't any pain. Only pleasure.

Unbelievable, immense pleasure.

My pussy is still pulsing with release.

I was halfway through an orgasm when he split me in half with his cock.

I claw at the back of his neck. "Nathan."

"That's right, Beautiful." He pulls out farther, then slams back in. "It's me inside you." He does it again. "And you're taking me so good."

He tries to pull back, but I hold him tighter.

Nathan chuckles, but it sounds strained.

Lips press against my temple. "You okay?"

His tone is sweet, but he rolls his hips as he asks, lodging himself even deeper.

I drag my nails up the back of his neck and grip his hair. "So okay."

I feel his lips pull into a smile against my cheek. "Think you can give me another?"

I tilt my hips, meeting his strokes. "Another?"

Fingers move between us, his hand back where our bodies meet. "You can give me another."

He doesn't ask it this time.

He just starts playing with my clit.

I squeeze my eyes shut. My oversensitive flesh immediately responds.

His body moves over mine.

His hips lifting and lowering.

His cock sliding in and out.

Stretching. Impaling.

Lips move against mine.

Warm, demanding lips, that I'm starting to know, are claiming my own.

Pressure builds in my core and in my eyes.

It's too sweet.

Nathan's kisses are too sweet.

They promise too much.

A tear drips down the side of my face as I open my mouth and swipe my tongue across his lips.

Nathan groans.

His hips move faster.

His tongue pushes into my mouth.

And he's all I can feel.

He's all I know.

"Say my name." He breaks the kiss to growl his demand. "Say my name when you come."

Fingers strum my clit.

His chest hair rubs against my pebbled nipples.

His cock drags against that spot inside me.

And I'm there again.

Sensations and emotions overtake me.

And my body implodes.

SIXTY
NATE

Rosie's pussy clamps down around my length.

"Nathan!" Her cry is hoarse.

Her voice cracks on my name.

And I feel the first pulse of my own release shoot deep inside her channel.

I jerk my hand away from her clit and grip my cock as I pull out of her heat and keep coming.

Her hands slip from my hair, and I push myself up on my free hand so I can jerk off onto her sweet body like I promised.

A rope of release splatters across her belly.

Another across her tits.

But then I aim back down to her perfect little pussy.

Painting her curls and pressing my tip against her clit.

Rosie's body twitches, but she doesn't push me away.

I drag my hand up and down my cock one last time, then I sit back and take in the woman beneath me.

Rosie is a mess.

Cum all over. Her own pleasure coating her thighs. Makeup smeared.

And a smile on her face.
She looks like mine.

SIXTY-ONE
ROSALYN

The mattress jostles as Nathan collapses onto his side next to me.

"Holy fuck." He's panting as hard as I am.

His eyes look glazed. His body is gleaming with a sheen of sweat. His hair is sticking out in every direction.

He looks like perfection.

We lie next to each other for a long moment, catching our breath.

I can't believe we just had sex.

I can't believe I broke my dry spell with famous football player Nate Waller.

I roll my head to the side to take him in again.

I can't believe my best friend from twenty-five years ago grew up to be a famous football player. Who is *built* and knows how to use it.

Another smile pulls across my lips.

He really is something.

A breeze from the ceiling fan overhead ghosts over my skin, making me shiver.

The chilled air has felt good until just this moment. And now, as my body cools, I'm becoming more and more aware of the stickiness. Everywhere.

Nathan notices my reaction to the cold and pushes up onto his elbow.

And good lord, there's a reason they put athletes on magazine covers. Nathan, who has been retired for a couple of years, is still so goddamn muscular.

I can't pull my eyes away from his biceps.

His arm moves, and he reaches out to trail a finger across my stomach. He drags a line of stickiness with his fingertip, and I shiver again.

"Come on," Nathan grunts as he sits up.

I stare at his back muscles while I drape an arm over my bare breasts. "Come where?"

Nathan looks back over his shoulder at me with a smirk.

I roll my eyes. "Oh my god, you're still twelve."

He barks out a laugh and stands from the bed.

"Sometimes feel like it. Unless you're talking about my hips, then I'm eighty." I frown. He smiles wider. "I'm just teasing. It's only like seventy-five."

He reaches a hand out to me, and I take it.

I don't think he's kicking me out, not that I'm going to stay the night, but I have no idea what he's thinking.

Nathan helps me sit up, then grabs my other arm—pulling it away from covering my chest—and uses both arms to drag me to the edge of the bed.

When my feet hit the ground, I stand.

"Now follow me." He turns and heads for a darkened doorway. "A shower is going to be the easiest way to clean up the mess you made."

"The mess I made?" I take a step to follow him, one hand

going back across my chest, basically holding my boobs in place, and the other hand dropping down to cover my vagina.

Nathan might be comfortable walking around bare-ass naked, but I'm not quite there.

He steps into the bathroom and flips on the overhead lights.

The room becomes so incredibly bright.

I hurry the few steps to follow, and once I'm past the doorframe, I flip the light back off.

Nathan lets out a chuckle. "What are you doing?"

I stand with my back to the wall. "It was too bright."

He hums in response, and I listen to his steps cross the room.

Then there's the soft scratching sound of a match being struck.

Flame flickers to life, and the image of Nathan lighting a candle is reflected back at me through the mirror.

He drops the match into the sink, then repeats the process twice more until he has a trio of candles burning between the two sinks on the long vanity.

The glow is the perfect amount. Enough to see by but not enough to illuminate every inch of everything.

Nathan crosses over to the shower stall and slides the frosted glass door aside so he can reach in and turn on the water.

He then opens a cabinet and shakes out a clean towel before he hangs it on the hook next to the shower. "The hot water is pretty much instant, so you can get in." Nathan gestures, then smirks as his eyes travel along my body. "You do recall that I, quite recently, saw you naked, right?"

I huff. "I recall. I'm just not as wildly comfortable walking around nude as you seem to be."

"You should be." He takes a step toward me. "Now get your

ass in the shower and hurry up. If you take too much time, I'll join you. And I'm not sure you're ready for that."

The ache between my thighs throbs, reminding me that no matter how much I enjoyed it, I'm going to be sore tomorrow.

And probably the day after that.

I rush past Nathan and into the shower.

"The body wash is in the black bottle. Since it's hard to read the labels in the dark." Nathan reaches into the shower and slaps my ass.

I swat at his hand and shut the shower door.

It is rather dark in here with the door shut, so I appreciate his tip about the bottles.

I pour some of the body wash into my palms, then lather them together.

The scent is masculine. And expensive. And rubbing the suds all over my body feels like I'm getting an olfactory hug from Nathan.

I do a once-over and rinse, then I snag the loofah hanging off the faucet handle and squeeze more soap onto it.

I didn't want to get a bunch of... stuff on Nathan's loofah. But this round is for me, because this shower is really nice, and I want to enjoy it.

Unfortunately I didn't bring a hair binder with me, and I can't bring myself to ask Nathan for one because I don't want to know if he has stuff from other women around here, so I'm careful to keep my hair behind my shoulders and not get it wet.

Nathan is moving around the bathroom, but I take my time scrubbing myself down, even washing away most of my makeup.

Once I'm rinsed again, I turn off the water.

Nathan opens the shower door before I can, handing me the towel he hung up.

I take it wordlessly and wrap it around myself.

Then I look down.

This is the biggest, fluffiest towel I've ever used.

It almost wraps around me twice. The exact opposite of a hotel experience.

I squeeze myself with it. "Thank you."

Nathan nods. "I have some clothes here for you too." He lifts a small pile, then crosses the room to set them on the vanity.

"Um, I have clothes," I say slowly, the *obviously* left unsaid.

Though I do recall Nathan putting my underwear in his pocket... so I don't think I'll be getting those back.

Nathan shakes his head. "You can't sleep in those."

I blink at him. "I don't need to sleep in them. I need to sleep at home."

He shakes his head again. "Not yet. I'm mostly sober now, but I need a nap before I drive you home."

"Nathan," I say with exasperation, though I'd honestly forgotten we'd been drinking. The euphoria of what we just did overtook my buzz. "I don't need you to drive me home."

"I do. Now get those pajamas on and come to bed."

"Nathan."

He yawns loudly, drowning out anything else I might want to say.

I huff out a breath as he closes the bathroom door.

If I really wanted to, I could walk out of his fancy penthouse and order my own ride.

But... A groan leaves me, because I know I'm not going to do that.

I use Nathan's extra-large towel to dry myself off quickly, then pull on the pair of too-long sleep pants and plain black T-shirt.

It's not exactly a sexy look, but thankfully the waistband is stretchy, and everything is comfortable.

And comfortable is good, because I guess I'm taking a nap with Nathan.

SIXTY-TWO
NATE

I folded Rosie's clothes—minus her panties—and set them on the chair in the corner of the room.

I can see them right now.

They're still there.

But I still half expect her to walk out of my bathroom fully dressed—in the clothes I can see—declaring that she'll find her own way home.

The door clicks open, and I try to stay relaxed.

I'm lying in bed, one arm bent back behind my head against my pillow, the other resting on my chest, wearing a pair of gray pajama pants, same as the ones I gave Rosie.

She steps into the bedroom.

I didn't turn any lights on, but I didn't shut the curtains either, so I can still see her.

And the sight of her in my clothes causes something to shift inside me.

"Come here." My voice is scratchy.

She hesitates, but it's only for a moment.

Rosie crosses to the empty side of the bed, the closest to the bathroom, and pulls the blankets back.

Six years.

I swallow.

If she hasn't slept with a man in six years, then she hasn't *slept* with a man in six years. Because there's no way a warm-blooded male would be able to share a bed with Rosie and not fuck her.

Rosie is giving me so much by staying. Even if she thinks I don't understand.

But I do understand. Even without her telling me. I know her staying is a big deal.

After another second of hesitating, she climbs in.

I wait, but she settles against the pillow, facing me.

"I said come here." I pat my hand against my bare chest.

She huffs, but I lift the arm closest to her, making room.

Slowly, Rosie shuffles closer until her front is against my side.

I lower my arm until it's around her shoulders, then I pull her even closer.

Her exhale is warm on my bare skin.

I move my other arm out from behind my head so I can reach across and palm the back of Rosie's.

I apply a small amount of pressure, and she finally relaxes her muscles and rests her head against my chest.

A satisfied moan rumbles in my chest, and I slide my hand down her hair, down her shoulder and arm, stopping when my fingers find hers.

I hug her even tighter against me with the arm around her back as I wrap my fingers around hers, holding our hands together on my stomach.

This moment feels surreal.

More surreal than when I had her under me.
Than when I was inside her.
This feels more... personal.
Intimate.
This feels like Rosie belongs to me.

SIXTY-THREE
ROSALYN

I squeeze my eyes shut.

I'm the one cuddled against Nathan, but he's the one holding me like I might disappear.

Like he can't let me go.

I inhale deeply, letting his scent fill my lungs.

He's acting like this is the beginning of something.

But I'm the one who knows this won't last.

It can't.

Vibrations wake me.

I crack an eye open.

The room isn't as dark as it was, but it's not light out either. It's that time right before dawn, before the world wakes up.

The vibrations continue, and I blink as I realize there's something heavy and warm on my back.

During the night, I slung my leg up over Nathan's thigh,

and I draped myself farther over his chest, my arm draped all the way across his body.

His arms are wrapped around me, in a hug tighter than I thought possible for a sleeping person. But his arms aren't vibrating.

I lift my head from Nathan's chest and arch my neck to look behind me.

A pair of eyes looks back at me.

I squeak, then try to hold very still.

The cat's face is inches from mine. A cute little orange face, but we haven't been properly introduced, and I don't want to be swatted by startled claws.

"Good kitty," I whisper, trying to remember the cat's name.

Nathan grumbles something, and the arms around me tighten. Then the cat starts purring again, and the vibrations finally make sense.

Not a bad way to wake up.

I give myself a mental shake.

I need to get home so I can spend the day cooking. And I need to leave before I get used to this cozy little wake-up scene.

Nathan was nice enough to let me—a.k.a. make me—stay here so he could drive me home safely, but I won't read into it. He's just a nice guy doing nice guy things.

And I'll admit the sexual tension between us has been real since the moment we first saw each other again. But we've done the deed. We've broken the spell.

Time for me to get back to life.

I look at the cat again.

He looks back at me.

"Excuse me." I stick to my whisper. "But I need to get up."

The cat just blinks at me.

"Please." I lift my shoulder, jostling him a bit.

He lowers his head and licks his paw.

"Stubborn little thing." *Just like his owner.*

Nathan makes another sound, then he starts to move.

Still asleep, he shifts toward me, rolling me onto my back.

"The cat!" I shriek, not wanting to crush him.

Nathan jolts at my outburst, but he's already on top of me.

And the cat, as I should have known, jumped out of the way.

"What?" Nathan's voice is full of sleep, and it's stupidly attractive.

"The cat was on me," I explain, but my words are muffled because Nathan's heavy weight is pressing down on my chest.

He lifts his head to look down at me, then plants a hand on the mattress and lifts some of his weight off my ribcage. "Cat..." He glances past me to where I assume the feline is on the floor. "Oh, sorry about that."

"What? No, I didn't mind the cat. I just didn't want you to smoosh him." I plant a hand against Nathan's chest. "Like you're smooshing me."

Nathan leans his body back against mine, trapping my hand. "Can't have any smooshing." Then he presses his lips to my forehead.

Something tightens around my lungs, and it has nothing to do with the body on top of mine.

Forehead kisses are playing dirty.

The cat meows loudly.

Nathan groans and rolls off me, flopping onto his back. "Dude, it's literally hours before your breakfast time."

The cat meows again.

It's different from the first one, and I have a feeling he's disagreeing with his human.

I push myself up to sit and look down at the gorgeous animal. "What's his name again?"

"Charles." Nathan yawns. "The animal shelter had listed his name as Caramel, but I could tell he didn't like it."

I bite down on a smile as I study the cat and find I have to agree. Charles is much too sophisticated to be a Caramel.

As though he knows what I'm thinking, Charles sits up straighter in what can only be called a *regal* posture.

I sigh.

I need to leave before I never want to go.

"I've always wanted a cat." The admission is out of my mouth before I can stop it. "Ever since I can remember."

Nathan rolls his head toward me. "Yeah?"

I nod.

"Why didn't you get one?" Nathan asks the obvious question.

Because my mom was allergic.

Because after my mom died, my dad would scream at me anytime I mentioned getting one.

Because even after my dad died, I wasn't sure I'd be around to take care of it.

Because sometimes I still worry about my past catching up to me.

Because a part of me doesn't feel like I deserve the unconditional love of a pet.

"Because I work too much." Sadness drips from my words, and I clear my throat. "Speaking of..." I start to climb out of the bed. "I should get going."

Honestly, I could sleep for a couple more hours and still get everything done on time. But I'd rather leave before the light of day.

It'll be better that way.

Nathan lets out another yawn. "Alright. I'm up."

Charles stands and comes over to weave between my feet.

"I'll just order a ride. You don't need to drive me. Go back to sleep." I reach down and run my fingers down Charles's back. His fur is so soft beneath my touch.

"No dice," Nathan says with a stretch as he stands opposite the mattress from me. "You're not getting a ride with a stranger at..." He glances at the clock. "Five in the morning."

I do my best not to stare at the morning wood tenting his pants. "Nathan—"

"Not budging on this, Rosie." His tone is serious.

"Fine." I widen my eyes at him. "Be unreasonable and start your day stupid early."

He smirks. "Glad we agree." He tips his head side to side, cracking his neck. "Just let me brush my teeth, then I'll make us some coffee."

I almost tell him I don't need coffee, but that would be a giant lie.

I always need coffee. Now more than ever.

Charles lets out another loud cat shout and trots after Nathan, who is striding across the room.

They have a similar swagger, and as they disappear into the bathroom, I can't recall ever seeing anything cuter.

I fully intend to use some of Nathan's toothpaste when he's done, but while he's occupied, I'm going to hunt down my underwear.

Except when I circle the bed, I can't find his pants anywhere. Or any of his clothes.

I know he threw them on the floor, same as I did when we first got here. But where my outfit is folded nicely on the dresser, his clothes are nowhere to be seen. Meaning my panties are gone with them.

I'd crouch to look under the bed, but I'm sure they're not there. And the ache between my legs has pulsed with every movement I've made, reminding me exactly what we did last night. And crawling around on the floor isn't going to help that.

Accepting my fate, I pick my clothes up with a frown. I'm really not looking forward to putting these pants on without underwear, but I'm not willing to ask Nathan if I can wear his clothes home.

Not only do I not want my neighbors to see me like this, but I also don't want Nathan to feel obligated to see me again. And taking his clothes home would do just that.

Bundle in hand, I walk through the open bathroom door just as Nathan turns off his electric toothbrush.

He makes eye contact with me through the mirror as he spits into the sink.

The ache between my legs intensifies.

That should not be hot.

I look away and rush across the tile floor into the small toilet room, shutting the door behind me.

SIXTY-FOUR
NATE

I'm pouring coffee into two travel mugs when Rosie emerges from the hallway.

She's no longer in my clothes, and even though she looks fine as hell back in her outfit from last night, I kind of hate it.

Charles bumps his head against my elbow, and I look down, seeing I'm seconds from overflowing my cup.

I set the pot back on the warmer and pat Charles on the head.

Some people think it's gross to have a cat on the counter, but Charles is more than a cat. And I don't limit his freedom.

I scratch behind his ears, and we both watch Rosie as she looks around my condo, taking it in.

It was pretty dark in here last night when we arrived. And I didn't exactly pause to give her a tour. But now, with the kitchen lights on, and with the sky just starting to lighten beyond the glass wall, she can see the space clearly.

Maddox gave me so much shit when I hired an interior decorator, but I have zero regrets. Everything is exactly how I want it.

The light wood floors.

The soft white walls filled with art in tones of green and tan.

I see when her eyes catch on Charles's space.

I press my lips together, wondering what her reaction will be.

Charles is my best buddy, and I'm not embarrassed that I had a custom cat tree built out of real branches that's seven feet tall with half a dozen padded perches for him to sleep on.

It's against the wall of windows, and some could say it's blocking part of my million-dollar view, but I'd argue that Charles deserves the sunshine more than I do.

Rosie's mouth pulls into a wide smile, and I let out a breath of relief.

I don't know what I'd do if she didn't like Charles, but now I don't have to worry about it.

"That's pretty impressive," she says, still looking at the cat tree.

Charles purrs under my hand. "Thanks. Charles wanted a bigger one, but I told him we'd start small."

She shakes her head, the smile still on her face. "Good of him to compromise." She turns her attention toward me and the kitchen.

"How do you take your coffee?" I ask, but I've lost her attention.

Her lips are parted, and her eyes are wide.

I'm not a good cook, hardly passable, but I did want my home to have a chef's dream kitchen. And from the look on Rosie's face, I think I've accomplished that.

The island is... large. It seats eight comfortably on the white and gold stools across the white marble top from where I'm standing.

The base of the island and the cabinets are all a dusky blue, and all the hardware is gold.

Behind the massive stove, the marble goes all the way up the wall to the ceiling in the most over-the-top backsplash ever.

"Is it Rosalyn Restaurant approved?" I ask, breaking her trance.

Charles slips out from under my hand and struts across the counter toward Rosie.

Rosie stops on my side of the island and turns to me. "It's fantastic."

Her tone is so serious it makes me chuckle. "Is it really?"

She nods and absently reaches out to pet Charles. "It's like you plucked my dream kitchen straight out of my mind." Rosie looks down at Charles. "Cat and all." Charles purrs louder. "Can I pick him up?"

Her question is quiet. Hesitant. And it takes me a moment to reply. "Charles? Yeah, he loves being held."

Rosie holds her hands out to him. "Is that true, big guy? Can I give you a little hug?"

Charles steps between her outstretched hands, and Rosie scoops him up.

My no-loyalty cat goes boneless in her arms, and Rosie hugs him to her chest.

I can't hear what she says as she rocks him side to side, mumbling something while she presses her face into his fur. But my heart still melts into a globby puddle inside my ribcage.

My cat and my girl.

I clear my throat. "How do you take your coffee?"

Rosie looks up at me, her cheek still pressed to Charles. "Black is good. But could you add an ice cube so I can drink it right away?"

"Sure thing." I turn to the freezer and pull out two ice

cubes, one for each of us. "I should really make some of those coffee ice cubes I see people do online."

Rosie hums. "I did them once for a summer brunch event. They wanted those big drink dispensers filled with lemonade and cold brew. Worked so nothing got watered down."

I lift my brows as I gently drop the cubes into the coffee. "Genius."

Rosie rolls her eyes. "It's not like I came up with the idea."

"Don't care." I twist the lids onto the travel tumblers. "You still executed it."

"I froze some liquids," Rosie deadpans.

I move closer, holding our coffees. "You don't take compliments well, do you?"

Rosie shrugs, then nuzzles her nose against my cat one more time.

She sets him back on the counter. "Bye, Charles."

She sounds so fucking sad when she says it.

My brows lower.

Does she think she'll never see him again?

Can she really believe this is a one-night thing?

SIXTY-FIVE
ROSALYN

Clutching the coffee to my chest, I turn away from Nathan and circle around his giant island.

Leaving that damn cat has me way too close to crying.

I lift the tumbler to my lips and try to mask my sniff with a sip.

Maybe I could get a cat. I've just always felt so guilty about leaving them home alone on my long days, but maybe they'd be okay. And I could make up for being gone with all the days I'm at home cooking.

Nathan joins me by the front door, and we put our shoes on in silence. And I finally notice that he's dressed the same as last night too. Minus the hoodie.

He hands me my purse from where I dropped it on the floor, and I try not to blush remembering our hurry to get to the bedroom.

The silence continues in the elevator and as we walk through the below-ground parking ramp.

Nathan leads me to an all-black midsize SUV.

It's nice. Like really nice, but I still somehow pictured him in some snazzy sports car, not something so... practical.

Nathan reaches around me to open the passenger door. "Don't forget to buckle up."

I make a humming sound and avoid eye contact as I slip past him.

He closes my door for me, and I use the time it takes him to round the back of the vehicle to quickly buckle my seat belt, setting my purse on my lap and resting my coffee on top of that.

I'm making it weird.

I know I am, and I don't mean to, but I just feel so... melancholy.

Everything has felt so easy between us.

The drinks. The kissing. Talking.

And that fucking cat.

More of that sadness twists around my heart.

Last night was the perfect reminder of why we were such good friends twenty-five years ago. Even as kids, our personalities just... clicked.

Nathan opens the driver's door, and I force my body to relax. I don't want to end our time together with awkward silence.

Turning my head to look at him, I hold up my coffee. "Thank you for this."

The side of his mouth pulls up in a partial smile. "You're welcome."

He sets his drink in one of the empty cupholders between us, buckles in, and starts the engine.

Nathan pauses with his hand on the shifter. "Wanna put your address in the GPS?"

My fingers flex around the cup in my hands.

I don't really want to do that. Giving him my address seems a little too... hopeful.

But my horny ass agreed to let him drive me home, so there's literally no way to avoid it.

I reach out to the screen on his dashboard and start to type in my address.

Before I can finish, the radio clicks on, and voices fill the car.

"Oops." Nathan lifts his hips off the seat and shoves his hand into his pocket.

I can't tell if they're the same jeans from last night, but instead of pulling my panties out, he pulls out his phone.

A second later, the voices stop.

"Podcast," he explains.

"What one?" I ask, curious, as I type in the rest of my address.

When I'm done, Nathan reaches up and rubs at the back of his neck. "Uh, it's the *Pretty Cat* podcast."

I roll my lips together. "Oh."

He glances at me as he starts to reverse the vehicle. "It's about cats."

I nod, trying not to laugh. "I gathered."

Out of the parking spot, Nathan puts his vehicle in drive. "It's actually really interesting. And it's not just about house cats. They talk about big cats too. Like tigers and shit."

A chuckle finally breaks free, and he darts a look at me as he drives up the ramp toward the street.

"I'm not laughing at you," I tell him. "Just at your delivery. You sound so serious."

His cheek twitches. "Cats are serious business."

"Absolutely." I use a sober tone. "Tigers and shit."

Nathan smirks. "You're a little turd."

I snort a laugh, and that's all it takes to break through the funk.

As Nathan pulls out onto the mostly empty street, I stretch my arm out and hit the play icon on the screen.

The podcast starts up again.

I'm curious to hear what they're talking about. And if it's also a way to avoid making conversation for the next eighteen minutes, then so be it.

I relax into my seat and sip my coffee.

Then ten minutes later, I'm listening raptly as to why bobcats don't have tails.

SIXTY-SIX

NATE

I keep glancing at Rosie, watching her react to the podcast with varying facial expressions.

"See?" I turn to face her when I'm forced to stop at a red light.

She grins at me. "You were right. Serious business indeed."

I nod. "Charles is an apex predator."

Rosie huffs. "Is that your takeaway?"

The light turns green, and I take my foot off the brake. "Usually is."

"Uh-huh." Rosie takes another drink of her coffee, then sets it in the empty cupholder next to mine. "Good thing he has his tail, though, with that mountain-size cat thing you have."

"To my knowledge, he has yet to fall off it."

"Well, if he ever does, don't give him a hard time about it."

"Maybe I'll show him some YouTube videos of Siberian tigers hunting. So he can learn some tips." My tone loses its humor as I talk because I'm getting distracted by the neighborhood.

It's not bad. But it's not great either.

And no matter how capable the woman sitting beside me is, I don't like her living here alone.

"I bet he'd like that." Rosie carries on with the cat discussion.

I take the final turn onto Rosie's street.

The streetlamps are still on, but they don't seem bright enough. Because even with the sunrise creeping onto the horizon, the buildings are still covered in shadows.

She sits up straighter. "It's up on the left. The second apartment building."

Her tone has changed too, and it makes me feel like an asshole. I don't want her to think I look down on where she lives. It's not about luxury or wealth. It's about safety.

She points. "You can pull in there."

I turn the wheel and pull into the tiny parking lot in front of her building.

Spotting a van with her business logo, I tighten my grip on the steering wheel.

She lives alone, and her van announces exactly where to find her.

There's an empty spot two down from her van, and I pull into it.

"Thanks for the ride." Rosie unbuckles her belt. "I, uh, it was nice to see you."

I put the vehicle in park and turn to face Rosie.

She has one hand holding her purse in a white-knuckle grip, and the other hand is on the door handle, like she's ready to jump out.

"It was nice to see you too." I tell her the truth.

She gives me a soft smile, then she opens the door and slips out.

Rosie pauses, one hand on the door. "Bye, Nathan."

The words feel like daggers.

Like she's saying goodbye for good. Cutting me from her life.

I want to shout. Want to ask her why she's acting like this.

Why she's been acting like this since I first saw her.

Ask how she can act like the hottest night of my life meant nothing.

I want to ask her why her eyes are full of secrets.

But mostly, I want to tell her I want to see her again.

That I want to see her every day.

That I haven't felt this sort of connection with anyone before. Only ever with her.

But then she shuts the passenger door and walks away.

I clench my jaw, but I don't get out and follow her.

I'll give her some time to think. She clearly needs it—for some reason.

Then I watch her reach out and turn the handle, opening the front door of her building.

No key. No lock. It just fucking opens.

Dammit, Rosie. You need me just as much as I need you.

And I won't quit until you realize it.

SIXTY-SEVEN
ROSALYN

I'm breathing heavier than normal when I finish climbing the two flights of stairs to get to my apartment. And as I unlock my front door, I pretend it's because it's early. Or because I need to work on my cardio. Or that I'm just tired from lack of sleep.

I don't acknowledge that it has anything to do with the fact that Nathan didn't say goodbye.

The fact that he didn't say anything at all.

I shut the door behind me and turn the deadbolt.

I went into last night strongly assuming that it would be a one-night thing. So I don't know why I have this crushing sense of disappointment over that assumption being true.

Everything went exactly as I thought it would.

Liar.

I can't even think those thoughts without my subconscious calling me out.

I figured drinks might lead to sex, considering what happened in that pantry and the sexual tension I felt at the picnic.

But I hadn't counted on the conversation.

Hadn't counted on the way I felt so comfortable around him.

How sitting with our legs pressed together at the bar felt right.

And I never imagined that our sex would be... like that.

My thighs clench as I drop my purse on my kitchen counter.

I continue to my bedroom and think about everything that came after the sex.

The shower. The borrowed clothes. The cuddling. The cat. The coffee.

As soon as I reach my room, I start to strip.

It wasn't supposed to be like that.

Our night together wasn't supposed to feel so... fated.

With my clothes on the floor, I walk into my bathroom and turn on the shower.

I want nothing more than to crawl into bed and sleep through my own personal little pity party.

But I can't.

Because I have work to do.

And because Nathan is now back where he belongs.

In the past.

Charles greets me at the door, and as soon as my shoes are off, I bend down and scoop him up.

He meows.

"I know. I like her too."

He bumps his chin against my chest.

"I'll text her. Just not yet."

Charles lets out a scratchy meow.

I sigh. "I'm not playing games. If anyone is playing games, it's Rosie." I shift Charles in my arms and stride toward my bedroom. "It's like she can't just be happy around me. I get these moments. These glimpses of her smiles, two seconds of a laugh, but then she's back to being shuttered."

The furry body in my arms rumbles with a purr.

"I don't know what the deal is."

Charles purrs louder.

"Dude, I said I'd text her."

He kneads his front paws against my chest, and I change my grip to hold him at arm's length.

"Fine. You win."

I set Charles down on the bed and pull my phone out of my pocket.

SIXTY-NINE

ROSALYN

I stare down at my phone.

> Nathan: Drinks, same time, same place.
> Friday?

I just finished making myself another cup of coffee after my quick shower. And Nathan is texting me, seeing if I want to go out again next weekend, after not saying anything at all when I got out of his car.

> Me: I'm working Friday night.

He replies immediately.

> Nathan: Saturday night then.

> Me: I'm working Saturday night too.

> Nathan: Meet me after.

I drag my teeth over my lower lip.

> Me: Do I get to see Charles?

My question implies we'll end up back at his place. But I figure that's a given, so I don't feel bad about being so forward.

> Nathan: Let me ask him if he'll be home.

I picture Nathan turning to his cat and asking him the question out loud. And I know I'm screwed.

I'm going to say yes to drinks. We'll have another mind-blowing night in his bed. And then, when this thing between us fizzles out, I'll only have myself to blame for my broken heart.

> Nathan: He has lunch plans but said he'll be home by the evening.

Instead of laughing, his response makes me want to cry. Because by the end of this, I'm going to be just as attached to his fucking cat.

I close my eyes and take a breath before replying. Dooming myself to heartache, but unable to stop.

> Me: I'll meet you there.

SEVENTY

Four Hours Later

Nathan: Did you get all your cooking done?

Rosie: It's not even noon.

Nathan: Is that a no?

Rosie: I'm a professional, not a magician.

Nathan: Are you making meatballs today?

Rosie: Not if I keep getting interrupted.

Nathan: Mimes zipping lips.

Sunday - The Next Day

Nathan: How was your event yesterday?

Rosie: No complaints. No ambulances. Calling it a win.

Nathan: What flavor marshmallow did you make?

Rosie: Banana Cream.

Nathan: Banana? Rosie, how could you?

Rosie: What's your problem with bananas?

Nathan: Nothing. When they stay in their lane.

Rosie: There's a banana lane?

Nathan: Obviously. And it doesn't include soiling marshmallows.

Rosie: I'm rolling my eyes.

Nathan: Pics or it didn't happen.

Rosie: You're ridiculous.

Nathan: Your banana marshmallows are ridiculous.

Rosie: They were Banana Cream. And I had a pie crust crumble on top, so basically a banana cream pie in marshmallow form.

Nathan: *snickers at cream pie*

Rosie: Rolling my eyes even harder.

Nathan: Do you have any left?

Rosie: Patience? No.

Nathan: Cute. But you know I'm asking about the marshmallows.

Rosie: Every last one was eaten. Because they're so good.

Nathan: Hmm. How hard are they to make?

Rosie: My recipes are classified.

Nathan: Woman, I struggle making rice. I was not suggesting that I'd try to make them. I want you to make them. But I'm wondering if that's something we can do after the bar or if sobriety is necessary?

Rosie: Sobriety is not necessary.

Nathan: Good.

Rosie: BUT

Nathan: *groans in banana marshmallow*

Rosie: They need hours to rest before eating.

Nathan: So... breakfast marshmallows.

Rosie: You're impossible.

Monday

Nathan: I looked up a standard marshmallow recipe and ordered all the things.

Rosie: It's 7 a.m.

Nathan: But I don't know if you use real bananas or the fake flavor stuff. And I have creamer, but I don't know if that's the cream in banana cream.

Rosie: SEVEN

Nathan: And the recipe included nonstick spray, which is stupid because there are like a million options. So I got the regular kind, avocado, and grapeseed. Because grapes go with bananas.

Rosie: Nathan?

Nathan: Yeah, Beautiful?

Rosie: If you don't let me go back to sleep, I'm going to suffocate you with a sheet of marshmallows.

LOVE
LETTERS

Tuesday

Rosie: *sends picture of nonstick spray*

Rosie: I'll bring the banana.

Nathan: I feel like that's my line.

Rosie: Are you still 12?

I grin at my phone.

This is the first time since our night together that Rosie has reached out first.

I lean back in my office chair and reply.

Me: Perpetually.

SEVENTY-TWO

Wednesday

Nathan: Did you know it's believed that cats are the only mammals that can't taste sweetness?

Rosie: You don't say.

Nathan: Is that a tone I'm picking up? Are you trying to say you already knew that?

Rosie: I may have learned that fact earlier today.

Nathan: *Gasping* Did you listen to the Pretty Cat podcast?

Rosie: I've been batch-baking pastries all day. I needed something to entertain me.

Nathan: Rosie, you know what this means, right?

Rosie: I like podcasts now?

Nathan: It means you're a cat lady, just like me.

Thursday

Nathan: You home?

Nathan: Or at an event?

Nathan: Just tell me you aren't in that pileup on 494.

Nathan: Rosie, answer me.

Nathan: Don't make me track your phone.

SEVENTY-THREE
ROSALYN

I turn the faucet on with my elbow and stick my hands under the water.

I've been slathering and skewering chicken for the last thirty minutes, but I'm finally done.

The TV was playing some reruns in the background while I worked, but I'm pretty sure my phone vibrated with several texts.

Hands clean, I turn off the water and grab a hand towel.

I have a feeling it's Nathan texting.

Not that the pool of candidates is large, but I've messaged with Nathan every day this week.

It's been... unexpected. But at the same time, so Nathan.

I brush back the strands of hair that have escaped my ponytail and pick up my phone.

My pulse jumps at his first text, asking if I'm home, thinking that he might be on his way over.

Then I keep reading, and my heartbeat changes for a different reason.

He's worried.

Me: I'm home.

Me: Was elbow deep in raw chicken.

I read his last text twice.

Me: And what do you mean track my phone?

He can't really do that, right?

Nathan: Good.

Me: Nathan, can you track my phone? Is that what Catch Tech does?

Nathan: I'm going through a tunnel. You're breaking up.

I snort.

Me: You're absurd.

Nathan: Losing signal. I'll text you later.

SEVENTY-FOUR
NATE

I send the text, then lower my forehead until it's resting on my desk.

My heart has been racing for the past forty minutes, waiting for Rosie to reply.

I'm not this person.

I've never felt so irrationally worried in my life.

I inhale slowly.

I was in the breakroom filling my coffee when one of my employees mentioned a big accident on the highway.

They didn't know anyone in the accident. They hadn't even heard anything about anyone being hurt. They were just sharing the news.

But that didn't matter.

My brain instantly went to Rosie.

I tried to shake it off on my walk back to my office. There was no reason at all for me to think she'd be on that stretch of road. But with every second that passed, my nervousness increased, and I ended up sending off a string of messages without a single thought as to how I sounded.

There's a knock on my doorframe.

"Come in," I call, forehead still attached to my desk.

"Uh, Mr. Waller." Blake sounds like he's never seen a man having a mental breakdown before.

I sigh, keeping my face where it is. "Whaddya need, Blake?"

"He doesn't need anything." My best friend's voice booms into the room. I roll my eyes, even though no one can see it. Maddox is as quiet as a stampede. "Except maybe a drink."

I lift my head to look at him, but my view is blocked by a piece of loose paper stuck to my forehead.

I swat it away.

"I have no idea why you'd think that." I sit up straight in my chair. "And this isn't a TV show. I don't keep booze in my office. If I want to drink, I'll just go home."

Maddox grunts as he drops into the chair opposite my desk, Blake already out of sight. "It's nice to be in charge."

I reach into my desk drawer and pull out a miniature bottle of bourbon. "Cheers to that."

Maddox shakes his head, looking up at the ceiling as I take a pull off the bottle. *"If I want to drink, I'll just go home."* He mocks me.

I try not to cough as I swallow down the mouthful.

"Want some?" I set the bottle on the desk.

Maddox leans forward and grabs the bottle. "Of course I do. I'm not going to let you drink alone in your misery."

Maddox, owner of his own whiskey label, doesn't so much as clear his throat after taking a pull.

I take the bottle back from him. "What makes you think I'm in misery?"

"Well, Hannah told me you were sweet on a girl. Then I come in here and find you trying to osmosis your face into your desk." He lifts a brow. "Doesn't scream of a real good time."

"I want you to know this next shot is because your wife has a big mouth, and since I have no recourse against her, I've been pushed to drink." I tip the bottle up.

Maddox smirks. "Her mouth is the perfect size."

I yank the bottle away from my lips, another cough building.

Maddox takes the bourbon out of my hand and sits back.

"You did not just say that." I pound a fist against my chest to get the alcohol out of my lungs. "I don't want to hear that shit about my sister."

Hannah isn't my sister, but Maddox is closer to me than my own brother, so she might as well be.

Maddox replaces the cap on the bottle, essentially cutting me off. "If you don't want to talk about my wife, let's talk about yours."

He's just trying to get a rise out of me by throwing out the *W* word.

But that's fine. He can be a dick. Because while he's smirking, I'm thinking about the fact that I fingered my girl in his pantry, next to his favorite hot sauces, and he has no idea.

Something must show on my face because Maddox narrows his eyes.

I lean back in my chair, pretending my throat isn't still seizing from the straight booze. "Was there an actual reason for your visit?"

"Lunch." Maddox lifts a shoulder. Since his wife works for me—long story—Maddox spends half his lunches over here at my company. "And... I was told to find out the backstory between you and the caterer."

I let my shoulders slump. "Can't you two find something to talk about other than me?"

"Sorry, but it's because we love you," Maddox says with a completely straight face.

I throw the piece of paper at him.

But it's still a flat page, so it goes about four inches before it floats back to my desktop.

"That should cost you at least one of your rings." Maddox shakes his head like he really believes it.

"I was a wide receiver, not a fucking quarterback." I push up to stand. "And if you agree to wait to ask me about the caterer until next week, I'll pay for lunch today."

Maddox stands too. "I didn't say you were invited."

I roll my eyes. "I'm always invited."

SEVENTY-FIVE

Friday

Nathan: What sort of event are you working tonight?

Rosie: A third birthday party for triplets.

Nathan: For real?

Rosie: For real.

Nathan: So... what sort of food do they have?

Rosie: Everything has a theme of three.

Nathan: How does that work?

Rosie: *sends pic of food table*

Nathan: Are those melon balls?

Rosie: Yep. Watermelon, cantaloupe, honeydew. And since it's not good to have toothpicks around a bunch of kids, I had to make my own out of a watermelon rind.

Nathan: Even Charles is impressed.

Rosie: I'm blushing.

Nathan: What flavor marshmallow did you make?

Rosie: Birthday cake. Not the most original, but I used a number 3 cookie cutter to stamp them out and covered them with sprinkles. The kids seem to like them.

Nathan: My birthday is in February. In case you forgot.

Rosie: I didn't forget.

Saturday

Nathan: Do you want to just come over here and skip the bar tonight? Since we have those banana 'mallows to make?

Rosie: I still can't believe you bought all that stuff.

Nathan: Believe it, Beautiful.

Nathan: And you didn't answer the question. We can order in some takeout... I'd offer to cook for you, but my specialty is microwaving frozen meals.

SEVENTY-SIX
ROSALYN

"Earth to Rosalyn," Presley singsongs.

I shove my phone into my pocket. "Sorry."

We're standing at the back of my van, between the two open back doors, putting the empty food containers back.

Today's event was a family reunion. And it was in a nice area with plenty of street parking, so we found an empty section of the block, giving us plenty of space for loading and unloading our wagon.

Presley props her hands on her hips. "Instead of apologizing, how about you tell me if the person on the other end of that phone is Nate Waller?"

My cheeks start to heat, giving Presley the answer she wants.

"I knew it!" She fist pumps.

I shake my head. "It's—"

"Let me stop you right there." Presley lifts a hand and counts off her fingers as she goes. "Complicated. You're busy. You have history."

"How did you know we have history?" I ask, wanting to know what gave it away.

She grins. "I was just guessing, but thanks for confirming." I roll my eyes. "But seriously, the way you two were, pardon my French, eye fucking each other at that picnic, it's obvious there's something there. Not to mention the absurd amount of money he tipped."

When Presley saw the money I sent her, I told her Nathan insisted I split it with her. If she knew it was simply my guilty conscience, she would have rebuffed it.

I grab a container out of the wagon, preparing to turn to put it into the van. But I freeze.

There's a car driving toward us.

The speed limit here is low. They aren't going fast.

But... the car is starting to veer out of its lane.

Toward us.

They'll correct.

The car keeps coming.

They'll slow down.

They don't slow down.

They're getting closer.

They aren't stopping.

Then I see the driver. Slumped against the wheel.

"Presley!" I drop the container.

"Wha—"

With no time to explain, I turn and shove her as hard as I can.

Presley yells something as she stumbles back, falling onto the sidewalk.

I feel a little bad. But she's out of the way.

Safe.

I try to follow her.

Try to get out of the way.

But then the sound of metal meeting metal fills the air, and I know I'm out of time.

I have one moment to feel fear.

Then all I feel is pain.

SEVENTY-SEVEN

Nathan: How do you feel about Greek food?

Nathan: I can order ahead of time if you let me know when you think you'll be done.

Nathan: Or I can be patient and wait for you to tell me what you're in the mood for.

Nathan: Okay, fine, I'll leave you alone so you can finish working, but Charles already knows his order.

SEVENTY-EIGHT
NATE

I drum my fingers against the couch armrest.

It's still early. Not quite the time we agreed to meet. But late enough that Rosie should be done with her event by now.

I drum my fingers again.

Maybe I should just order food.

Another moment ticks by.

I pick up the remote and turn off the TV. I'm not watching it anyway.

I stand and start to pace.

I already put the mixing bowls and all the stuff we'll need for marshmallows on the counter. But now, as I think about it, maybe it's a stupid idea. Rosie literally spends all day cooking, and then I ask her to come over and do more...

I'm an asshole.

My feet change direction, and I head into the kitchen.

I'll put everything away, and if she really wants to make them, then I can take everything back out.

My fingers wrap around the rim of a mixing bowl when my phone vibrates with a call.

Thinking it's Rosie, I drop my hold of the bowl and yank my phone out.

It's not a number I have saved in my phone.

Usually I wouldn't answer, but...

I hit accept.

"Hello?"

"Hi, um, is this Nate Waller?" a female asks.

"Who's calling?" I ask instead of answering. The caller's voice sounds vaguely familiar, but I can't place it.

"This is Presley. I'm the one who works with Rosalyn." Coldness twists around my heart. "You gave me your card at that picnic and said to call if Rosalyn ever needed anything."

I brace my free hand on the counter. "What happened?" My throat is tight.

"Um." Presley's voice trembles, and I lean harder against the counter. "We—Someone—She's gonna be okay." She stops to suck in a noisy breath.

"Presley." I try to snap her name, but it comes out as a whisper.

"Sorry, sorry. She's okay. But... she's hurt."

That coldness crackles through my veins. "Where is she?"

"The hospital."

"Which one?" I push away from the counter, willing my legs to keep me upright.

My Rosie is hurt.

"Just wait, okay."

"Where's Rosie?" My voice is stronger now.

I stride toward the front door.

"Let me explain."

"Explain what?"

"She's gonna need your help." Presley's voice cracks again. "You said to tell you if she needs help."

Her words slice through me.

My girl is hurt and needs my help, and I'm just standing here.

"I'll do anything for her. Just tell me where she is," I grit out.

Presley's exhale is rough. "They're taking her back for a CT scan, or something like that, in just a moment. So even if you raced here, you wouldn't see her."

I stop walking and close my eyes, forcing a slow breath. "Tell me what happened."

"I promise she'll be okay, but I'm a crier. So I'm going to cry while I tell you this, but it doesn't mean anything bad." She finishes on a hitch.

"Okay." I keep my eyes closed. "My mom's a crier too."

She sniffs. "So, we were loading the van, and some guy driving down the road had, like, a medical emergency or something behind the wheel." My heart rate trips with each word out of her mouth. "Rosalyn, she... she saw them and shoved me out of the way." Presley's voice cracks.

My eyes open as I listen to her take another choppy breath.

I need her to keep talking.

I need her to tell me what happened.

But even though I understand criers, I can't ignore the emotion in her voice.

"Are you okay?" I ask.

"Yeah. Sorry. She just... Rosalyn saw the car, and she just pushed me. I scraped my elbow on the sidewalk when I landed. But... but she didn't have time." Presley sucks in a breath. "The car hit her."

A sound of distress that I don't recognize leaves my throat.

"She's okay," Presley says again. "But she hit her head pretty bad and has some scrapes... and her ankle... They don't know if it's broken or just sprained."

"But she's okay?" I whisper.

Presley said it already. But I need her to say it again.

"She's going to be totally okay. The doctors said it was all treatable, and she'll be fine once she heals. But... she needs a place to stay. Her apartment is a walk-up. I don't know if you've seen it, but she can't go there. Even if someone could help her up the first time, it's not safe for her to be stranded up on the third floor if—"

"She'll stay here." I don't need to hear any more reasoning.

"I'd have her stay with me, but I already have two roommates, and there's no extra space."

"She'll stay with me," I repeat.

Presley exhales. "I'm sure she'll fight you on it. She never wants to accept help. But you're the only person I could think of to call. She doesn't have an emergency contact."

Another hit to my chest.

Rosie doesn't have an emergency contact.

I remember her mom died when she was young.

I remember she was an only child.

I remember her dad being scary.

I already know she works too much.

And now I know she doesn't even have an emergency fucking contact.

I tighten my grip on the phone. "She has me."

"Good. Okay, good." Presley's breathing evens out. "We're at Health Place in St. Paul."

"I know where it is." I continue toward the door.

"You need to go to Rosalyn's place first."

"What? Why?"

"She'll need to go from the hospital right to your place. If you take her to her apartment to get her stuff, she'll insist on staying. So go there first and get clothes and... whatever else."

"Good point," I admit.

I hate the idea of going anywhere but straight to Rosie's side. But Presley is right.

"Do you know where her apartment is?"

"Yeah."

"Okay. Oh, and she won't have to do stairs in your house, right? I didn't even think—"

"No stairs. And there's an elevator up to my condo."

"Thank fuck." Presley's relief is thick through the line. But even if my house was made of nothing but stairs, I'd rent out a place that wasn't. "I'll text you her room number. They said only family could visit, so I lied and said she was my sister. But they'll probably let you in since you're... you."

"I'll get in," I say with confidence.

"Oh shit, you'll need her apartment keys."

"I'll get in," I repeat, still meaning it.

"How...?"

"I know a guy."

"Okay. Just make sure the locksmith doesn't break anything. I don't want Rosie getting in trouble with her building."

I think of my buddy Tony Stoleman.

Not a locksmith.

Then I head for the door. "We won't make a mark."

I hold open the front door of Rosie's building, and Tony walks through.

"Nice security." He lifts a brow.

"I know."

But I can't think about that fucking unlocked door right now. That's a problem for later.

Tony jogs up the stairs, and I follow him.

As soon as I hung up with Presley, I called my friend.

We met a decade ago through some random mutuals on the West Coast, but he's actually from around here. Tony's in the process of finding a house to buy in Arizona, but luckily for me, he's back home house-sitting for his parents while they travel.

Tony rounds the top of the stairs and starts up the next flight.

He's a good guy.

The best sort of friend.

But he's also shady as fuck.

I don't ask questions beyond what he offers, but I know he

can get me into Rosie's apartment quicker than I could track down her keys.

"So." Tony looks back and forth across the short hallway. "Which one is hers?"

"Fuck me." I clench my jaw. Two apartments occupy the third floor, and I didn't ask which one.

Tony holds up his hand, small metal tools glinting under the overhead light. "I can just open both."

I roll my eyes.

A good guy but one who doesn't always think about the consequences.

"You can't just open someone's door. What if they're home?"

He shrugs. "I'll tell them I had the wrong number."

"You're an idiot." I look back and forth between the doors.

"Do you have a better idea?" Tony leans his shoulder against the wall.

"I do." I lower to the floor and crawl over to the closest door.

"The fuck are you doing?" Tony sounds like he's trying not to laugh.

I ignore him, put my nose to the bottom of the door, and sniff.

"I need you to appreciate my restraint right now," Tony says flatly. "If this were any other situation, I'd be recording this."

"Uh-huh," I say absently.

I don't know if I expected to smell scents of her cooking or her shampoo, but the inhale of incense is an even better answer. If she lived here, I would've smelled that on her.

I point to the other door as I lean back onto my heels. "That one."

Tony pushes off the wall, and by the time I've gotten to my

feet and crossed the hall, he's pushing open the now unlocked door.

He steps aside, and I walk into Rosie's apartment.

I'm tempted to look around. To touch everything. But I need to get her stuff and get to the hospital.

The fucking hospital.

The apartment is small, and I can see the door straight ahead that must lead to her bedroom.

I stride for the door.

"I'll wait here," Tony calls out as I hear furniture creak under his weight.

I don't answer. And alone, I step into Rosie's bedroom.

Turning on the light, I stand in her room and take a heartbeat to calm myself.

On the way over, I thought through what sort of clothes Rosie will need. I just need to focus and find all the comfortable things.

I start with the dresser under the window.

I pull the top drawer open. Underwear.

Reaching in, I grab a handful, then drop them because I need something to carry everything in.

Cursing myself for not bringing a suitcase, I turn to Rosie's closet.

The doors fold open to either side, revealing a standard closet with one shelf up top and a bar to hang clothes on.

Shirts and dresses hang from the single bar, and plastic storage bins line the floor—stacked three high.

I huff out a breath, then spot the large duffel bag on the top shelf.

Good enough.

I grip the side of the bag and drag it off the shelf.

Dropping it on the bed, I unzip the duffel and find another similar bag inside.

I pull out the second bag and set it on the bed next to the first.

Whether it's a break or a sprain, Rosie will have to stay off her ankle for weeks. So I should probably take as much of her stuff as I can fit.

I unzip the second bag and find a shoe box inside.

It's plain, with a rectangular lid that comes all the way off, printed with a brand that's no longer in business.

Trepidation settles around me as I lift the box out of the duffel.

I should set it aside.

I should put it back up on the shelf.

It was hidden inside two bags for a reason.

It's old.

It's none of my business.

But there's something about it that feels impossible to ignore.

Carefully, like the contents might be fragile, I set it on the nightstand.

"Forgive me," I whisper. Then I lift the lid.

Paper.

Folded letters.

The entire box is filled with folded pages, tucked together, propped upright with the long edge resting on the bottom of the box.

The folded paper fills the box end to end.

Slowly, I drag my fingers across the surface, the top edges dancing under my touch.

There are dozens.

But they aren't all the same.

The pages are different shades of white. Some lined, some not. But all folded the same in the perfect tri-fold of a proper letter.

Except the first one.

The one at the far end of the box is different.

I hesitate, then I reach for the sole envelope.

As I lift it, I turn it so the front faces me.

And nothing in the world could have prepared me for what was written there.

My mouth opens, and every molecule of air slips from my lungs.

It's a child's handwriting.

And I know it's hers.

Nathan Waller
323 Kendel Way
Cleveland, OH 44111

But it's not the writing that makes my hand shake. It's the bright red ink.

It's the UNDELIVERABLE that makes it impossible to breathe.

I stare at the envelope in my hand.

She wrote to me.

She got my letter. And she wrote to me.

But the address is wrong.

Dread.

Dread like I've never known locks my feet to the floor.

Rosie is meticulous. Even back then. Even twenty-five years ago, Rosie wouldn't have made a mistake.

It had to have been me.

I must've written it down wrong.

I left her. Moved away. And when Rosie wrote to me, it got sent back to her.

I swallow, feeling like I'm going to be sick.

I turn the envelope over and lift the torn seal.

There are two pieces of paper inside.

I pull them both out.

When the first paper is half unfolded, I recognize my handwriting. The letter I left for Rosie the night before I moved.

And even though I don't want to look, I do.

> DEAR ROSIE,
> I'M SORRY I WAITED SO LONG TO TELL YOU...

I force my eyes down to the address.

The incorrect address. I messed up the numbers.

My heart breaks a little for myself.

I thought she didn't get the letter. Or ignored it.

I was sad she never wrote me.

I trace my fingertip along the edge of the page.

It's worn. Soft. Like it's been handled many times.

Like someone has run their fingers across the paper over and over.

"Fuck." My curse comes out broken. "Fuck."

I refold the letter and slide it back into the envelope.

Then I look at the one still left in my hand.

This is *my* letter.

The one she wrote to me.

So I won't feel bad about reading it.

But as soon as I start, I wish I hadn't.

> Dear Nathan,
> I'm sorry too. I never even asked you how you felt about moving.
> And I'm sorry for crying so much. And for not saying goodbye.

I wish I would have asked you for a hug before you left.

A hug would be really nice.

I hope your new house is nice.

If you send me your new phone number, I can call you. But don't call me. My dad won't like that.

I miss you.

Your best friend,

Rosie

Heat builds in my eyes as I fold the letter and put it back into the envelope.

My dad won't like that.

I haven't forgotten about him.

Haven't forgotten the franticness that laced Rosie's sobs when I told her I was moving.

Haven't forgotten her answer when I asked if he hurt her.

Not like that.

"Rosie." I say her name like a prayer.

I slide the envelope back into its spot at the end of the row inside the box.

Is this why I see that sadness in her eyes?

Because she tried to write to me, but I fucked it all up?

Because eight-year-old Rosie wanted to ask twelve-year-old me for a hug.

I pull in a deep breath.

My best friend writing me because she wanted a fucking hug.

But I wasn't there.

My eyes trail over the rest of the folded letters.

They have to be something else.

A collection of letters from something else.

But the longer I stare, the worse I feel.

And I need to know.

I pull out the next folded piece of paper.

And when I open it, I feel the weight of it on my sternum.

It's to me.

I glance at the box, and I know.

All these letters are to me.

> *Dear Nathan,*
> *I know I can't send you this letter. But I can't*
> *stop myself from writing it.*
> *I miss you a lot.*
> *Like so much.*
> *And I keep wondering if you miss me too.*
> *Love,*
> *Rosie*

I suck in a breath.

I missed her too.

I'd missed her so fucking much, and I couldn't tell her.

Didn't tell her.

That fucking day.

That fucking day I told her I was moving. How I'd waited because I was a coward. How if I'd told her sooner, maybe we could have talked about it, and I could have gotten her the right address.

How different all this would be if I'd just gotten that first fucking letter.

I put the paper back in the box and pick up the next.

And the next.

And the next.

They're all to me.

And they're all sad.

Only one letter hasn't been sad.

Just one.

> Dear Nathan,
>
> I saw a bunny today. I was sitting in the woods in our spot, and I was still for so long that he hopped right up to me.
>
> I wanted to feed him a marshmallow, but I don't think they're supposed to eat them. So I guess I'll have to finish the bag myself.
>
> PS It's a new bag I bought for myself with a five I found on the ground in the park. I finished the bag you left a long time ago.
>
> Love,
>
> Rosie

I can picture it. Her sitting quietly in the woods.

I fold the page and put it back.

There are so many letters.

And I read them.

Because they're mine.

I pull out another.

After the first few, she started dating them. And the date at the top of the letter in my hand is four years after I moved.

To the day.

> Dear Nathan,
>
> He hit me today.

My knees give out, and I drop onto Rosie's bed.

"No." The paper trembles in my hand.

He's never hurt me like that before.

It was always just words.

Do you remember when you left? Do you remember asking me if he hurt me?

I wish I'd told you then. I wish I'd told you how mean he was.

But it was always just words.

Tear marks stain the page, and I feel like I'm going to throw up.

He wasn't always like this. But ever since Mom died...

It's been bad, Nathan.

I wish I'd told you.

I wish I could've gone with you.

But that's just not how my life works.

I miss you.

Rosie

I drop my head forward.

The bastard hit her.

She was twelve. She was the age I was when I moved away. And her dad fucking hit her.

I can't even imagine.

Memories of my own family drag through my mind.

Laughter. Dinners at the table. Homework. Movies.

I lived in comfort while my Rosie was living in hell.

As I slide the paper back into the box and pull out the next, a part of me understands that I was just a kid too. I'm not responsible for her dad. But if I'd known... If I'd seen the signs or asked more questions, I could've told someone.

My parents would have done something.

That uselessness I felt walking into this room has nothing on the way I feel now.

I might have been a kid. But I still hate myself for what I unknowingly let happen.

I open the next letter.

> *I fell asleep in the woods today. I didn't feel like going home.*

And the next.

> *I broke my arm. I had to tell the doctor I fell.*

Another and another.

I read them until my vision is blurry.

Until my tears fall onto the pages, mixing with Rosie's.

And I can't stop.

I need to know.

I need to read them.

I owe her that much.

I owe her the friend she lost.

I feel like years have passed when I pull out the last letter. The final one in the box.

She was nineteen when she wrote it.

> *Dear Nathan,*
> *It's time to let you go.*
> *You don't know it, but you've been saving me for years.*

I pretend you read these letters.

I make up your responses in my head.

I pretend you understand.

Pretend you think of me when I think about you.

I pretend a lot of things...

But today is different. Because my dad died today.

It was a long time coming. And I feel like I can finally breathe for the first time in my life.

While I was in the waiting room at the hospital, I saw you.

You were being interviewed after a game for catching the winning touchdown.

Your eyes are the same, you know?

Somewhere inside that athlete's body, you're still that sweet boy from down the street.

The one who befriended me when no one else would.

I'm so proud of you. And I still miss you. But I'm finally free.

And I need to be free of you too.

Because you don't read these letters.

Because I don't send them.

Because even if I could, you probably don't remember me.

Maybe you've forgotten all about me.

And that's okay.

But I need to stop pretending now.

Goodbye, Nathan.

I'll always love who you were to me. But this will be my last letter.

Your friend,

The girl from the woods

Something splits inside me.

I drop the letter on top of the box and press my palms into my eyes.

My blood feels like it's on fire.

I feel like this sense of failure is going to pull me through the floor.

Because she's right.

I didn't read her cries for help.

And I wasn't thinking of her when she was thinking of me.

Because I'd forgotten.

Like her last letter said. I'd forgotten all about my Rosie.

She was all alone, and I was living out my dreams.

I didn't help her.

My lungs struggle to inhale.

I didn't help her.

No one did.

"We gotta take care of somebody?" Tony's low voice comes from the doorway.

He's never sounded so serious. And it's like I'm hearing the real him for the first time.

Because I know exactly what he means, and I kinda love him for it.

I shake my head. "He's already dead."

Tony grunts.

"I wish he wasn't," I whisper. "Whatever end he got... It wasn't enough."

EIGHTY
ROSALYN

Everything hurts as I open my eyes, and I wish I was still asleep.

At least the room is dark.

Lying in the partially inclined hospital bed, I turn my head toward the door.

It's closed, but the glass top half of the door is letting in light from the hallway. Enough to see by, but not so much that my concussed brain screams at it.

I wiggle my toes and groan.

The doctors said it was a miracle I didn't break anything. And I'm glad for that. I am. But a miracle would be not getting hit by a car in the first fucking place.

But miracles aren't really my thing.

Foolishly, I try to flex my ankles.

My left protests at the attempt, the plastic brace cold on my skin as pain radiates up my leg.

I want another blanket.

I want to go home.

I slowly roll my head away from the door so I can stare at the ceiling.

A tear rolls down my temple.

This...

I close my eyes again.

This isn't how today was supposed to go.

I wasn't supposed to end up like this.

Hurt.

Alone.

With no one to help me. No one to rely on.

Another tear slips free.

They won't let me leave by myself.

Said they can't discharge me from the hospital unless I have someone to pick me up.

But I don't have anyone to pick me up.

I just need an Uber. Or Presley can give me a ride when she gets back from retrieving her car.

I'll crawl up my stairs if I have to.

It's not like I can afford to stay in a hotel for weeks until my sprained ankle is better.

And I can't afford to miss weeks of work either.

Another tear.

I wish Nathan was here.

I don't like hospitals.

There's a creak in the room, and I open my eyes again.

Maybe Presley fell asleep in the chair.

I turn my head toward the covered windows, where the pair of chairs are for visitors.

And one of them is occupied.

I try to narrow my eyes to see the person better.

They're leaned forward, elbows on their knees.

"Nathan?" My question is quiet, like maybe I'm seeing things.

His head jerks up to look at me. And he's close enough that I can see his eyes.

They're red rimmed and full of pain.

His throat works, like he's trying to talk, but he just ends up shaking his head.

I want to ask how long he's been here.

Want to ask if he's alright.

If that look on his face is for me.

But then someone walks past the door, causing the light to shift in the room. And my attention is drawn to the other chair.

To the shoebox sitting next to Nathan.

It's like a mirage.

A terrible mirage.

Because I know that box.

My heart clenches.

No.

No, no, no.

He can't have those.

"Those—Those aren't for you," I whisper.

Nathan shakes his head. "They are for me. You wrote them for me."

My heart feels like it's about to stop.

He...

I think about everything I wrote in those letters.

I think about all the awful secrets I've kept for so long.

The shame.

Maybe he didn't read them all.

But I know he did.

Of course he did.

"I'm sorry." Nathan's voice breaks. "I wish I'd known... The address."

He sounds shattered.

And I hate it.

All my fears.

All the reasons I tried to keep my distance.

They all come crashing down around me.

His voice hitches, and it's everything I didn't want.

I didn't want him to take on my darkness.

I never wanted to put this on him.

"You weren't supposed to read those." I can't raise my voice above a whisper. "They're nothing."

"Don't," he snaps. And it's loud in the silent room.

I wince, the noise too loud against my pounding skull.

"Fuck." Nathan drops his voice to a whisper. "Fuck, I'm sorry. But don't pretend they're nothing."

Nathan slides off the chair, his knees landing on the hard floor.

"Careful." I try to lift my arm to stop him, but my limbs are too heavy.

Nathan shuffles forward, putting us eye to eye.

"I'm not going to be careful, Rosalyn Kay Edwards. I know we just found each other again. But I'm here now, and I'm not going to be fucking careful." He grips the edge of the bed, leaning toward me, our faces inches apart. "I'm here. And I don't want you to pretend anymore. Please don't pretend anymore."

I think about that first moment when I opened the door and saw it was him.

How I pretended not to know him.

How I pretended seeing him wasn't exactly what I needed.

How I pretended my past wasn't awful.

How I pretended to be okay with casual.

How I pretended that just being near him wasn't healing something inside me.

"I'm sorry," I choke out, my voice loud to my own ears as my words turn to sobs.

My head throbs with each beat of my heart, but I finally get my arms to move, and I cover my face with my hands.

"No, Beautiful. No apologizing." Warm fingers wrap gently around my wrists. "You have nothing to be sorry for."

His kindness only makes the tears come faster.

He never changed.

In all this time, with all his success, he never changed.

Nathan slowly pulls my hands away from my face. "Please stop crying. Your head has to be killing you."

It is.

I try to shake my head, to deny it, but it hurts too bad to move.

"Shh." He guides my hands down until they're resting on my stomach. "I've had enough concussions to know what your head feels like right now. Shut your eyes."

I do as he says. Then I feel his fingers ghost over my temples, lightly brushing away my tears.

EIGHTY-ONE
NATE

It only takes a minute for her breathing to even out. For her features to relax.

I lightly place my hand over her heart, feeling it beat beneath my palm as I lean my forehead onto the bed beside her.

EIGHTY-TWO
ROSALYN

The low rumble of masculine voices pulls me out of sleep.

There's a lamp on in the corner, and without turning my head, I can tell it's dark beyond the curtains.

I don't know what time it is. But it's late.

Focusing on the voices, I see Nathan talking to the doctor when my eyes adjust.

They're standing just inside the doorway, bodies angled toward me, but they're both looking down at the clipboard the doctor is holding.

Nathan is leaning in, with a look of concentration on his face, and I imagine the doctor is going over my diagnosis, or medication, with him.

It seems like that's breaking some sort of rule. Like the doctor shouldn't be sharing my information with some random man in my room.

Some random man.

If it wouldn't hurt so much to scoff, I'd do it.

The man in my room is more than my long-lost childhood friend. He's literally a famous football player.

The doctor surely recognized him.

As I watch the two talk, I think about Nathan being here. And there's only one way he'd know to come.

Presley.

I don't know how she got a hold of him, but she's the only one who even knows about the accident.

She's also the one who rode in the ambulance with me. Holding my hand and crying the whole time. Saying she owed me her life.

She doesn't owe me anything, but she's the best sort of over-the-top friend, and I appreciated her being with me.

My eyes trail down Nathan's frame. To the shoebox tucked under his arm.

My heart throbs all over again at the sight of it.

I was too stunned when I first saw it to even think about *how* he found them. And the times I've woken up and dozed back off since finding Nathan in my room, I've been too out of it to try and figure out what happened. But lying here, watching this man I know talk to my doctor like it's his job, I can picture it all perfectly.

Presley calls him. Tells him about the accident. Tells him to stop by my place and bring some clothes—since I'm pretty sure my pants were cut off...

And if he went to my apartment and opened my closet, he'd have thought it was a good idea to use one of my duffel bags. And just like that... shoebox.

He shouldn't have opened the box.

It's obviously personal.

But if I'm honest, if our roles were reversed, I'd have opened it.

Presley must've given him the keys to my place. But I still think about that comment Nathan made the other day—about tracking my phone—and I wonder if his tech company can break into houses.

I pull my eyes away from the box and look back toward the chairs.

Under the second one is the duffel I expect to see.

But it looks awfully full for one change of clothes.

"Miss Edwards." The doctor's voice pulls my attention back to the men.

I lift my hand. "I'm up."

Nathan crosses to me in four strides, standing in the same spot he was kneeling when I fell asleep.

He sets the box on the chair behind him, then wraps his fingers around mine. "How're you feeling?"

"That's my line." The doctor chuckles as he comes around to the other side of my bed.

"Sore," I tell them both. "But I'd like to go home."

My experiences with hospitals haven't been great. And no matter how nice this doctor is, I don't want to stay here longer than I have to.

The doctor nods. "I was just discussing that with Mr. Waller. He assumed you'd want to leave when you woke. We're completing the discharge papers now, then you're free to leave under his care."

Under his care.

I open my mouth to ask what that means but then assume I'm getting released because now I have a ride home.

"Thanks, Doc." Nathan rubs his thumb across my wrist.

"Would you like a nurse to help you get dressed?" the doctor asks me.

I start to shake my head, then stop when I remember my horrible headache. "No, thank you." I flit my gaze to Nathan, silently asking...

"I'll help her."

The doctor nods. "I'll have pharmacy deliver the medications in about ten, then you should be good to go."

I wait until the door closes behind the doctor. "Nathan..."

He shakes his head. "We'll talk at home." Nathan lets go of my hand and turns away to grab the duffel. "We're getting you dressed first."

"Thanks for driving me," I tell him.

I want to tell him he doesn't have to, but that'd be a lie. I need someone to help me.

I thought maybe Presley was coming back to drive me home, but she had to take an Uber from here to go home—where her car is—and she must've fallen asleep.

Thankfully there aren't any parking restrictions where the van is still parked, so my battered baby will be okay for a day or two until I can figure out how to get it back to my place.

In the meantime, I'll accept the ride.

Nathan sets the open duffel on the edge of my bed. "Do you want pajamas since it's late?"

I stare at the bag.

It's full.

Like completely full of my clothes.

"Why... Why is there so much?" I ask, hardly believing my eyes.

"So you don't have to do laundry every other day." He pulls out a thin pair of navy sleep pants. "How about these?"

"They're fine. But what do you mean about laundry?"

Nathan pulls out one of my sleep tank tops. "I have a sweater in here too if you're cold. But I think the tank top would be best to avoid the scrapes on your arms."

I look down at my right arm.

I was afraid I'd need stitches, but the cuts were small enough that they were able to just use those butterfly bandages.

When the car hit me, it threw me against the back of my van.

The simultaneous collision with the corner of my van's bumper kept the car from crushing me. But my shoe snagged on a crack in the road, and the push was enough to twist my ankle. It's a grade three sprain, which apparently means lots of pain, an ankle brace, and crutches.

I tried to catch myself but just ended up scraping my arm on my own van. And the pavement. And then the side of my head cracked against the sidewalk.

So, all in all, not a miracle, but I'm still lucky it wasn't worse.

And the instructions for recovery seem pretty simple.

Do as little as possible for the next few days for my concussion. Then continue to take it easy for the next couple of weeks.

Keep my bandages dry for three days.

Keep on the crutches for up to three weeks.

The body aches and bruises should start to fade in a few days.

And then I'll be good as new.

Stress fills my body.

The instructions might be easy, but I need to work. I can't take three weeks off. And I can't run events on crutches.

"Want help sitting up?" Nathan's words are soft.

"Yes, please."

"How's your back?"

I take a moment to think about the answer, furrowing my brows as I concentrate on how my back feels. "I think it's fine."

"Alright." Nathan leans down and slides a hand under my back. "Slowly now."

With his help, I sit up, and then, with more help, I get my legs over the edge of the bed.

My ankle hurts, and with it hanging down, the extra blood flow is making it throb.

"Shirt first," Nathan tells me. Then he reaches around me in a loose hug and unties the back of the hospital gown I'm wearing.

I slide my arms out but hold the front of the gown up.

I know he's already seen my boobs, but I'm feeling about as vulnerable as I ever have, so I keep myself covered.

Nathan's fingers graze over my elbow. "Arm."

He guides one arm, then the other, through the straps, letting me hold the gown up each time. Then, when the tank top is carefully moved over my head, I drop the gown.

Nathan pulls the gown away and kneels in front of me.

The sleep pants have wide legs, so he's able to get it over my new plastic ankle brace.

He helps guide the pants up my hips as I shift side to side.

By the time my pants are on, I'm exhausted.

Still kneeling on the ground, Nathan reaches up and zips the duffel closed.

"Why did you bring so much?" I ask, looking at the bag.

"Why didn't you tell me?" We're both whispering.

When I lift my eyes to meet his, I know he's talking about the letters.

A weary sort of heaviness settles around me. "There was no point."

"No point?" He jerks back. "You don't think I'd want to know?"

"I knew you would. But all that stuff." I lift a hand to gesture at the box. "It was a long time ago."

Nathan holds my gaze. "It was hours ago."

The pain and rage in his expression presses against my chest.

"This is why I didn't tell you." I lift my hand to his face and trace the side of his mouth. "I never wanted to make you feel like... this."

EIGHTY-THREE
NATE

I never wanted to make you feel like this.

I close my eyes and lean into her soft touch.

"Rosie." Her name comes out gruff.

"I didn't want to tell you because it's all done." Her hand slips away, and she sets it in her lap. "And even if you'd never moved away, my home life wouldn't have changed. None of that was your fault."

"It would have changed!" I say it like I believe it. "I would've... Rosie, if I'd known he..." I have to swallow. "I would've done something. If I'd have known he was hurting you, I would have done something."

Her breath hitches at my words, and tears trail down her cheeks. "I was never your problem. Please don't take this on."

I was never your problem.

And it hits me.

The truth of it.

Rosie's never had anyone to trust.

Her mom might have treated her okay, but she died when Rosie was young.

Died and left her with a monster.

Then I left. And from the letters she wrote, that left her with no one.

That thick taste of guilt coats my tongue.

I came back.

I found her again.

But I've been acting like nothing changed between us. Except everything changed.

I'm not a kid anymore. And Rosie stopped being a kid long before me.

She never had a chance.

"Is this why you're always looking at me like it'll be the last time you see me?" I finally ask the question out loud. Because I finally understand what I've seen in her eyes.

Acceptance in the defeat.

Her hands move to press against her stomach. "You were never supposed to know."

"I'm glad I know." I pull her hands away from her body and hold them in mine. "You're not alone anymore, Rosie. I'm not leaving."

EIGHTY-FOUR
ROSALYN

A sob breaks through, and I watch Nathan's features crumple.

He's saying everything I've always wanted to hear.

I never wanted to be alone.

Never wanted to be scared.

Never wanted to do what I've done.

"I'm sorry." He lets go of my hands to lightly hold my sides. "Please stop crying. I can't watch you cry. Especially when you're hurting."

"I'm okay," I croak.

I'm not okay.

"No more pretending, remember," Nathan murmurs. "Promise me."

I nod my head once, slowly. "I promise."

Nathan slides his hands off my body and presses them to the mattress, pushing himself up with a groan.

I pull up the edge of the blanket and wipe the dampness from my cheeks. "You shouldn't kneel on the ground like that."

"I'm fine." Nathan cuts his gaze to meet mine. "See? I can lie too."

I drop the blanket. "Except you're not good at it."

He narrows his eyes at me. "Well, you'll have lots of time to teach me your ways over the next three weeks."

I narrow my eyes back. "What do you mean?"

Nathan pats a hand on top of the duffel bag. "I packed all this, plus another bag in my vehicle, because you're coming home with me."

Nathan's SUV pulls up to the sidewalk, and the nurse who pushed my wheelchair down from the room guides me through the automatic front doors.

It's dark out. I've lost all track of time. But I find I don't even care if it's closer to dusk or dawn. All I want to do now is sleep again.

Nathan rounds the front of his vehicle as we reach it and opens the front passenger door.

The wheelchair felt unnecessary, but I can accept that it would've been a long way to use crutches for the first time.

Especially since I still feel like I've been hit by a car.

I snort at my own silent joke, then wince because snorting hurts my head.

"Let's get you in the car before full delusion sets in." There's a smile in Nathan's voice.

I look up to see his smile is soft, but his face shows exhaustion.

I frown. "You don't have to do this."

His smile drops. "Woman, you're going to start hurting my feelings if you keep saying that. Now keep your weight off your left foot and let me help you into the fucking car."

Sighing, I take my feet off the little footrests on the wheel-chair, and I let Nathan help me into his vehicle.

Nathan grabs my seat belt and reaches across me to clip it in. "Watch your arm," he tells me, then he shuts the door.

My eyes close, and as my body gently throbs, I let unconsciousness pull me back under.

EIGHTY-FIVE
ROSALYN

"Little Rose." The deep voice rumbles through my body.

"Hmm?"

"Rosie, I need you to wake up for just a moment."

I crack my lids open. "What?"

Nathan's mouth pulls up on one side. "You gotta get out of the car."

Turning my head, I look past Nathan to the wheelchair waiting beside him. "Did you steal that?"

He scoffs. "I *borrowed* it."

I roll my eyes. "More like you sweet-talked the nurse into it."

The other side of his mouth pulls up to make a full smile. "No idea what you're talking about. Now help me help you, or else we're just gonna sleep in the car. And that will make Charles very cross."

Charles. The reminder of his cat waiting upstairs is the motivation I need.

I unbuckle, and Nathan uses his hands on my hips to help me turn so my feet are out of the vehicle.

"I'm gonna guide you," Nathan tells me as he pulls me toward the end of the seat. "Just remember to keep your foot up."

I grip his shoulders and do as he says.

When my right foot hits the ground, Nathan reaches behind him and swings the wheelchair around so it's right beside me.

By the time my butt hits the seat, I'm back to being achy and tired.

Nathan shuts my door, then disappears around behind me.

I hear him open and close another door before he reappears.

He has an overstuffed duffel bag on each shoulder, the shoebox under one arm, and the crutches tucked under the other.

I hold my hands out. "Give me something. You look ridiculous."

Nathan looks at the shoebox but makes no move to give it to me. "Can you take the crutches?"

Reaching out, I take them and settle them between my knees and onto my shoulder so they won't catch on doorways. "You can just set everything in my lap."

"Not gonna happen." Nathan moves behind me, but it's obvious to all involved that it's going to be difficult to push my chair with that shoebox under his arm.

"Give me the... box. It's light."

He hesitates. "You won't try to do anything to them, will you?"

I sigh. "Nathan, even though those letters are mine and I can do whatever I want to them, I'm not going to magically set them on fire while they're sitting in my lap."

He makes no move to give them up.

I lift a hand to my chest. "Swear on my love for Charles that I won't do anything to damage them."

"Fine," he huffs and sets the box in my lap.

Draping my arm over the box, I nod to Nathan.

The parking garage is empty of people as Nathan pushes me down the row.

And in the quiet, I think about how staying here is too much to ask.

We may have been close all those years ago, but as adults, the reality is that we just met a few weeks ago.

I feel the weight of the box in my lap.

And now that Nathan's read the letters, it's like we just met all over again.

The elevator doors open, and when Nathan pushes me inside, I look at his blurry reflection in the back wall.

He looked so fucking sad when I woke up and found him with the letters.

I never wanted to make Nathan sad. He's only ever brought happiness into my life.

I let my eyes drift closed as the elevator takes us up.

And it's nearing the middle of the night. Nathan is probably as tired as I am.

I'll argue with him about going home tomorrow.

EIGHTY-SIX
NATE

Rosie's asleep by the time I get the blankets pulled up over her.

Charles jumps onto the bed—having meowed and bumped against my legs the whole way across the condo—and moves to stand beside Rosie.

"I know, bud." I pass a palm down his back, applying pressure when he arches into my hand. "She'll be okay."

I try to believe my words as I go through the motions of getting ready for bed.

Physically, she'll recover.

But the things she's been through...

I leave a trail of clothes across the closet and grab the first pair of sleep pants I can find.

From the way she worded things in those letters... I don't think she's told anyone.

I don't think anyone knows how much she's suffered.

My fists clench.

I broke my arm. I had to tell the doctor I fell.

Her dad shoved her to the ground, and she had to fucking lie about it.

I can't imagine how that must've felt. To be in pain, surrounded by a hospital full of people, but to still be alone.

Those doctors failed her.

Society failed her.

I turn off the lights and cross to the bed.

I failed her.

I get into bed as slowly as possible, not wanting to wake her.

Under the blankets, I roll onto my side, facing my Rosie.

She's on her back, face turned away from me, hands folded on her chest.

I scoot closer.

I need to touch her.

When she let me help her change, I had to grit my teeth at all the bruises and scrapes that covered her body.

The side of her thigh.

Her knees.

Her arms.

Her ankle.

I wanted to scream at the injustice of it all.

Hasn't she been through enough?

I slide my hand across the inches between us, then gently rest it on her stomach. The one place I know it's safe to touch.

And with my shame hidden in the darkness, I cry.

I did earlier.

Couldn't stop myself when I was reading those fucking letters.

But I was still trying to hold back.

I still had things to do.

But now, with her in my bed, with her visible wounds treated, I let out the pent-up rage.

The panic.

The sorrow.

The fucking guilt.

Charles clunks his hard skull against mine.

I grunt.

He does it again.

I lift a hand toward him. "Five more minutes."

Teeth lightly close around my pointer finger.

I open my eyes. "What the fu—"

But then I stop chastising my cat because I see *her*.

Rosie is draped across me.

Her hair is spread across my chest. The deep red strands look perfect against my bare skin.

Her left knee is hitched up over my thigh, and I can feel the edges of her new ankle brace against my shin.

She has a hand wedged between her body and my side, and I can only hope it's comfortable for her.

I don't know when we changed positions, but my arm is tucked around her back. The subconscious part of me just as aware of the fact that I need her close.

I flex my arm, just a little, to hold her closer.

Her back rises with a slow inhale.

I lift my head and press a kiss to the top of her hair, and Charles drops his hold of my finger before he steps up onto my stomach.

He's already purring when he curls up on my body. Just above Rosie's knee.

With the arm not around Rosie, I reach down and scratch Charles behind the ears.

This damn cat is getting just as attached to Rosie as I am.

I open my eyes.

The buzzing continues, and my brain finally clicks on.

I dart my hand out to grab my phone off the nightstand and tap the screen to send the call to voicemail.

The phone stops vibrating, and I look down at the woman still sprawled across me to make sure she didn't wake up.

Once I confirm her breathing is still steady, I relax.

Charles, however, is staring at me out of one eye.

Sorry, I mouth to him.

In response, he stretches his front legs, flexing his paws and jabbing me with his little claws.

I slip my phone under his paws, stopping the attempted stabbing.

Bitch, I mouth this time.

My phone buzzes once, and I snatch it back away from my body, not wanting the vibration to somehow transfer through my body and wake up Rosie.

I look at the screen.

> **Hannah:** I know you're off today, but we have that call with the potential merger people in ten.
>
> **Me:** I'll be there.
>
> **Hannah:** I emailed you a breakdown of all the numbers.
>
> **Me:** Appreciate it.

Fucking hell. I forgot all about that damn call.

I look back down at my sleeping girl.

No part of me wants to get up. But if I cancel the call, I'll just have to reschedule it—probably within the next few weeks while she's still here. So if I can do it while Rosie's sleeping, then that's probably the best option.

Using the top edge of my phone, I nudge Charles.

He doesn't react.

I nudge him again, and he turns his head away from me.

I nudge him harder. "Get up, you furry fuck," I whisper as quietly as possible.

Charles yawns.

I pull out the big guns.

"Hungry?"

His head pops up.

That's what I thought.

I gesture with my chin for him to get up, and he finally listens.

He stands on his little orange paws, slowly turning around and swooshing his tail in my face before jumping off the bed.

The attitude on this feline.

With one obstacle out of the way, I start to slide myself away from my warm Little Rose.

She makes a small noise but doesn't wake as I replace my body with pillows. Tucking one under her cheek and another under her knee, leaving her in the same position.

Charles bonks his forehead into my leg, reminding me I promised him food, then with my phone in hand, I stride out of the room, famished cat in tow.

EIGHTY-SEVEN
ROSALYN

Nathan's voice comes from somewhere in the condo, so I do my best to stay quiet.

He'd help.

He'd insist on it.

But I have to pee, badly, and I don't want help doing that.

Plus the bathroom is *right there*.

Every inch of my body aches when I sit up and swing my feet over the side of the bed.

The crutches are propped against the nightstand, so I'm able to reach them.

It's a little bit of a struggle to get to my feet, balancing only on my good leg, but I manage.

The first step on crutches is sketchy.

So is the second and the third. But then I finally get the hang of it and make it into the bathroom.

I don't want to turn the lights on, but I also don't want to trip on anything, so I squint my eyes and flip on the light.

Of course there's nothing in the way. I should've remembered that the floor in here is pristine, like the rest of Nathan's home—as far as I can tell.

My head is throbbing by the time I make it to the little toilet room, water closet, whatever it's called. But as I pull the door shut behind me, I feel pride at making it on my own.

There's another light switch inside this room, and I turn it on, then notice the dimmer and slide it to its lowest setting.

The glow is just enough to see by and perfect for my headache.

After leaning my crutches against the closed door, I push my sleep pants down my hips, so they drop to the floor, then lower myself onto the toilet.

My knees sting, and my thighs are sore, but nothing can take away from the relief of going when you really have to go.

Finished, I'm reaching for the toilet paper when I hear a sound.

I freeze, trying to listen, and that's when the door handle jiggles.

Like all the door handles in this place, it's a lever—not a round knob—and it starts to lower.

I didn't lock the handle. Didn't think I had to. Because it's not like anyone else would be using the bathroom.

"Um, I'm in here." I feel like an idiot saying it out loud, but seriously, what is Nathan doing?

Instead of a response, the handle jerks all the way down, unlatching the door.

"Nathan!" I shout, mad he'd invade my privacy like this.

Then several things happen at once.

The weight of my crutches pushes the door open.

They clatter loudly against the tile floor.

Charles lets out a yowl as he leaps out of the way.

And my own shriek mixes with the cat's.

But there's no Nathan.

No human on the other side of the door.

Just Charles.

The cat in question picks his way over the downed crutches and walks into my little room with a noisy purr.

"Jesus Christ, Charles." I try to huff out a laugh, but all those loud noises have amplified my headache.

My sliver of humor is quickly cut off by the sound of running feet.

"Rosie!" Nathan's voice echoes through the condo.

Oh god.

"Rosie!" He's closer now.

"I'm fine!" I try to shout back, but my headache spikes.

"Rosie, where are you?" His voice has entered the bedroom.

"I'm fine. Please go away," I say at a normal speaking voice, knowing he can hear me now.

But he doesn't listen.

He's a man. Of course he doesn't listen.

"Rosie." Nathan appears in the doorway, wearing sleep pants and a white T-shirt.

I slap my hands over my lap and slam my knees together, causing pain to zip up and down my limbs.

"Nathan. Get out."

"Are you okay?" His eyes jump from Charles to the crutches to me. To my hands. "What happened?"

"Your cat opened the door." I press my legs together tighter.

"But you're okay?" His eyes roam over me. "Do you need help with..." He gestures toward the toilet paper.

"Oh my god." I strive for a calm tone. "I appreciate the concern, but I need you to go away."

He sighs, like I'm the one being absurd. "Rosie, I hate to have to remind you, but I've already seen those pretty little curls between your legs." He drops his eyes to my lap, then back up to mine. "And when you're feeling better, I'm going to put my mouth on them. So there's no need to cover yourself."

I blink at him once.

The thought of Nathan going down on me is appealing.

Very appealing.

But not when I'm currently sitting on a toilet. With my pajama pants pooled around my feet.

"Nathan, if you ever want to have sex with me again, you will get the fuck out of the bathroom. Right. Now."

His eyes rove over me once more, his expression turning more serious. "Come to the living room when you're done."

Crouching, he picks up my crutches and leans them against the wall of the toilet room where I can reach them.

He takes a step back. "C'mon, buddy." Nathan pats his thigh, and Charles lets out a sound of assent, then follows his human out of the bathroom.

Pinching my eyes shut, I don't move until I hear the main bathroom door shut.

EIGHTY-EIGHT
NATE

Only a few minutes pass before Rosie crutches her way down the hall and into the great room.

She eyes the wall of windows.

When the sun started rising and the light started filling the condo, I realized it would be too bright for my concussed girl, so I had the hidden shades roll down to filter the light.

"On the couch," I direct her.

I want to help her. Want to scoop her up into my arms and carry her.

But I won't.

Because she's still not ready for the amount of attention I plan to give her.

Staying on my side of the island, I watch her move and try not to think about her scraped-up knees.

When I heard her yell from the bathroom, I nearly had a damn heart attack.

And then when I saw the cuts and bruises on her legs... I got pissed at the world all over again.

"Shouldn't you be at work?" Rosie asks as she drops down onto the end spot of the couch.

"I called in," I answer while she shifts the extra pillows I piled up for her.

Rosie makes a humming sound but doesn't comment more.

When Charles jumps up on the cushion next to her, she immediately reaches out to pet him. "When'd you learn to open doors, huh?" she says to the cat.

"He's been doing that since I got him," I tell her as I carry over a tray holding a bowl of sugary cereal, a small plate of scrambled eggs, and a glass of orange juice. "Think he might be a prison breakout."

It's a joke, but my tone doesn't come out right.

Rosie eyes me as I set the tray on the end table next to her armrest. It's not the greatest combination of food, but I wanted to give her choices.

"Eat. Then you're going back to bed," I demand.

She just got up, but she looks exhausted.

Rosie doesn't reply, but she doesn't argue either.

I go back into the kitchen and grab my own eggs and a mug of coffee rather than juice.

Her gaze is on me as I sit on the opposite end of the couch from her.

She looks from me to my mug. "Can I have coffee?"

I set the mug on the coffee table and shake my head. "No. Not for a few days."

She digs her teeth into her lower lip.

I set my plate next to my mug. "Don't do that."

"Do what?" Charles walks onto her lap, and she wraps her arms around him.

"Bite your lip," I tell her. "Don't do it."

She lowers her face to Charles's fur but eyes me over his back. "Are you... mad at me?"

"What?" I shift forward until I'm perched on the edge of the couch and turned to face her. "No. Rosie, I'm not mad at you." I force my jaw to relax. "I'm just... I'm mad at fucking all of it. And..." I suck in a deep breath. "I feel like shit. Every time I think about what you wrote in those damned letters... I feel like fucking shit."

Rosie lifts her head from Charles's side, and that goddamn sadness is back in her eyes.

I fucking hate it now more than ever. Because now I know what put the sadness there.

"I'm sorry." Her voice is soft. "I never meant to upset you."

"Don't apologize." Anger bubbles inside me. "You went through hell. None of that is your fault. You have nothing to apologize for."

"I never should have written those letters. It was stupid, and I'm sorry if they weirded you out. I wasn't obsessed with you. I just..."

"You don't have to explain. I get it." I do get it. She'd had no one.

I'd been her best friend, then I left.

And things got worse.

She's shaking her head, not listening to me. "No. I shouldn't have let you bring me here."

"Don't," I growl, knowing where this is going and already hating it.

She lifts Charles off her lap and sets him down next to her. "I know we have history. And you'll always be important to me, Nathan." *No.* That now familiar lump in my throat starts to form. "But none of that means you're responsible for some... fling."

"Fling?" I shove up to stand and stomp the few feet over to her. "This isn't a fucking fling for me, Rosie. You mean something to me."

I drop down onto my knees before her.

Rosie reaches out and tugs on my shirt. "Stop doing that."

"I can't stop caring about you."

She tugs on my shirt more. "I mean, stop kneeling on hard floors, you dummy."

I lean into her space. "I will always kneel before you." I lightly grip her wrists. "And you're just proving that you care about me too. Even if you don't want to admit it."

"Of course I care about you!" she practically shouts as she throws her hands up pulling out of my grip.

Then she winces.

The bubbling anger inside me pops, morphing into guilt.

"Shit." I gently cup her cheeks. "Just hold still and let me tell you something."

"Tell me what?"

I ghost my thumbs over her cheeks. "We're dating."

EIGHTY-NINE
ROSALYN

"We're... what?" I stare into his eyes, sure I heard him wrong.

"We're dating. This isn't a fling. It isn't casual. You're my girlfriend."

My mouth opens. Then closes. "You want to date?"

He shakes his head. "Don't want. We are. And we're going steady."

"But you—"

"Swear to god if you say something about obligation or me being famous, I'm going to lose it." He takes a slow breath. "Tell me you understand."

I shake my head the smallest bit. "No one says going steady anymore."

The side of his mouth lifts. Just a little.

Then it drops.

He brushes his thumb over my cheek again. "I want to kiss you."

"You can." I rest my hands on his forearms. "I might be a little banged up, but I'm not broken."

I refuse to be broken.

"I don't want to hurt you," he whispers.

I lean forward. "You're not."

"Tell me you'll stay." Nathan moves closer, leaving only inches between us.

"I'll stay," I tell him. Even if it's just for a few days.

His fingers flex, like he knows what I'm thinking. "For the three weeks you're on crutches."

"Nathan," I sigh.

"Rosie."

"Three weeks is a long time," I try to tell him.

"It's a blink," he replies. "Now agree you'll stay."

It's ridiculous, and...

"You really want to date?"

Nathan groans. "Pretty Rosie, I know you're a clever girl. And I know you heard me the first time."

"Isn't it weird to have your girlfriend of like, what, a week, live with you?"

He shakes his head. "First, you and I go way back. You're not just *some girlfriend*. And second, the beginning of a relationship is always the most sex-filled." My brows lift. "I know I need to give you some time before I fuck you into the mattress again." He slides one of his hands down from my cheek to palm the side of my neck. "But as soon as you're ready, I'll be making use of the fact that we're under the same roof. And in the same bed."

I roll my eyes, like my body isn't thrumming at the idea. "Do you promise not to barge in when I'm on the toilet?"

He nods solemnly. "Unless you scream my name again."

I give him a flat look. "Sorry, I hadn't assumed it was *the cat* opening the door."

"Never underestimate the cat."

I roll my lips together and take in the man before me.

He's so handsome.

And has such a mouth on him.

He's kind and generous and a good cat dad.

And he's practically begging me to be with him.

A part of me knows that we can never be. Not forever. My baggage is too heavy.

But I can have him for now.

I can have him for at least three weeks.

"Okay." I nod against his hold on me.

"Okay?" His eyes search mine.

"Okay, I'll stay. Okay, I'll be your girlfriend." My mouth pulls into a smile at the look on his face. I tip my chin up. "And I believe you said you'd kiss me."

Nathan grins. "That's my girl." Then his lips are on mine.

They're warm, and he presses them firmly against my own.

My body relaxes, and muscles I didn't realize were tense release.

I lean into the kiss.

But Nathan pulls away.

"Eat your food."

I blink my eyes open. "You're a tease."

He snorts, then reaches down to adjust himself. "I am not without punishment."

I bite down on my laugh, knowing it will only make my head hurt more.

Nathan braces his hands on either side of me. "I'll grab your painkillers, but you gotta eat something."

I look over at the bowl of cereal, taking in the little shapes floating in some sort of milk. "Marshmallows?"

"They're no Rosalyn's Restaurant's. But they help feed my newly rediscovered marshmallow obsession." He holds my gaze. "Because it seems I've become obsessed."

My eyes stay on him as he stands and strides away.

Because I've become a little obsessed too.

NINETY

ROSALYN

Go to bed with Nathan beside me.

Wake up sprawled across him.

Eat.

Nap.

Repeat.

For two days.

Maybe three.

Time has begun to blur.

Another nap.

Another meal.

Someone knocks on Nathan's front door, and he gets up from his end of the couch to answer it.

He's been keeping his distance, physically. Not touching me, except for in sleep. But he hasn't left the condo since we got here.

Always nearby to offer help.

Always telling me to rest and feeding me.

And always keeping our topics of conversation light.

He's been... perfect.

I smile into my bowl of canned soup. Happy to know there's at least one thing he's not good at.

When he apologized for it being canned, I made an offhand comment about having a bunch of homemade soups and casseroles in my freezer back home. And it wasn't until Nathan perked up that I realized I probably shouldn't have said that. It didn't work out well the last time he went snooping around my apartment. But I am glad I can bring something to this *relationship*, even if it's just my cooking skills.

But as my eyes roam around the condo, I concede that this isn't such a bad deal.

Living in a penthouse.

Having a super fine man waiting on me around the clock.

I set my bowl on the side table as Nathan opens the front door.

There's no need to glance down at myself to know I'm in a bit of a state.

My hair is oily and pulled back into a loose ponytail since I want it out of my face, but a tight bun still makes my head ache.

I'm wearing the same set of sweatpants and T-shirt I went to bed in last night. And the little body wipes Nathan gave me have only done so much.

All in all, I feel and look disgusting, and I can only hope this visitor won't judge me.

"Thanks." Nathan's voice carries through the apartment, then he shuts the door.

Okay, not a visitor.

When he turns back, he's holding three paper shopping bags in one hand, and in the other, he has a stool with a plastic top and metal legs.

He lifts the stool, showing it off. "Care for a shower?"

My mouth drops as I look at the item again. "You bought me a shower stool?"

"Technically, yes." He smirks as he carries the bags over to the island. "But I can't promise that I won't take a seat on it next time I'm tired in the shower."

A shower stool should hardly make me want to cry.

I have no idea how expensive they are, and with Nathan's bank account, I'm sure he didn't blink at the price. But the thought...

I lift the collar of my shirt and try to discreetly wipe at the corners of my eyes.

The stool is practical.

A tool to use in managing my hygiene.

And yet, it's the most thoughtful gift anyone has ever bought me.

When I leave, I'm bringing it home with me. I don't care if it will take up half of the tub in my bathroom.

"Want to use it now?" Nathan is still in the kitchen, but his tone has changed, and I suspect he caught me wiping my eyes.

I nod and scoot forward on the couch, grabbing my crutches from where I left them leaning against the coffee table.

I don't bother trying to grab my dirty dishes—Nathan has scolded me enough for that—I just make my way toward the bedroom.

NINETY-ONE
NATE

I feel stupid for not buying Rosie the shower stool sooner.

And truthfully, it was Maddox who suggested I get one, but I'll keep that to myself. Because as soon as he said it, I wanted to smack myself in the face. I've been injured enough over the years to know showering with an injured leg is hard. I've just always lived in places that have the built-in shower seat, so I never had to buy anything special.

Something special. It's a fucking shower stool.

And it made her cry.

"You need anything else?" I ask, standing in the bathroom door.

Rosie eyes the dining room chair I put outside the shower stall. "Please tell me you aren't planning to sit there watching me."

I look at the chair, then to the opaque glass of the stall. "If the glass was clear..."

Rosie huffs. "Nathan, I appreciate you, but I'd like to do this alone."

I hold my hands palms out. "You're the one who brought it

up. And, Miss Pervy, that chair is for you to use while you're taking on and off your clothes. Unless you'd rather I help..."

She purses her lips, assumably at her new nickname. "Thank you, but no." Then she glances at me. "Not this time."

That sparks my interest.

I take a step forward into the bathroom. "But another time?"

She lifts her shoulder in a casual shrug, and the days of denying myself physical touch gather like a weight around my balls.

I take another step closer. "I can be gentle."

A flash of humor crosses her features. "I'm sure you can. But I'm gross."

"You're not gross." I immediately argue.

"Nathan, I haven't showered in days. I feel grimy and disgusting, and I can smell myself." She makes a face as she says the last part.

When she looks like she'll try to take a step backward on her crutches, I stop advancing. "Fine," I tell her. "But I'm leaving the bathroom door open. If you need anything at all, just yell."

The look Rosie gives me says she won't be yelling for help, but as I back out of the doorway, I decide to stay close by.

NINETY-TWO

ROSALYN

Feeling relaxed and squeaky clean—after three rounds of body wash—I decide to pull on the fluffy pink robe that magically appeared on the back of the bathroom door yesterday.

I didn't ask about it, sure it was purchased for me and uncomfortable with the fact. But now that I have it on, it's definitely coming home with me, along with that shower stool and possibly a bottle of Nathan's shampoo.

Nathan left the bathroom door open like he said he would. But he didn't mention that he'd be waiting in the bedroom.

On the bed.

Lounged back on the pillows.

Reading a book.

I stop just inside the room. "What are you doing?"

He looks up at me, his eyes traveling over my robe-clad body. "Waiting for you."

His black T-shirt clings to his body, and his sweatpants should be illegal.

He's been wearing lounge clothes all week, and I don't

know if it's out of solidarity or if he really dresses like this at home. But either way, I appreciate it.

And I appreciate it even more now because *damn.*

Nathan lowers a hand to his lap.

"What exactly are you waiting for?" I ask as I take a step closer to the bed.

Instead of answering my question, Nathan sits up and pats the bed next to him. "You need to take a rest."

"A rest?"

Nathan stands and circles around the foot of the bed, not stopping until he's right in front of me. "A rest."

Nathan takes my crutches and rests them against the wall. Then he wraps his arms around me in a hug and lifts me, carrying me to the edge of the bed.

He sets me on my feet, and I keep just the toe of my bad foot on the ground for balance.

Letting go of me, Nathan leans in, lowering his voice. "And if you listen like a good girl... I'll treat you like my good girl."

Something heated rolls down my spine, settling between my thighs.

We've been so close to each other. Waking up wrapped together. But not touching beyond that... And fuck if I'm not ready for more.

"You gonna do that for me, Rosie?" he whispers. "You gonna give me that control you hold on to so tightly?"

I swallow.

I never wanted to be the way I am.

Rigid. Paranoid. Scared.

And as I look at the man in front of me, I understand.

I don't have to be this way.

Not with him.

My fingers move to the tie at my waist, and I pull it free.

The robe parts, exposing my nakedness. And I shrug it off, dropping it to the ground.

A noise rumbles in Nathan's chest, but instead of stepping into me, he steps back.

To look at all of me.

I still have scrapes.

Still have bruises.

Still have a plastic brace on my ankle and wet hair lying across my shoulders.

I still have the same soft body I did a month ago.

Heavy tits and stretch marks and parts I've never wanted a man to see in the light.

But all that disappears when Nathan looks at me.

Because he's not looking at me like he sees my insecurities. He's looking at me like he's memorizing me.

"On the bed. On your back," he demands.

I lower myself to sit on the edge of the mattress, then shift so I'm lying fully on the bed.

Nathan steps to the foot of the bed, bends, and picks up the large wedge pillow off the floor.

I eye him as he carries it back to my side. "What are you doing?"

"You're supposed to be elevating." He shifts the pillow to one arm, then hooks his other arm under my knees.

With no apparent effort, Nathan lifts me by the knees, raising my ass off the mattress so he can shove the wedge pillow underneath my butt, leaving my ass several inches in the air above the mattress.

This pillow is meant to keep my leg elevated, but since I've just been putting my ankle up on Nathan at night, at least we're making use of it.

Nathan lowers me, then steps back again.

I keep my knees lifted, and even though they're pressed together, so much of me is still exposed.

He groans and palms the front of his pants, which are now tented from his body.

Letting him be in charge, I don't say anything.

I just watch as he squeezes his dick once more before letting go and shoving his pants down.

As soon as his cock is freed, it bobs in the air.

I expect him to pull off his shirt and climb onto the bed. But instead of grabbing his hem, he wraps his hand around his length.

And he starts to stroke himself.

My blood sizzles at the sight.

Eyes on my body, with his hand on his dick, Nathan is the most divine thing I've ever seen.

He hasn't touched me.

Hasn't even kissed me.

But I'm so ready for him.

So ready I have to do *something*.

Needing some sort of contact, I reach up and grab my breasts.

"That's it," Nathan moans.

He's gripping his cock so hard I don't know how it doesn't hurt.

I roll my head to the side so I can stare at his dick.

There's no point pretending I'm not watching him jack off.

With the hand not on his cock, Nathan grips the hem of his shirt and pulls the material up.

His stomach muscles flex. And a shiver of excitement coats my body as I admire his strength.

I shift my fingers until I'm pinching my nipples.

"That *is* being a good girl." He makes a sound in his throat, then pulls his shirt off all the way.

He keeps stroking himself, and I keep staring as his tip starts to glisten.

"Legs open," he demands.

I drop my knees apart.

"Foot on my shoulder."

I lift my gaze from his dick to his face.

"What?" I ask, but he's already climbing onto the bed.

Between my thighs.

He's on his knees, and I think he's going to shuffle forward so he can line up with my exposed entrance. But he doesn't shuffle, he bends.

One hand presses into the mattress next to the pillow—which is lifting my core to mouth level—and the other hand hooks around my knee, guiding me until my ankle brace is resting on his back.

"Nathan—" I start to protest because that hard plastic can't feel good on his bare skin.

"Elevate. Remember?" he states, then lowers his open mouth to my flesh.

My eyes snap closed, and I arch my neck.

Nathan flattens his tongue, swiping it up the length of me.

Then he reaches my clit. And he devours it.

Sucking while simultaneously pressing the tip of his tongue against my bundle of nerves. And it's all my primed body needs.

Embarrassingly quickly, my core contracts.

A moan is ripped out of me, and I tangle my hands in Nathan's hair.

His lips part, and he gives my pussy an open-mouthed kiss as I continue to come.

"Holy—" I pant.

He shifts lower, plunging his tongue inside me. His nose bumps against my clit, sending a shudder through my body and making my knees automatically press together, trapping his head.

"Nathan," I gasp.

He lifts his eyes to look at me, pulling his mouth back just enough to speak. "That's one. I need at least one more."

Then he lowers his mouth.

NINETY-THREE

NATE

Her taste has me closing my eyes.

It's her essence. Her slick. The proof she's enjoying this just as much as I am.

Nails scrape across my scalp, and I moan into her pussy.

I curl my tongue into her. Fucking her with my mouth.

She's writhing. Moving and moaning. And I need to make her come again so I can leave her boneless and resting.

But knowing she's sensitive, I give her clit a break.

Just for the moment.

Licking at her slit, I bring one hand up and trace my finger over her seam.

Rosie reacts by squeezing my head harder between her thighs.

I feel precum drip from my tip.

I want to have every part of her.

I trail my finger down.

I want to have every hole.

I circle her tight rear entrance.

I want to consume this woman.

Rosie lifts her hips toward my mouth.

I want to own her.

Because she already owns me.

"Nathan."

Hearing her pant my name is like a shot of adrenaline to my nuts.

I press my finger just a little bit more, then I pull it away.

Rosie curses. And I shut her up by clamping my lips back on her clit.

Her curse turns into a moan.

And I lower my hand back down to my aching dick.

NINETY-FOUR
ROSALYN

He's too good at this.

The teasing.

The touching.

All my muscles tense and flex.

As he laps at me, I roll my head side to side.

I've never had a man go down on me like this. And never had one try to make me come twice in a row with his mouth.

His exhale is hot against my blazing skin.

He drags his tongue down my whole length again, down to *that spot*, and my eyes fly open.

No one has ever paid this much attention to my ass. I've never even considered allowing anyone to. But all this teasing...

Movement catches my attention, and that's when I see it.

Our reflection.

I open my eyes wider, to soak in the details.

And my breath catches.

Watching Nathan jerk off standing next to the bed was one thing, but this.

My mouth opens so I can pull in more air.

The tall mirror in the corner of the room is angled toward us, and the view...

I let go of Nathan's hair to grab my breasts again.

Nathan is kneeling on the bed, bent over, one arm supporting his weight, with his mouth on my pussy and his other hand stroking his cock.

The hottest man I've ever met is jerking off while eating me out.

I want him to fuck me.

I want to feel him stretching me.

But more than anything, I want to watch him come undone.

Keeping my feet on his back, I stop squeezing his head with my knees and lower them apart.

In the reflection, I can see Nathan shift so he can look at me.

I keep watching the mirror. "I want you to come on me."

Nathan's tongue pauses against me. And I watch his hand stop too.

I shake my head. "Keep going. Please. Keep going."

NINETY-FIVE

NATE

I groan into her sweet pussy.

"I want to feel you come on me again." Her voice is husky with lust. "It felt so good."

I squeeze my fingers tighter around my dick as I start to stroke myself again.

Rosie's dirty talk is so fucking hot I'm ready to blow.

"It was so warm." She moans. "I like you marking me."

I was already planning on getting myself off—without fucking her. She needs to recover more before I do that. But to hear her ask for it... To want it...

She rolls her hips beneath my mouth.

"I'm so close. Nathan."

My jaw is starting to ache, and my tongue is tired, proving I'm out of practice, but no force in the world could make me stop now.

I press my tongue against her clit.

She's starting to tense, digging her heels into my back. And I'm sure she's putting too much pressure on her injured ankle.

I could pull my mouth away from her sweet little cunt to tell her to stop.

Or I could just make her come.

I hum.

And my Little Rose explodes.

The sound that leaves her fills me with pride. And the wetness against my chin sends me over the edge.

I lever myself up and shuffle forward.

With my hand no longer holding my weight, I reach down and rub my thumb over her clit just as Rosie pushes her tits together.

"You ready for my cum?" I grunt, stroking myself.

Rosie nods, whiny sounds of pleasure filling the room around us.

"Say it," I demand.

"I'm ready." Her eyes flutter open. "Come on me, Nathan."

My body obeys.

And my release splashes across her skin.

NINETY-SIX

ROSALYN

I'm still breathing heavily when Nathan pulls the blankets over me after wiping me down with a warm cloth and pulling the wedge out from under me.

I tuck the blanket under my chin as I roll so I'm facing Nathan's side of the bed.

He climbs onto the mattress, equally naked, and matches my position.

There's a look on his face, like he wants to say something, so I stay quiet.

"How did you go six years without sex?"

I snort, not expecting that to be his question. "It's pretty easy, really. I just didn't date."

He hums. "Before that?"

"Do you really want to know about my ex-boyfriends? Because I'm telling you right now, Mr. Waller, I don't want to know about any of your exes."

Nathan smirks. "Mr. Waller. I think I like that."

I roll my eyes. But I don't hate the idea of calling him that. In the right situation.

"How long was your relationship before the half-dozen-year hiatus?" he asks.

"How do you know I had a relationship before that? It could've been a one-night stand."

He shakes his head. "It was a relationship."

I wait a second, then sigh. "I was with him for three years."

"That's a long time."

I shrug.

Nathan presses his lips together, then decides to ask, "What happened?"

I shrug again. "He took a job in another state. Didn't ask me to come. I didn't ask to go."

"So he's fucking stupid."

His tone is so serious it makes me laugh. "That's the consensus."

"And you just decided to stop dating after that?"

"I was kinda over men, ya know?"

"I know." Nathan nods seriously. "That's why I have Charles as a roommate."

I smile. "He's a good roommate."

"The best." Nathan agrees.

I know I shouldn't ask. I just said I didn't want to know. But... "What was your longest relationship?"

He closes an eye. "The name or the time?"

"The time." I reach out under the blanket and shove at his chest. "I don't need to know her name."

He grins and catches my hand under the covers, holding it against his bare skin. "Longest was about a year and a half, I think."

"What happened?" I ask the same question he did.

He rubs his thumb over the back of my hand. "She wanted to get married."

"And you didn't?" It takes work to keep my voice even. The

thought of some bitch trying to marry Nathan makes my stomach hurt.

"It didn't feel right."

"The timing or the girl?" I can't help myself.

"Both." He lifts a shoulder. "I mean, we were exclusive, but I still saw it as a casual thing. Then one day she tells me she loves me and asks when I think we'll get married..."

I try not to smile. "I take it you didn't respond the way she wanted."

He chuckles. "Yeah, apparently wide eyes and dead silence weren't what she was looking for."

"I can't imagine why."

Nathan smirks. "I'd never had someone tell me they love me before. Or, well, you know, someone outside the normal people."

My nose scrunches. "Who are the normal people?"

"Family, friends, whatever." Nathan says it so casually.

Normal.

Because it's normal to have your parents tell you they love you.

Normal to have siblings or friends or cousins who love you.

My time with Nathan has made me forget.

I fight to keep my features neutral as his comment sweeps open the curtain I've been drawing over my past, revealing the hole in the center of my being.

The one that should be full of good memories.

Should be full of happiness.

Should be full of love.

But it's empty.

I try to pull my hand free of Nathan's grip. But he tightens his hold.

NINETY-SEVEN
NATE

I see it on her face.

What I've taken for granted my entire life, Rosie has never had.

No loving family.

No one to tell her they love her.

And it makes my fucking heart ache.

I hold her hand tightly.

It's right there, sitting on my tongue, to tell her I love her.

That I'll be her normal.

But I need her to believe me when I say it, and it's not time yet.

I inhale slowly.

And since I've already ruined the mood, I bring up another bad topic.

"How did your dad die?"

Her gaze lowers to my chin, and she presses her lips together before answering. "The final diagnosis was heart failure."

"Like a heart attack?"

She nods.

"Was it at home?"

"Yeah."

"Were you there?"

She nods again.

I squeeze her hand a little more.

She was nineteen when she wrote to me on the day her dad died.

Nineteen.

I can't imagine losing your only parent at that age.

And I can't imagine the mind fuck of that person also being your abuser.

The relief of them being gone but the unknown of being on your own.

"I'm sorry." I scoot a little closer to her. "I'm not sorry he's dead. But I'm sorry about... him."

"Thanks, Nathan." She shuffles her body a little closer to mine.

Fuck it.

I let go of her hand and grab her sides, dragging her to me.

Our naked bodies collide, but I keep pulling her until she's half draped across me, like how we wake up.

I wrap my arms around her firmly and kiss the top of her head—her hair nearly dry now.

"Nathan?"

"Hmm." I nuzzle her hair.

"I need to use your kitchen."

"Whatever you need." I close my eyes and relax into the change of topic. "What do you want to make?"

"It's not for me. I need to cook for an event."

My eyes open. "Rosie, you can't work yet."

"Nathan." She tries to lift her head from my chest, but I press my chin down, holding her in place.

"We can argue like this." I hold her tighter. "But you're also not going to win this argument. You can't work an event when you're on freaking crutches."

"One." She taps a finger against my side. "I literally became my own boss so no one could tell me what to do. And two." She dances her fingertips up my side this time, making me jump.

I slap my hand down on top of hers.

Rosie snickers. "Two, I can let Presley do all the running around."

"I don't care if you have help. Your legs and your arms and your everything will be killing you by the end of the night." I picture holding my weight up by my armpits for hours and pull a face.

"I need to work, Nathan."

"I'll give you whatever money you need."

She groans. "I appreciate that, but I'm going to pretend you didn't just offer me money."

"Why?" I ask, genuinely perplexed.

"Because I don't need money," she huffs. "I can pass off most of the jobs I have for the next three weeks and still pay my rent. But I need to keep a few. Presley can cook for most of them, but there's one in two days, and I need to do it myself."

"Why?"

"It pays well, which is part of the reason I don't need you offering me money. And the artist hosting the event is the sister-in-law of a woman who plans lots of fundraisers each year, and I'd like to make a good first impression."

I hate that she has good reasons. And I hate that I can't just tie her to the bed to keep her from working.

"What sort of artist?"

"She's a painter, and she's auctioning off a special collection for the fundraiser." Rosie inhales deeply. "Her work is amazing, and to be honest, I've been a fan forever, so really, I just want to meet her."

Any urge I had to argue dies with Rosie's admission. I can't stand in the way of her meeting someone she admires.

Instead of showing my defeat, I ask one last question. "What's her name?"

NINETY-EIGHT

ROSALYN

"You're a lifesaver," I tell Meghan.

"You saved my ass just the other week," she points out, referring to the night Nathan walked back into my life. "I owe you."

"One event versus eight. Not exactly the same."

She makes a noise through her lips. "Yeah, I'm gonna cry all the way to the bank over the discrepancy."

I laugh. "Well, I appreciate it. I'll email my clients now, copying you in."

When we hang up, I reach over to the nightstand and grab my laptop.

After Nathan and I had our post-sex cuddle chat, we got dressed into pajamas.

I chose to camp out in bed for my call to Meghan's Moments to see if she could take the events off my hands. And Nathan said he had some work to do before bed and that he'd do it in his office to give me room for my call.

He's been great company, but I really should find a way to

make him go into his actual office. I'm sure he's missing a lot, and it's because of me.

NINETY-NINE
NATE

"Hello?" A stranger answers the phone.

"Orlando?" I prompt.

"Yes?"

"Sweet. You the guy who owns the studio doing that Savannah Vass fundraiser in a couple of days?"

This time when he says yes, he drags it out into a question.

"Can I talk to her?" I ask.

"Uh, she's not... here."

I roll my eyes. "Can I have her number?"

"I don't, uh, I can't do that."

"Some sort of privacy thing?" I should have figured.

"More of a scary husband thing."

That makes me laugh. "Okay, well, can I talk to her sister-in-law or whoever is in charge of planning?"

"That just makes him the scary brother." He snorts.

"Okay, well, can I have you pass along my number?"

"And why do you want to talk to her?" Orlando asks.

"I just need to talk to someone about the setup." I could probably just tell this guy that Rosie needs a chair to sit in. But

I don't want to chance the paying clients showing up and demanding it be removed.

I give him my number.

"And your name?"

"Nate Waller."

There's a pause.

Then Orlando clears his throat. "Like... *the* Nate Waller?"

I grin. "The one and only." He's definitely gonna pass my number on.

Five minutes later, my phone rings.

"This is Nate," I answer.

"Care to tell me why a famous wide receiver is trying to get a hold of my wife?" a deep voice replies from the other end of the line.

The scary husband.

I bite down on my chuckle. "Is this Mr. Savannah?"

The man chuffs. "It is. Now explain yourself."

My brows lift at his directness, but I played pro ball, so I'm used to being around intense dudes. "I'm reaching out because my missus is catering the event your missus is hosting in a couple days." Missus is close enough to the truth. "But my girl is in rough shape."

"Sick?" he asks.

"No. Hit by a car."

"The fuck?" Shock fills the man's voice.

"My reaction too. And yet she's insisting on working."

The man sighs in a way that tells me his woman is stubborn too. "Christ, man, we can hire someone else."

"Yeah, I can't let you do that. She's excited. A fan of your wife's work. And obstinate."

"I know the type." I swear I can hear him rolling his eyes. "But if you don't want us to hire someone else, what do you need?"

"I need to make sure no one will bother her for sitting or take away the chair I'm going to insist she uses the whole night. And I need to make sure no one will try to kick me out since I plan on assisting her. Most likely against her will."

"No one will say shit to you," he says confidently, and I believe he's telling the truth. "Just make sure to spend some of that game money while you're there."

"Deal."

And after I hang up, I make one more call.

ONE HUNDRED
ROSALYN

"Nathan, what's the address here?" I call across to the kitchen.

"What for?"

I look up from my place on the couch. "Kidnap much?"

He smiles as he pours two cups of coffee at the island, and I'm grateful we're past the days of Nathan telling me I can't have caffeine.

"I'm ordering groceries," I explain.

"Beautiful, I told you I'd get you whatever you want."

There he goes. Using that damn nickname.

"It's not for me." I focus on the conversation. "I need to do a bunch of prep today for that fundraiser tomorrow night." I remind him of the conversation we had last night.

He hums. "Was everything you need on that menu spreadsheet?"

My mouth opens and closes. "I'm sorry, what?"

Nathan sets the coffee carafe down and looks at me. "I sent the girls to the store with the list." He glances at the clock on one of his ovens. "They should be here any minute."

I look at my laptop, sitting on the cushion beside me. "That spreadsheet is on my laptop. It's password protected." I'm saying this mostly to myself. Because the laptop is also password protected.

"If there was something else you needed, we can order it." He ignores the whole *breaking into my laptop* thing. "And they're both good in the kitchen, so they can help you, since Presley is out of town visiting her mom."

"Nathan Waller." Using his full name gets his attention. "Who are these girls you're talking about? And why are you talking to *my* Presley?"

"Rosie Posie." He fights a smile as he carries both coffees toward the living room. "Presley called me to see how you were doing because she doesn't trust you to tell her the truth." He lifts an eyebrow at me, and I don't bother responding. "And the girls"—there's a knock on the door—"are here."

He turns back around and deposits the mugs on the island.

"Nathan," I hiss as I climb to my feet. "I'm not dressed for company."

"You look perfect," he says without even looking at me.

"I look like a troll," I grumble under my breath. And Nathan smothers a laugh.

I'm wearing a pair of black leggings under my ankle brace, which is fine. But my soft, no-padding bralette and strappy gray tank top are not company appropriate. My girls require a lot more support if they're going to be around other people.

Not to mention, I've had zero beauty routine, beyond using Nathan's deodorant, since I got here.

I watch Nathan's ass as he walks toward the door in another pair of sweatpants, and I have to think those aren't for company either.

Freaking perfect Nathan.

I've never felt more comfortable around anyone before in my life. But I've also never felt more possessive.

I reach up and tighten my ponytail, thankful I've at least showered in the last twenty-four hours.

Nathan opens the door, and I squeeze the handles of my crutches, prepared to be confronted by beautiful women in business suits or dresses or something. But that's not who enters.

"Mama Ruth. Smidge." Nathan holds his arms out. "You two are the literal best."

A woman in her sixties, dressed in loose-fitting jeans and a Biters T-shirt, steps into the condo first. She's followed by a girl with dark brown hair, green shorts, and a tie-dye tank top, who must be somewhere between a tween and a teen.

The elder of the pair steps forward to accept Nathan's hug. "Oh, Nate. You're always such a sweetheart."

The girl next to her rolls her eyes. "We're not supposed to fall for the charms of men. Remember, Grandma."

The woman/grandma/Mama Ruth steps back with a chuckle. "That rule is for young people."

Nathan holds out his fist. "To never falling for men."

The girl bumps her fist against his. "Deal." Then the girl reaches behind her. "Now make way. We have cold stuff out here."

Nathan backs up, holding the door wide, and the girl drags a wagon into view.

It's overflowing with grocery bags and has to weigh twice as much as she does, but instead of the teen crankiness one might expect, this girl is grinning.

I want to say something, maybe introduce myself, but I feel so awkward that I just stay put. Frozen in front of the couch.

Until Nathan swings the door shut behind *the girls* and gestures toward me. "Ladies, please allow me to introduce you to my girlfriend, Rosie."

The gasp that comes out of the older woman would make

me laugh if my body wasn't too busy reacting to Nathan calling me his girlfriend.

He told me we were dating.

I agreed.

But hearing him say it...

I roll my lips together, then work on forming my mouth into a smile. "Hi."

"Oh my gosh."

That's all the warning I get before the older woman is hustling across the great room toward me.

"You are so pretty." Her voice catches, and I think she might be crying.

I freeze, completely unsure of how to react. But the woman isn't deterred.

Sturdy arms wrap around me, trapping my arms at my sides —where I'm still clutching my crutches.

"I didn't know our Natey Boy had a girlfriend!"

I look at Nathan over her shoulder and mouth *Natey Boy*.

He rolls his eyes, but the effect is lost since he's smiling.

"Rosie, this is Ruth, Hannah's mom." Nathan walks toward us. "And the little gremlin setting up in your kitchen is Chelsea, Hannah's niece."

Still stuck in the embrace, I look over to where the young teen is putting the groceries on the counter. Now that Nathan's introduced them, I remember seeing them both during the party at the Lovelace house.

And then my cheeks flash pink because of how I ended the night at the Lovelace house.

"Nice to officially meet you both." I repeat their names in my head so I don't forget.

"It's our pleasure." Ruth steps back and squeezes my upper arms before letting go and wiping at her eyes.

Nathan clicks his tongue as he steps up beside Ruth and

puts his arm around her shoulders. "Now, now, stop acting like I was never going to find a woman."

Ruth swats at him with a sniffle.

"There's a difference between finding and keeping," Chelsea points out from the kitchen.

I bite my lip to keep from laughing.

Nathan winks at me, then turns to face the girl, slapping a hand to his chest. "Do you doubt me, oh wee one?"

Chelsea lifts a shoulder. "Just saying."

"Uh-huh. Just saying my ass."

"Nathan," I scold, not sure if he should be swearing in front of this girl.

He grins at me. "I put a hundred in her swear jar at the beginning of every month."

I look at the girl. "That true?"

She nods.

"Well, fuckity shits on a stick." I turn back to Nathan. "Give her another hundred."

The girl lets out a whoop.

"I like her," Ruth says while looking at me.

It's the simplest of compliments. She doesn't even know me. But Ruth radiates a sort of maternal warmth that I want to curl up in.

I want to let her like me.

"Thanks," I whisper.

Nathan's expression softens, and he closes the distance between us, placing his palm on my spine. "Come on, Girl-friend. Let's get you all set up."

ONE HUNDRED ONE
NATE

"Is it time?" I ask Rosie.

She bites her lip, like she's trying not to smile, and nods. "I think so."

Gripping the back of her chair, I wheel her over to the dining table.

After the initial introductions, the three ladies crowded around the island to sort the groceries and go over the recipes.

I know Rosie was uncomfortable at first, but she never questioned the fact that one of her helpers was a thirteen-year-old girl.

Not that she should. Chelsea could cook most adults I know under the table.

Within the hour, they were all chatting and chopping produce, seasoning meat, sorting ingredients...

Ruth ran her own flower business for a long time, so she's good at task management. And Chelsea spends most of her time in the kitchen when she's not at school. And despite her great comebacks, she's actually really good at taking direction.

And based on the questions I heard Chelsea asking Rosie, Smidge is impressed with my girl's catering business.

I pull the chair to a stop once Rosie is tucked into the table.

She fought me on the office chair—of course she did—but I insisted. And I'm glad I did, because there's no way she could've been on her feet this long.

"Okay, Sensei, teach me your ways of the 'mallow."

Rosie shakes her head, but her smile is genuine. "I can't believe you bought a hot plate for this."

I look at my setup on the kitchen table, feeling oddly proud.

I ran the extension cord from the far side of the table so no one would trip on it.

Set up the stand mixer, pot, candy thermometer, sugar... Everything I purchased last week for the banana marshmallows. Only the hot plate is new.

I can't help but think about the night we were supposed to have but didn't, because my Rosie got hit by a fucking car.

I bend over the back of her chair and wrap my arms around her in a hug.

She makes a small sound of surprise but relaxes as I squeeze her.

"You're really excited about these marshmallows." Her murmur is just for me.

"I'm really excited that car didn't fucking kill you."

Rosie laughs, and it's a light, breathy sound. "I'm excited about that too." She pats my arm. "Little looser, Catcher."

I'm beaming at her new nickname for me before I realize what she said. "Oh, sorry." I loosen my hold so I'm no longer strangling her neck.

Then, because I can, I plant a noisy kiss on the top of her head.

"Gross." Chelsea's voice comes from behind us in the kitchen, and it just makes me smile more.

This is not a time for sappy sadness. This is a time for sugary pillows of joy.

I take a seat at the table, and Rosie walks me through each step.

She's patient and forgiving. And we make our personal batch of banana cream marshmallows first—so I can practice on the ones that aren't for the client. And then Chelsea joins us for the second batch, which is peach bellini flavored.

"I'm impressed with us," I say around a mouthful of banana-flavored sugar.

"I'm impressed with you too." Rosie leans back in her chair and looks around the kitchen.

Everything that needed to be prepped has been.

All the surfaces have been cleaned and set back to rights. And all the food is put away.

The appliances are stuffed to the max, but it worked. And I wonder how she's done this out of her much smaller kitchen.

Rosie is a fucking wonder.

"I can't thank you two enough," Rosie says, turning her attention to the two who made this possible. "I'll, of course, pay you for—"

"Absolutely not." Ruth cuts her off. "Nate here is family, and family doesn't pay each other for help." The woman only pauses long enough to lower herself into a chair opposite us at the table. "And I won't hear anything about payment tomorrow either."

"Tomorrow?" Rosie repeats.

Ruth nods. "You're going to need help cooking everything, and I have nothing better to do."

Rosie glances at me. But I just lift a shoulder. "There's really no use arguing with her."

Emotions war in Rosie's eyes.

She doesn't want to accept help.

She's overwhelmed by the offer of help.

And she's accepting that I'm right, that there's no avoiding it now.

My girl sighs. "You've already done too much." When Ruth opens her mouth, Rosie holds up a hand. "But you're right. I would really appreciate your help again tomorrow."

"Anything you need, dear." Ruth rests her hand on the table.

"Anything?" Rosie repeats.

I drop into a chair next to Rosie, eyebrows raised since it sounds like she's going to ask for something more.

Ruth also perks up. "I feel a sense of intrigue all the sudden."

Rosie chuckles. "Nothing too exciting, I'm afraid. I just need a dress and some makeup picked up from my apartment."

"Of course," Ruth answers without even asking where the apartment is.

"I can do it," I interject. I'm glad Rosie is willing to ask Ruth, but I have time to go over there.

Rosie turns to me. "How familiar are you with bronzer brushes?"

"Uh, what?" My brows furrow.

Rosie nods and turns back to Ruth, dismissing my offer. "You at least have to let me pay for gas or something."

Ruth shakes her head. "Maddox keeps telling me to use my driver more often, so we'll just stop and pick up what you need on our way over tomorrow. I'll give you my number before we leave."

Before she can say more, Ruth's phone rings, and she answers it.

While she's talking, Rosie turns to me. "Should we offer to order dinner or something?"

I can see how exhausted she is, and I'm sure her social

battery is damn near dead, but she's still thinking about feeding the people who helped her.

A fucking wonder.

Reaching up, I brush my thumb across her cheek.

I've never really thought about bravery. All the examples that come to mind are of famous battles or movies with actors like Drake Daniels doing wild stunts. But every day with Rosie, I learn a little more about what it means to be brave.

Being brave is being a girl facing the day, knowing it's going to hurt.

Being brave is betting on yourself when no one else will.

Being brave is putting your heart out there and doing things you don't want to do because you know they'll make someone else happy.

Being brave is being Rosie.

I look at her like I already love her.

Because I do.

ROSALYN

"What is it?" I whisper.

Nathan brushes his thumb across my cheek again, and his throat works on a swallow.

I reach up and grip his forearm.

His mouth opens.

"They're here," Ruth declares, setting her phone back on the table.

My attention snaps back to Ruth. "Who's here?"

"Hannah and Maddox." She beams. "They've brought dinner from this Greek place near our house. You're gonna love it."

I blink at her. "Here?"

Ruth rolls her shoulders out. "Don't know about you, but I don't really feel like cooking dinner after all that."

"Well, no. But you have to let me pay for dinner," I try to insist.

"Give up the fight, Beautiful." Nathan drapes his arm over the back of my chair. "Plus, it's Maddox's money. That fucker has more than he needs."

I bite my cheek, remembering what I'm wearing.

Ruth and Chelsea have been nothing but chill, but Hannah and Maddox are the definition of a power couple.

Making the excuse of needing to use the restroom, I let Nathan roll me down the hall into the bedroom in his office chair.

He parks the chair in front of the bathroom door and hands me my crutches.

But before he goes, he bends down and presses his lips to mine.

They're warm and soft, and I close my eyes to soak in the moment.

When he pulls away, he taps his fingertip on the tip of my nose. "They already love you. So stop stressing."

They already love you. So stop stressing.

The *L* word and a demand to stop stressing. Two things that are beyond my capability right now.

I lift my arm and apply more of Nathan's deodorant.

As much as it pained me to ask Ruth to go to my apartment, the thought of having to send Nathan there unsupervised was sending me into a spiral.

I understand how he found the letters the first time he went there. He needed a bag for clothes... the box was in the duffel bags... But now that he has a nose for snooping... I can't take the chance.

And it's a simple truth that Ruth will be better at packing the *girly things*.

I secure the cap back on the deodorant and put it in the cupboard.

In all honesty, I'll probably still use some of Nathan's things while I'm here.

It's nice being surrounded by his scent.

Voices carry in through the open bathroom door, signaling the arrival of Hannah and Maddox.

Knowing I'm out of time, I grab the shirt I snagged out of Nathan's closet and shrug it on.

The sleeves are too long, so I roll them twice. And instead of buttoning the shirt up, I tie the bottom ends together at my waist. It's still open, but the tied bottom means that the shirt stays mostly in place and covers my unsupported boobs. It also covers the scrapes that are still healing on my arms.

I cringe a little at the *morning after* look wearing Nathan's shirt gives me, but it's the best thing I could think of without changing my whole outfit. Not that I think Ruth or Chelsea would comment on a wardrobe change... I'm just trying not to make it weird. And now, other than my ankle brace, you really can't tell I was injured.

Reminding myself that I've met these people before, I try to stop caring about my appearance.

It's not like I'm trying to impress or entice anybody; I just want to make a good impression as *Nathan's girlfriend*.

Grabbing my crutches, I take a deep breath and leave the bathroom.

ONE HUNDRED THREE
NATE

"Here she is now." I hold my arm out, gesturing to Rosie's arrival as I hear her crutches approach. But then I turn, and my mouth goes dry.

Because Rosie is wearing one of my work shirts.

And she looks like a fucking advertisement for late-night sex and bad ideas.

"Hello," she says quietly. Shyly. And it's like a dinner bell for my genitals.

I clear my throat. "Hannah, Maddox, you remember Rosie."

"She's Nate's girlfriend," Chelsea calls out.

"That she is, Smidge." I close the distance to Rosie so I can place a hand possessively on her back. "Rosie, you know Hannah and Maddox."

Her muscles relax under my palm, and a sense of pride fills my chest.

I did that.

I made her feel comfortable.

"Sit, sit." Ruth, ever the mother, directs everyone to the table after the round of *hello*s is finished.

Rosie takes the closest chair, and I help her scoot in.

The office chair was useful, but I left it in the bedroom, assuming she wouldn't want to use it for dinner.

Plates are passed out, and Maddox uses the serving utensils to start dishing out food.

Chelsea chatters away about all the food they made today, telling Hannah every detail of every dish.

Maddox lifts a brow at me, and I just shrug. The girl has an excellent memory.

Happy to listen, I shove spanakopita into my mouth.

"I've been meaning to ask all day." Ruth turns to Rosie. "How did you two meet?"

Rosie glances at me, but my mouth is too full to reply.

She sets her fork down, and I wonder if she's going to tell them the whole truth or say we met at the party.

"We, um, actually go way back," she tells Ruth.

My heart gives a little squeeze.

I don't know why I thought she might not want to admit that, but a part of me did.

"Really?" Maddox drags out the word, but I refuse to look at him.

I gave him so much shit over not telling me about Hannah when she reappeared in his life that I know I have a good reaming coming.

But instead of facing the music, I just fill my mouth with more spanakopita.

"You two dated before?" Hannah asks.

Rosie shakes her head. "No, nothing like that. We were friends when we were kids."

"Really?" Maddox repeats, slightly louder this time.

Rosie glances at him, probably thinking that he struggles with the English language. Which isn't entirely incorrect.

Rosie turns her attention to Maddox. "Nathan lived at the other end of the street from me."

"In Ohio?" Maddox asks. I keep avoiding his gaze.

"Wisconsin," Rosie corrects.

"Wisconsin?" Maddox sounds like he's thinking *really hard,* and I have to stop myself from sighing.

"I didn't know you lived in Wisconsin," Hannah says, sounding like she can't believe it.

"It was a long time ago," Rosie reasons, her cheeks turning pink. "Nathan, Nate, moved away to Ohio when he was twelve." She looks over at Maddox. "I was his best friend first."

My smile is so sudden and so wide that a piece of food falls out of my mouth.

"Gross." Chelsea scrunches her face at me.

I open my mouth wider, showing her the rest of the mashed-up food on my tongue.

Chelsea looks at Rosie. "Was he like this as a kid too?"

Rosie nods. "Worse, even."

Maddox leans forward. "Okay, *best friend,* why haven't I heard of you?"

Rosie's expression falters, and I've never wanted to punch Maddox more in my life.

"We lost touch," I say before Rosie has to answer. "You know how it is." I hold his gaze as I say it. Maddox should know better than anyone how that feels, and my tone should tell him not to push it.

He lifts a brow but doesn't pry.

"So when you saw each other at our reception..." Hannah prompts.

Rosie's cheeks get even pinker. "That was the first time... in a long time."

Maddox stares at me. "Interesting."

"Very." I nod slowly. "Now, can someone pass me the rice?"

"Tell Rosie I'll text her in the morning," Ruth whispers to me with a wave.

"Will do," I whisper back. "Thanks again for all the help."

Ruth shakes her head, then starts toward the door where Chelsea and Hannah are putting on their shoes.

Rosie will no doubt feel bad about not saying goodbye, but after hearing the story of the car accident, no one would let me wake her.

I look down at the woman tucked beside me.

She's in her usual spot at the end of the couch, only with her back against the armrest, her side against the back of the couch, and her legs up over my lap.

After dinner, we all made our way over to the living room, and after we were forced to tell a handful of childhood stories from the woods, Rosie nodded off.

That's when I told them how she got hurt. Including the part where Rosie pushed her coworker out of the way, sacrificing herself.

Maddox was watching me the whole time like he knew I was leaving something out. But I wasn't about to talk about the letters in front of his whole family.

I love them. I know I can trust them. But that's not my decision to make alone.

If I have my way, Rosie will become close with them too, but I want to let her control how much she shares.

A hand smacks the back of my head, making me hunch my shoulders.

"Fucker," I hiss at Maddox over my shoulder.

He points at me. "You've got some 'splaining to do." He keeps his voice low so as not to wake Rosie. And as much as I want to backhand him in the nuts, I appreciate the consideration.

"Later." It's a promise and a warning.

Maddox dips his chin, then follows his women out the door.

I feel a little bad that Tony knows more than he does since he was there when I found those letters—and saw me weeping like a baby.

But that's the thing about Tony. He knows something fucked up happened. Offered to—I'm pretty sure—kill a guy. Then took my answer at face value. And hasn't asked a follow-up question since.

Maddox, however, would be nothing but questions. And right now, I just want to enjoy my time with my girl.

Because I have about two weeks to convince her to stay and never leave.

ROSALYN

"God damn!" Nathan's exclamation startles me into dropping my earring on the counter.

I slap one hand over my heart as I pick it back up. "Jesus, Nathan."

"Sorry." He whistles. "But. God. Damn."

I watch him approach in the reflection of the bathroom mirror.

His eyes are all over the place. From my head to my feet and back again.

The reaction seems like a bit much, but I still soak it in.

My hair is pulled back into a low bun, with a few loose strands curled into waves. My face is done up in a full routine of makeup. And I'm wearing the most sparkly thing I own.

The color theme of the fundraiser is gold, so I have a gold dress on.

I bought the thing last year for a New Year's party I was supposed to work. The event was canceled at the last minute, so I never got to wear it.

"What is this made out of?" Nathan stops right behind me, hands holding my waist, helping me balance on my good foot.

"No idea." I try to focus on putting my—also gold—dangly earring in. "I take it you like it?"

"Like it? Woman, I want to peel it off you with my teeth."

I smile. "That will have to wait until after."

Earrings secured, I run my hands down the front of the dress.

It's sleeveless with a V neckline. The underdress is a lighter gold that ends just above my knees. And then there's a sheer golden layer over top, covered in gold embroidery and fake crystals.

If I was going anywhere else, I'd say it's too fancy. But I think I can get away with it tonight.

Nathan uses his hold on me to turn me around and back me against the counter. "How am I supposed to be professional around you when you're dressed like this?"

I run my palms up his chest, noting he looks pretty fine himself in black pants, a black and gold belt, and a partially unbuttoned white shirt. "You could solve that problem by not coming."

Today was another day where Nathan surprised me with his kindness. But I think it probably says more about me and my trauma that I allow myself to be surprised when he's just being his usual nice self.

Nathan spent all afternoon helping Ruth and me in the kitchen.

He brought up all my travel tubs from my van. Which is parked downstairs. Because back when I was still in the hospital, he arranged to have it brought here—instead of to my house, where I assumed it was.

It still has a banged-up bumper, but it drives just fine.

Then, an hour ago, Nathan announced he'll be my assistant tonight.

I tried to fight it.

Tried to picture *the* Nate Waller acting as my catering assistant.

But no matter what I said, he insisted. He also claims to have cleared it with the event space.

So Nathan and I are about to head out, dressed up, with him driving my catering van.

I press my lips together and slowly inhale through my nose.

Nathan's support is the thing dreams are made of.

And before I wake up from this heaven, I need him to know.

"Thank you," I whisper. "You've already done so much... I can never thank you enough."

Nathan settles his hands on either side of my neck, his skin so warm against mine. "There's nothing I wouldn't do for you, Pretty Rosie."

I swallow.

Then I swallow again.

Because he just might be telling me the truth.

And that's as terrifying as it is wonderful.

ONE HUNDRED FIVE
NATE

"It's her." Rosie's fingers dig into my side.

"Who? The painter lady?" I look around the mostly empty art gallery, even though I don't know who I'm looking for.

"The painter lady." Rosie mocks me. "You mean Savannah Vass, one of the most talented painters I've ever followed."

I bite down on my smile.

I don't know how I ever thought Rosie was fangirling over me when I showed up at Maddox's house that day. Clearly, I had no idea what fangirling Rosie looked like.

"My bad," I say in a serious tone. "Which one is she?"

"Oh my god, she's coming over. Hold my crutches." Rosie, still clinging to my side with one hand, shoves her crutches at me.

I try not to chuckle. "Beautiful, you still need to keep your weight off your foot."

She presses the crutches against my chest. "I'll sit in that damn chair all night if you give me this."

In that case.

I take the crutches from her and reach back to rest them against the wall.

Her reaction to the chair was nearly as comical as her reaction right now.

When I told her I'd been trying to talk to Savannah directly, she looked like she might slap me. So the concession on using the chair is worth her being wobbly for this interaction.

"Thank you," Rosie says quietly. "Don't let me fall."

"Never." I place my palm on her lower back where the skirt of her dress flares out from her waist. Then I bunch my hand in the fabric, holding on tight.

She lets out a snort, and I smile down at her.

Then I mouth *You got this.*

Rosie presses her lips together and nods, then turns her attention forward.

Rosie quietly clears her throat, then she holds out her hand to the approaching woman.

I stay silent at her side as the women introduce themselves to each other.

The blond one—the artist—is in a sparkly gold jumpsuit, and the ice on her ring finger looks big enough to sink a ship.

After a few moments, Rosie introduces me as her *boyfriend and helper*, and I release her skirt long enough to shake Savannah's hand.

"Oh, before everything starts and my brain goes to mush, I have something for you," Savannah tells Rosie.

"For me?" Rosie's voice is full of disbelief.

The blonde nods and looks around before gesturing to a big man across the room.

The man lifts his chin and strides our way.

He's dressed in an all-black suit with a gold tie, and he looks about as chill as a puddle of lava.

I'm a big dude too. Still in decent shape even after retiring. So not many people intimidate me. But I'd be lying if I said this guy wasn't doing just that.

As annoying as Maddox can be, I wouldn't mind him at my side right now.

The man narrows his eyes at me, and I amend my previous thought. *Tony Stoleman would be a better backup option.*

I also don't miss the fact that this man is attractive, so I use my grip on Rosie's skirt to give her a tiny shake. Reminding her that I'm an attractive man too.

The big dude stops in front of me, holding my gaze. "The footballer, I take it?"

I release Rosie's skirt again and hold my hand out. "Mr. Savannah?"

The man grins—and I can't tell if it's friendly or not—as he takes my hand. "Everything to your liking?" He tips his head toward the chair beside the dessert table behind us.

"It is." I nod.

Savannah hooks her arm around her husband's. "Do you have the postcard?"

He reaches into his suit jacket and extracts a piece of rigid paper, tucked inside some sort of clear plastic wrapper.

Savannah takes it, then presents it to Rosie. "I heard about the accident and that you're a fan, so I wanted to give you a little something." Rosie takes the tiny painting with shaking fingers. "You pushing your coworker out of the way was pretty amazing."

My eyes move from the little painting to her husband, because I don't remember mentioning that detail.

He lifts a shoulder. "Traffic cameras."

My brows raise. I hadn't even thought to hack into those.

But then again, the idea of witnessing Rosie getting hit by a car might stop my heart completely.

"I... I can't possibly accept..." Rosie's breathless voice pulls my attention back to her, and I lay my arm across her shoulders, holding her to my side.

Her body is trembling.

This little piece of art clearly means so much to her.

I tighten my hold. "She'll absolutely accept it," I tell the artist. "That's really kind of you."

Savannah smiles up at me. "It was a fun little project last night, to take my mind off the fundraiser."

I flex my fingers on Rosie's shoulder. "Show me."

She holds it up.

Savannah called it a postcard, and that's about as big as it is, but the entire piece of paper is covered in shades of gold paint. The lines are smooth. The design is sort of circular. And it takes me a moment before I see the image. A rose, made of nothing but gold.

"Wow." I look back up at the blonde. "Impressive."

She does a little curtsy. "Thank you."

Someone calls her name from across the room.

"I'm sure I'll see you throughout the night, but if not, thank you again for the delicious food. I've already snagged a few things from your servers." Savannah smiles at Rosie.

Rosie presses the rose painting to her chest. "Thank you so much."

"Don't forget," Mr. Savannah says to me as they step back. "Spend some of those zeros."

I nod. With the way Rosie reacted to that tiny painting, nothing will stop me from buying her another.

ROSALYN

I wait until Savannah disappears around the corner, then I sag against Nathan.

He tightens his grip around my shoulders. "Whoa, there."

I hold the miniature painting up in front of me. "I can't believe she did this," I breathe.

It's so perfect.

So Savannah.

Letting Nathan hold me up, I carefully hold the postcard by a corner and trace my fingertip over the swirl of petals.

All the paintings on display tonight are done in shades of gold, with only a few spots of color added for impact. And all the subjects are items from nature.

The fundraiser is raising money to protect Minnesota's natural resources. So not only is this rose meaningful to me by name, but it also fits with the collection.

"It's pretty." Nathan leans his cheek against the top of my head.

I roll my lips together, trying so hard to keep my emotions in check. "No one has ever made me anything before."

Nathan's body expands with a deep inhale, followed by a heavy exhale. "That makes me really fucking sad, Rosie Posie."

I tip my head back to look at him so he can see my eyes are filled with happiness, not sorrow. "It just makes this even more special."

Nathan searches my gaze before dipping his head and pressing a kiss to my forehead. "Want me to go put it in the van so it doesn't get crinkled?"

This time, I have to dig my teeth into my lower lip to stop my eyes from filling with tears.

I nod.

"Then pick out a painting you want me to buy."

I sniff. "You don't—"

"I do." He kisses my forehead again. "The scary husband said so."

My mind wanders back to Savannah's very handsome husband. "Was he scary, or was he—"

Nathan spins so he's in front of me, his hands under my armpits in an instant.

"Keep your eyes on the artwork, Woman." He lifts me. "Or I'll carry you right out of this building and over my lap."

Nathan takes the few steps over to my chair, then gently sets me down.

I want to chastise him, but I'm smiling too hard over his ridiculous jealousy.

"Sit," he commands.

Gripping his forearms, I lower myself into the chair.

He starts to step away.

"Nathan?"

He pauses.

I lift my hand and point. "I think Charles would like that one."

ONE HUNDRED SEVEN
ROSALYN

Little feet walk up my side, bringing me out of my dream, away from a naked Nathan.

"You little butthole." I yawn through the insult.

Charles, unbothered by the name-calling, pushes his nose against my temple.

"Okay, okay, I'm up."

I roll onto my back and blink up at the ceiling.

"Seriously." I scratch the top of Charles's head. "What's a girl gotta do to get some dick around here?"

The cat meows.

"You're probably right."

I sigh.

The lack of sex is my fault. I've been so tired the last two nights I barely even remember going to bed. But I do remember the conversation we had last night on the ride home.

And melancholy tries to envelop me as I recall it.

Nathan has to leave for California today for some sort of week-long tech conference.

He apologized, which is ridiculous since it's for his job, and his job is running a tech company.

But what's even worse than him leaving is that he's heading to the airport from the office.

Which again, I can't begrudge him since he's been home with me since the accident.

Obviously, as the man in charge, he can delegate. But that doesn't mean work hasn't piled up for him.

Because of me.

Charles meows again, and I turn my head toward the dresser against the wall. And the painting resting on top of it.

"You like your painting?" I hold out my hand and let Charles rub his cheek against my palm. "I like it too."

The large canvas covered in golden cattails is perfect for Charles. The orange tones shine through in the morning light, mimicking his glossy coat.

And the five figures Nathan paid for it will help to protect some animal's habitat, so I refuse to feel guilty for telling him to buy a big one.

Cat paws press into my stomach as Charles climbs on top of me.

Looking at the clock, I see it's just after nine. "Are you hungry, boy?"

Charles kneads his paws into my belly.

Before he left this morning, Nathan woke me up long enough to kiss me on the cheek and remind me I can call anytime if I have questions about Charles. But I've watched him feed the feline enough over the past several days, and I know it's past his breakfast time.

Charles jumps off me, then stands at the edge of the bed, looking back over his shoulder at me.

I hold my hands up. "Keep your furry pants on. I'm getting up."

He makes a noise that I'm sure is telling me to hurry, then he leaps to the floor.

"You and your human." I huff. "You're always hungry."

I'm reaching for my crutches when I pause, struck with an idea.

ONE HUNDRED EIGHT
NATE

I hit send on the email I just finished, and my computer updates with five new ones.

"Fuck me," I groan.

I mostly stayed on top of things while at home. But I know from experience that I'll end up swamped by the end of this damn conference.

If I wasn't one of the speakers tomorrow, I wouldn't leave tonight.

And if I wasn't on a panel the final day of the conference, I'd come home early.

But alas, the universe is set on keeping me apart from my Rosie for too many days.

My Rosie.

This morning when I woke her up to say goodbye, she was so sleepy her eyes were barely open, and she was the sweetest sight I could ever imagine.

I want to wake up to that sight every day.

I want to have her warmth beside me every night.

And I have to figure out a way to ask her to stay without sounding like an obsessed stalker.

I open the next email and do my best to push thoughts of Rosie out of my mind. But somehow, she's even more distracting when she's not here than when she is. Working from home, I knew she was close. I didn't have to worry about what she was doing or where she was.

Rosie has her own career. Her own business. But I'm wondering if I can convince her to come share my office.

I could put a hot plate on the credenza behind me. And there's room in the cabinet over in the corner for a mixer...

There's a knock on the door, and I'm so lost in my daydream that I jolt in my seat.

I spin my chair to face the sound. "Yeah?"

Blake opens the door. "Um, Mr. Waller?"

"Yes, Blake?"

"The front desk called to let me know there's a woman here for you. But she doesn't have an appointment, and I'm not sure what I'm supposed to do."

"Well, did you get a name? Or what she's here for?" I ask, slightly exasperated.

We don't take solicitors, and I'm not expecting anyone, so I'm annoyed my thoughts of Rosie were interrupted by this.

"Uh, she said she's your girlfriend. But—"

"Rosie?" I sit upright in my chair.

Blake shakes his head, dousing my excitement. "I don't think her name was Rosie..."

"Rosalyn?"

Blake lifts his pointer finger. "That's it."

I bolt out of my chair. "She *is* my girlfriend."

Blake's eyes widen. "Oh, shit."

I almost grin at Blake finally swearing in front of me, but I'm too excited about Rosie being here.

Wait, why would she be here?

I rush around my desk toward my door.

Did something happen?

Blake jumps back out of my way, and I stride past him.

Our office space isn't huge, but there's a turn in the hallway between here and the front desk.

As my worry ramps up, I remember her crutches.

My feet stop.

Should I bring my office chair?

I turn back toward my office.

But that's backtracking.

I turn back around.

Should I grab someone else's office chair?

"Nathan?"

My head snaps up.

Standing there, at the end of the hall, with crutches under her arms, is a stunning little redhead.

Her hair is loose around her shoulders, she's wearing jeans and a tank top, and she looks just as stunning as she did last night.

Better even because she's here.

In my office.

"Rosie." I break out into a jog.

Her wide smile settles the nerves bubbling inside me, but I don't slow down.

I stop when there's only a foot between us, reaching up to cup her cheeks.

"You're okay?" I search her gaze.

Her smile drops. "I'm fine. Sorry, I... I didn't mean to worry you. I wasn't thinking."

I heave out a breath. "Don't apologize. It's not your fault that I'm apparently turning into my mother."

Rosie tries to shake her head. "Your mother must be very handsome."

I grin.

Then, because I can, I lower my head and press my lips to hers.

I feel her mouth pull up into a smile against mine.

When I back away, she clicks her tongue. "Such a bad boy, kissing me in the halls of your workplace."

"Key detail, *my* workplace." I look into her pretty blue eyes. "Are you just here because you missed me, or do you need something?"

We've been together round the clock for a week, but I've been missing her all morning, and as much as I don't want her unhappy, I hope she's been missing me too.

She lifts a shoulder. "I brought you lunch."

I stare at her. Stare into those fucking eyes that have captivated me completely.

"You brought me lunch," I repeat.

She nods, my hands still holding her face.

"What did you bring me?" I notice the reusable grocery bag over her shoulder that must be holding said lunch.

"A sandwich."

"Homemade?"

She lifts a brow. "Obviously."

I take the biggest inhale, then blow it out. "My girl brought me a sandwich." I shake my head. "That's it. I'm keeping you."

I drop my hands from her face and slip an arm around her back, hook my other arm under her knees, and lift her into my arms.

Her crutches clatter to the floor.

"Nathan!" Rosie squeaks, but she still loops her arm around my neck.

"Don't drop the sandwich," I tell her as I start back down the hall the way I came.

She swings the bag up onto her lap. "You're ridiculous."

A few heads pop out of office doors as we move down the hall.

I dip my chin in greeting but keep walking.

Rosie isn't an employee here. There are no rules against what I'm doing.

And even if there were, I'm in charge, so I could just change the rules.

As soon as we're in sight, Blake jumps up from his desk.

Before he can say anything, I gesture with my head back behind me. "Can you go grab Rosie's crutches? They're in the hall."

"Uh, okay." His eyes land on Rosie and widen. And it's like I can see the light bulb turn on that says *that Rosalyn.*

Rosie lifts her hand as we pass him. "Hi, Blake."

Blake isn't quick enough to reply before I step through my office door.

I pause.

If I'm not busy working, I like to wander. So I don't have a couch or big comfy chairs in my office like some people do.

Deciding my rolling desk chair is the best option, I cross the room and carefully lower Rosie into my seat.

She looks up at me like I'm absurd but doesn't protest.

Footsteps sound from outside the door, and I turn in time to see Blake appear with Rosie's crutches.

"Thanks." I cross the room and take them from him. "My girlfriend made me a sandwich for lunch, so consider me unavailable"—I glance at the clock and see it's just after eleven —"until noon." Then I close the door.

"Why do I get the feeling you terrorize that poor man?"

I chuckle but focus on more important things. "Tell me you

brought two sandwiches and that you plan to stay and eat yours with me."

Rosie nods while she uses her good foot to scoot the chair back. "Before we eat, though, I have something to tell you."

She sets the bag on the floor and pulls a hair binder off her wrist.

I approach as she secures her hair into a ponytail, and I have to assume she's not about to give me bad news if she's already prepping her hair to eat lunch.

Taking the opening she made, I move in front of her and lean back against the edge of my desk. "What is it?"

"It's just something I need to confess before you go." She scoots her chair forward, closing the space between us.

"You can tell me anything."

She nods, then reaches under the chair.

She pulls the lever I can't see, and the chair lowers.

Until she's eye level with my waist.

A tingle starts at the base of my spine, crawling up. "What do you have to confess, Little Rose?"

She holds my gaze. "That I *really* want to suck your cock."

"Fuck." I exhale the curse as Rosie reaches out and undoes my belt.

Rosie pauses to lift a finger to her lips. "Shh. We're eating lunch, remember?"

I grip the edge of the desk with both hands to stop myself from gripping her hair. "Did you really bring me a sandwich too? Or was that all a ruse because my girl is hungry for dick?"

"The sandwiches are real." She winks at me, then pulls my zipper down.

"Best fucking girlfriend ever."

When she tugs down the front of my boxer briefs, I lose the battle against my control.

ROSALYN

Nathan's fingers dig into my hair, messing up the ponytail I just made. And I love it.

I pull his dick free, and my core pulses at having him in my hand.

We've fooled around. We've fucked. He's come on me more than once. But I've never had a view like this.

Never had his cock in my mouth.

I grip his base with one hand and slide the other up his length.

"Jesus." His hips twitch. "Full disclosure, I'm going to come embarrassingly quickly."

I smile and roll my chair closer. "Sounds like a challenge."

I keep my eyes on his and open my mouth.

His gaze is hooded, and he tightens his hands in my hair.

Then I stick my tongue out and lick his tip.

He hisses.

I chuckle, because even though I'm torturing myself with this too, it feels good to cause such a reaction from him.

I lick again, tasting his excitement as I stroke his length.

"That's enough." He slides one hand around until he's palming the back of my head. "Time for you to suck."

My panties soak through at his tone as he drags my mouth onto his length.

The groan that rolls through his body is visceral.

I hum.

He pulls me closer, shoving himself deeper.

"That's it, woman." He grips my ponytail and drags my head back. "That's how you suck a cock."

My eyes start to close. His words of praise are so filthy. And I love them.

He pulls me forward.

The tip of his dick bumps into the back of my throat, and my muscles constrict.

He pulls me back. "We'll work on that." He drags me down his length again. "We'll work on getting my whole dick down your throat."

I hum again.

I want that.

I want to be able to take all of him.

But I'm also glad he's not going to try and force it.

"You like that idea?" With the hand not gripping my hair, Nathan reaches down to hold the front of my throat. "You like the idea of your throat bulging with my dick."

Holy shit.

He pulls my mouth off his dick and uses his hand on my throat to nudge my chin up. "Tell me."

I'm breathing so heavily that I take a second to reply. "I want that."

Nathan pulls my head back farther, then bends down and slams his mouth to mine.

He presses his tongue between my lips.

I let him in.

I let him taste himself.

I give back as much as I'm getting.

He growls and pulls away. "Touch yourself. Put my dick back in your mouth, then touch yourself."

I came here only intending to get him off.

I even wore jeans rather than something looser so I wouldn't be tempted.

But I'm so turned on there's not even a choice but to do as he says.

I close my lips around his tip, then let go of his dick with my hands so I can undo my pants.

It's hard to get my hand inside my jeans, but with some tilting of my hips, my fingers slide inside my panties.

As soon as my fingers make contact with my soaked clit, a shiver runs through my body.

"That's a good girl." Nathan pulls my head forward. "My good girl. Rubbing her little clit. Getting off on sucking me off."

He works me up and down his length. And I'm so close.

He pulls me deep again.

Nudging against my resistance.

I didn't know losing control could feel like this.

Could be this good.

"You're gonna be a quick learner," he grits out.

Back and forth.

Up and down.

"By the end of fall, you're gonna be swallowing me whole." He holds me in place. "And by the end of the year, you're gonna be able to take all of me in that sweet ass."

My pussy clenches, and I moan around him.

The idea should scare me.

Terrify me.

But I can't think of anything hotter than giving my body over to this man.

"God, you're fucking perfect," he groans. "I talk about taking your ass, and you moan around my cock."

My eyes flutter.

My clothes feel too tight.

My heart is racing.

"You close, Little Rose?"

I nod, taking him almost too far with the movement.

"Are you going to swallow?"

I rub my fingers faster over my clit and nod again.

I've never swallowed before. But I can't imagine pulling back now.

Can't imagine saying no to this man.

He tugs on my ponytail so that just the tip of his dick is in my mouth. "Come for me."

ONE HUNDRED TEN
NATE

Rosie's eyes meet mine, then hers roll back as her body shudders.

My perfect girlfriend comes with her hand down her pants and my dick in her mouth, and I couldn't stop myself from following if I tried.

Holding her head still, I flex my fingers around her throat and explode.

Pulse after pulse, I come in Rosie's mouth, and I feel every swallow she takes.

She jerks her hand out of her pants, and as I continue to come, I let go of her throat and grip her wrist.

Then I pull her hand up to my mouth and shove her shiny fingers between my lips.

A final jolt of my release fills her mouth. Then, with the taste of her pussy on my tongue, I finally drop my hold on Rosie.

She collapses back into my chair, her breathing just as labored as mine.

And when our gazes catch, she grins.

Needing another moment of connection, I bend down and seal my mouth over hers.

With her taste on my tongue and my taste on hers, I feel closer to her than I've ever felt to another person.

ONE HUNDRED ELEVEN
ROSALYN

Charles bumps his head against the corner of my laptop.

"I don't know either," I huff.

The cat looks at me. I look at the cat. Then I focus my attention back on the computer screen.

Yesterday, while we were eating my deviled egg salad sandwiches in Nathan's office, he asked me if I'd ever thought of writing a cookbook.

He said it between giant mouthfuls, just casually throwing it out there, as though the suggestion itself wasn't the most encouraging thing anyone had ever said to me.

And while I sat, stunned, he kept going. Suggesting that I could design it with handwriting in the margins, like the old cookbooks I liked to buy. Telling me it would feel more personal and that I could put a foreword, or an afterword, explaining about that first cookbook I found and how it started it all.

He might have picked up on my emotional reaction, but he just kept going. Talking about how I could have a whole section about marshmallows. And a section on the best way to make food for large parties.

It's not like I've never thought about it. Like I never dreamed about seeing my name on a cookbook cover. But that's all it's ever been.

A dream.

I look at the screen in front of me.

Realistically, I know it's still a dream. And the chances of me ever actually getting one published are as slim as slim can be.

But hearing Nathan talk about it with such excitement made me want to try.

Charles meows once, then jumps off the table.

I turn to watch him, wondering if there would be a way to incorporate a cat into the photos that would eventually need to be taken for the cookbook when he stops.

"What's wrong?"

Charles arches his back and lowers his head, and with a sound I can feel in my bones, he throws up.

"Oh my god!" My stomach rolls, even as worry grips my throat.

Charles makes a terrifying hacking sound, then pukes a second time.

"No, no, no, no. You can't be sick!" I plead with the cat that's already proven to be sick.

I push out of the dining chair. Crutches forgotten.

Standing, I dart my eyes around the condo.

I don't know what I'm looking for, but then something catches my eye, and I freeze.

Raw chicken.

I left a package of raw ground chicken on the counter to thaw because I was planning to use it for dinner tonight. But

I'm so used to living all fucking alone that I didn't even think about Charles trying to eat it.

I shuffle toward the island and can see that the corner of the package is chewed, but I can't tell if Charles actually ate any.

Raw chicken is bad, right?

I'm pretty sure it's bad.

I mean, he's a cat, but—

Charles walks a few feet and throws up a third time.

It's already making him sick!

Panic swallows me.

"It's okay. It's okay," I chant. "I got you. It's okay."

It's so not okay. I have no idea what to do.

I grab my phone off the table.

It's four p.m.

And that's what, two in California?

I don't know when Nathan's speech is.

I can't call him during that. What if his phone vibrating in his pocket distracts him?

My heart is galloping, and I try to focus.

Think!

I need help.

Need to get help.

I look at my phone.

I need to go *to* someone who can help.

I open the map app on my phone and search for emergency vets near me.

There's one four minutes away.

I hit start on the directions, then shove my phone into my pocket.

"Come here, Charles." I take a step toward him, putting my full weight on my sprained ankle without thinking.

It twinges.

It's sore.

But it's not horrible.

I take another step.

I can't carry Charles and use crutches.

And I'd choose Charles every day.

I take another step around the little pile of vomit, then I bend and scoop him up off the ground.

"You're a good boy," I tell him as I hug him close. "You're such a good boy, and you're going to be okay."

I pick up my pace, crossing to the front door.

My van keys are in a bowl on a side table next to the shoes.

I shift Charles into one arm, then snag the keys while shoving my feet into my sandals. My ankle brace easily fits in the loose footwear.

Then I pause for a second before also grabbing the bowl.

I'm pretty sure it's crystal, but if Charles has to puke again, I want to give him a place to do it.

I juggle everything into my arms, then remember my purse. "Fuck."

I've never been to an emergency vet before, but I'm sure it's not free.

My purse is back on the table.

I spin around too fast, and that's the movement that tweaks my stupid ankle.

"Fuck, fuck, fuck." I shuffle across the room as quickly as I can and one-handedly shove the little bowl and keys into my purse, then sling it over my shoulder. "Promise we're going now," I tell Charles. But then I look back at the gross spots on the floor.

Do I need to bring in a sample?

Forty-five seconds later, I have a sandwich bag on my hand, inside out.

I hold my breath, then bend over, twisting to keep my purse on my shoulder, and I pick up the slimy clump.

I gag.

This is so disgusting, but I have no time to spare.

Heaving out a breath, I hug Charles to my chest and awkwardly get the bag off my hand and sealed.

I gag again.

And I gag one last time when I shove the *vom bag* into my purse.

Charles blinks up at me like I'm crazy. But all I can think about is that he needs to be okay.

Charles has to be okay.

I wouldn't be able to handle it if he wasn't okay.

And if I was the reason something happened to him...

Hugging Charles tighter, I rush back across the condo and out the door.

His heart is beating against mine, and like this, right now, he feels fragile.

Tears burn as they fill my eyes.

This sweet, beautiful creature is sick because of me.

The tears fall as I enter the empty elevator.

This can't be my legacy.

I don't want to be a killer.

I can't be responsible for hurting an innocent.

I never wanted to cause anyone pain.

My tears turn to sobs.

I never wanted to hurt anyone.

Charles purrs, and the vibrations rattle against my ribs.

"It's okay," I whisper.

The doors open into the parking garage, and I rush out of the elevator, almost crashing into a man waiting to get on.

"S-sorry." My voice cracks.

He says something. Maybe yelling at me. Maybe asking if I'm okay.

But I can't make his words out over my pounding heart.

Four minutes.

All I need to get through is four more minutes.

Four more minutes, and we'll be somewhere that can help Charles.

I try to jog, but the jolt of pain that shoots up my leg almost makes me scream.

I choke on a breath.

If I injure my ankle further, then I won't be able to get Charles to the vet.

And waiting for an Uber would take too long.

I keep my steps as steady as possible and finally make it to the van.

Charles stays relaxed in my arms, and when I guide him onto the front seat, he goes willingly.

It takes some effort to get myself in, but when I get in and slam the door, I'm grateful that my right foot—my driving foot—isn't the one throbbing with pain.

"Hang on, buddy," I tell Charles as I shift into reverse and start backing out of the parking spot. "We'll be there soon."

ONE HUNDRED TWELVE
NATE

I don't recognize the number calling, but since it's from back home, I excuse myself from the table and answer. "Hello?"

"Hi, this is Lindsay from the Oak Tree Animal Clinic. Are you the owner of a cat named Charles?"

My fucking heart stops. "Yes." I have to press my hand to my chest. "What's happened?"

"He's totally okay." She immediately reassures me.

"Fuck me." My body sags in fucking relief, and I nearly collapse. "I think I need a defibrillator."

"Sorry, I didn't mean to alarm you." She's apologizing, but I swear I hear her trying not to laugh. "We just wanted to verify some information since the woman who brought Charles in didn't know anything about him. And we need to know what vet to call for his records."

The woman who brought him in.

"Rosie?" I shake my head. "Rosalyn? Did she bring him?"

The woman makes a sound of agreement. "She's okay now."

That makes my spine straighten. "What do you mean *okay now*?"

"She was, um, pretty upset when she got here. It took a few tries to understand what had happened."

"What *did* happen?" I try to keep my tone level, but I need this lady to start explaining.

"The cat threw up a few times, and Ms. Edwards was concerned that he might have gotten into some raw chicken, so she brought him in."

"Is raw chicken bad for cats?" I ask, thinking about all the raw food diet stuff I hear about.

"There can be a few reasons for concern, but generally, no. And we couldn't find any chicken in the sample she brought in. So there's a chance Charles didn't even eat any chicken, and his stomach discomfort was from something else."

"Sample?"

She clears her throat. "Of vomit."

I make a face. "But he's okay? I mean, he pukes sometimes, but he always seemed fine after."

The woman hums. "We've told her to keep monitoring him and to let us know if there are any changes, but we're comfortable sending him home. Could have just been a hairball or something else he ate, but his vitals are good, and he seems alert and happy. We just need his records so we can add them to our own for this visit. Do you have a vet we can call?"

"Yeah, we go to Nussen Veterinary," I tell her. "I'd have to look up the number."

"That's okay," she tells me. "We're familiar with him."

"Okay, good. And can I pay over the phone?" I don't want Rosie stuck with the bill.

"That's not a problem. I'll get you over to the front desk. There's usually a small charge for the cardboard carrier we're going to recommend, but we'll waive the fee. We just don't want her carrying him out in her arms without a leash or harness."

I have to sit with that for a second. "She... carried him in? Like just in her arms?"

"It happens."

As I get my card out to pay, I think about my Rosie and how scared she must have felt. And my heart aches.

ROSALYN

"Okay, Miss Edwards." The vet tech enters the little room. "You're good to go."

She sets a weird-looking box down on the exam table. It has holes in the sides and handles on top, and as I stare at it, I get it.

Embarrassment floods my cheeks, and I hug Charles closer to my body.

It's a cat carrier. Because normal people don't just carry their cat into the vet.

I press my lips together.

I fucked up again.

What if Charles had jumped out of my arms when I walked from the car into the clinic?

What if he'd run off?

I have the urge to pull the puke bowl out of my purse and use it.

Cats don't come when called.

Usually.

I look down into the feline eyes staring up at me.

You wouldn't have run away, right?

He blinks, and I know he's telling me he'd never dream of it.

My stomach settles a little.

The woman opens the top of the box. "This is for you to take home."

"Thank you," I say quietly as I stand.

My damn ankle twinges in protest, having been used far too much today, so I limp over to the table.

Shifting my grip on Charles, I hold him out over the box.

As I lower him, he sticks one paw out, slapping it down onto the top edge of the box.

Sorry, I mouth.

Traitor, he projects back.

The woman shows me how to secure the top, and I silently apologize to Charles once more before closing it.

"Thank you." I keep my eyes averted. "Do I pay you or on my way out?"

I came in sobbing.

I didn't know anything about Charles other than his name.

I carried him in like he was a bag of groceries and not a living creature.

And I've been shuffling around the exam room, my plastic ankle brace visible over my leggings, continually sniffing and wiping at my cheeks.

I really don't want to face anyone else here.

"Oh, um, Mr. Waller took care of it already."

My gaze jerks up to meet hers. "You talked to him?"

She nods, and I can't tell if the wary look she's giving me is because I'm generally pitiable or if Nathan was angry on the phone.

I was the one who gave her his information, so I shouldn't be surprised that she called him. But I guess I figured they just wanted it for the file on Charles. I didn't think—

I didn't think.

I hug the box to my chest.

"We, um, actually recommend using the handles," the woman says softly.

Of course they do.

Tears prick my eyes as I set the box back down on the table and pick it up by the handle.

The woman hands me my purse.

"Thank you," I whisper.

Holding the carrier at my side, I walk out of the room and out of the clinic.

ONE HUNDRED FOURTEEN
NATE

I watch Rosie's location, watch her move out of the vet clinic, watch her glowing dot move through the parking lot.

Watch it stop.

I was planning on waiting until she was home to call, but when her dot doesn't move for a solid thirty seconds, I decide not to wait.

ONE HUNDRED FIFTEEN
ROSALYN

With the AC blasting, I triple-check that my van doors are locked, then I twist in my seat and face the carrier in the passenger seat.

"I'll let you out, but you have to promise to go back in when we get to your building," I tell Charles through the holes in the side of the box.

I don't know what the rules are regarding guests at Nathan's building, but probably best if I don't draw a whole bunch of attention to myself.

Such as rushing off the elevator this morning and almost barreling someone over while crying hysterically with a cat in my arms.

I drop my head back against the headrest, remembering that they called Nathan.

He's not going to be happy.

I picture his handsome face.

Hear his gentle voice in my mind.

And remind myself that he won't yell at me.

He's not the type to scream when he's mad.

He won't hit me. Or hurt me.

I fill my lungs.

He won't do any of those awful things. But he'll still be upset.

I could've killed Charles.

Charles meows.

"Sorry, little man." I wipe the back of my hand across my cheek, then unlatch the top of the box and pull the sides apart.

Charles pops his head out of the box but doesn't jump out.

"Do you want to stay in there?" I reach out tentatively. Slowly.

Charles looks at me out of the corner of his eye, but when my fingers brush the top of his head, he leans into my touch.

His purr is so loud. So content. I break out into tears all over again.

Part of me expected him to hate me. But Charles is too good for that. Too magnanimous.

I reach into the box and haul him out and onto my lap.

"You're such a good boy." I hiccup into his fur. "The best boy. I love you so much."

He just keeps purring.

And I hug him tighter.

Then my phone vibrates with an incoming call.

"What if we run away?" I whisper against Charles, knowing who must be calling.

He meows again.

He gets it.

Resigned, I pull my phone out of my pocket.

I slide my tongue across my lower lip, my mouth feeling suddenly dry.

It's a video call.

I don't want to answer.

But I've spent so much of my existence doing things I don't want to do that I'm used to it.

I take another breath, then accept the call.

As it connects, I angle the camera so it's on Charles, showing he's okay.

"Aw, hey, bud." Nathan greets his cat with a kind tone.

Charles stretches his neck, releasing an extra loud purr.

Nathan chuckles. "Did you enjoy your field trip today?"

I keep my face out of view.

"You gave our Rosie quite the scare, huh?"

Our Rosie.

I sniff.

"My poor baby."

I peek over Charles's head at the phone and see Nathan's handsome face filling the screen.

But he's not looking at Charles; he's looking at me.

"I'm so sorry." I nearly choke on the words.

"Rosie—"

"I wasn't thinking. And I endangered Charles. And I-I." I suck in a jagged breath. "I'm so sorry, Nathan." I squeeze my eyes shut and press my face into Charles's back.

"Rosie." Nathan's voice is so soothing that it makes the tears come faster.

I know how much he loves this cat.

And I know he'll be nice about it if he asks me to leave.

But *nice* is somehow making it all worse.

I lift my head and force myself to face the consequences.

"Are you okay?" Nathan's question is quiet.

And I... I don't understand it.

"Me?" I mostly mouth the word.

He nods. "I should've warned you that he sometimes scarfs his food too fast and... does what he did. I'm sorry he scared you. And even if he got into the chicken, he'll be fine."

I stare at him. This boyfriend of mine. I don't deserve him.

"You're not—You don't want me to leave?"

Nathan's brows furrow. "What?"

I curl my fingers into Charles's fur. "I'd understand if—"

"No." He shakes his head. "No, Rosie, I don't want you to..." Nathan presses his lips together.

"I'm sorry," I whisper, not sure what I'm apologizing for this time but feeling the need to do it.

"Rosie. Listen to me. Okay?"

I bite my lip and nod.

Nathan takes a big breath. "I need you to really hear me when I tell you that I don't want you to leave. Charles doesn't want you to leave. You've done nothing wrong. The chicken was an accident, and it sounds like he didn't even have any. But even if he did, it was an accident. And you..." He shakes his head again. "You carried my cat in your damn arms straight to the emergency clinic."

On cue, Charles stretches his neck up and licks my cheek.

Nathan's smile is so soft. "Neither one of us wants you to leave, Rosie. And if we have our way, you'll never go."

I watch his features. He seems serious.

"You're not mad?" I have to ask. Need to make sure.

He shakes his head slowly this time. "I'm not mad, Rosie. Not a bit. Not at all. I'm grateful for how you handled it."

I watch him. Watch for clues that he's lying. But he doesn't seem to be.

"How's your ankle?" He looks at me knowingly. "I know there's no way you'd be able to carry him and use your crutches. So tell me, Pretty Rosie, how is your ankle?"

This man.

This fucking man is better than any hope I've ever had.

I rub my palm over my cheeks and answer him honestly. "It hurts."

"My poor girl." He gives me a sad smile.

Before he can say more, a loud, unmistakable rumble sounds through the phone.

My eyes widen.

My mouth opens.

And a laugh comes out.

I turn to look at the stall wall separating myself and the man who just ripped the loudest ass I've ever heard. "Dude, are you alright?"

"Sorry," someone with a deep voice grumbles.

I look back at the phone. "That wasn't me."

The dismay I feel over the man on the next toilet over fades when I hear Rosie's laugh.

"Where are you?" She's smiling at me over Charles, and I feel the brightness of her features in my soul.

I must have shifted too much because the toilet I'm sitting on starts to flush, the automatic sensors having been triggered.

I jump up with a curse, not wanting toilet water on the ass of my pants. "I was just trying to find somewhere private to talk," I explain.

Using my foot, I kick the four layers of toilet paper I lined the seat with into the bowl.

"Were you...?" Rosie holds Charles higher to cover her mouth.

I hold the phone out and tip it down, showing my body and the fact that my pants are on and secured. "I was just sitting."

"If you say so."

I open the stall door and stride out. "Hand to Charles." I stop at the sink. "But still, let me wash my hands. One second."

I slide the phone into my pocket and quickly soap up my hands.

Someone I recognize but couldn't name walks in.

"Hey, Nate." He greets me.

And my pocket meows back.

He tilts his head as he walks past me.

Charles always has the worst timing.

Hands dry, I exit the bathroom and pull my phone back out of my pocket.

Rosie has her hand over Charles's face. "Could you hear that?"

"Oh, the whole bathroom heard that," I deadpan.

She snickers. "Bad kitty."

A guy lifts his hand my way as he walks by. "Waller, how's it going?"

I dip my chin at him.

When I look back at the phone, Rosie's smile is gone. "I'm sorry. This is why I didn't call you. I didn't want to interrupt your work stuff."

"No more apologizing. And you're not interrupting anything. There just isn't any privacy, and I didn't want to walk the freaking half mile across the convention center back to my room." I turn a corner, then lean my shoulder against the wall. "I need you to promise me a few things before I go."

Rosie nods. "Anything."

Her instant acceptance calms me even further. "I need you to drive straight home. I need you to walk so very carefully to the elevators. Then I need you to be just as careful walking into the condo."

"I promise."

"After you get your crutches, I need you to get an ice pack out of the freezer, pour a water, and grab the painkillers from the bathroom." I pause, and when she doesn't say anything, I prompt her. "Say you promise."

"I promise."

She looks like she's fighting a smile.

Good.

"Then." I hold a finger up so she can see it. "You're going to go lie in our bed." Her gaze flickers when I say *our*, and I feel a sense of satisfaction when she doesn't argue. "You're going to elevate and ice your ankle. And you're going to elevate it for the rest of today. Icing three more times."

This time, when I pause, she answers. "I promise."

"And you're going to do that again tomorrow. I'm serious, Rosie. I'm going to randomly FaceTime you every day that I'm gone, and if you're doing more than moving from the bed to the couch, I'm going to get upset."

ONE HUNDRED SEVENTEEN
ROSALYN

"I promise."

Nathan dips his chin. "That's my good girl."

I hold Charles up a little higher, covering the bottom half of my face as I admit, "I like when you say that."

My boyfriend smirks at me through the phone screen. "Oh, do you?"

I nod.

"You hear that, Charles? Our girl likes to be praised."

"Nate." A feminine voice sounds from somewhere on Nathan's end of the line.

Charles turns his head toward the phone, and we both narrow our eyes.

The cat meows.

I agree.

Yes, Charles, who the fuck is that?

"If you need to go..." I prompt, feeling a little bit petty after he's been so nice to me but unable to help it.

Instead of looking annoyed at my attitude, Nathan grins. "Green looks good on you, my pretty Rosie."

"Nate?" The voice sounds again.

Nathan looks away from the screen, and his grin shifts to something more neutral. "I'll be with you in a moment." He looks back at the screen. "Sorry, Honey. I think one of the planners is summoning me for a session."

I lift a brow.

I don't think that's what's happening at all. But I think this might be his way of blowing the woman off.

"Oh, I'm not..." the woman cuts in, sounding awkward but not awkward enough to walk away. "It's me, Cindy."

I lift my face from behind Charles and mouth *Cindy*.

ONE HUNDRED EIGHTEEN
NATE

Cindy steps closer, intruding, even though she can clearly see I'm on the phone with someone. And the fact that I'm on a video call should tell her it's personal, which is even less of a reason to interrupt.

I keep the phone facing myself but lift my eyes to meet hers. "Oh, hey. I'll be just a minute."

It's vague and will probably annoy Rosie, making her wonder what I'll talk to Cindy about, but if she's annoyed, then maybe she won't be so sad. I'll take her irritation over her guilt.

"Of course." Cindy smiles. "Didn't mean to intrude. Just thought we could catch up."

I look back down at my phone and see the scowl on Rosie's face.

"I'll let you go," she says flatly.

Her words sting because I never want Rosie to let me go. But I know that's not what she means, so I wink at her.

"Don't forget your promises," I tell her.

Rosie continues to glare at me, and Charles turns away from the screen. "Have a nice catch-up."

She really is just as obsessed with me as I am with her.
And knowing that, I decide to distract her even more.
"Bye, Beautiful. Love you." Then I hang up.

My jaw drops. And the screen goes blank.

Did he...?

I look down at Charles, who is looking up at me. "Did that motherfucker seriously just say he loves me?"

Charles purrs.

And I burst into tears.

ONE HUNDRED TWENTY
NATE

I slip my phone into my pocket and feel victory at both the look on Rosie's face before I hung up and the uncomfortable look on Cindy's face now.

I don't want to talk to Cindy.

We've flirted some in the past—I flirt with everyone—but that's all it's ever been, because I don't fuck where I work.

My mind flashes back to yesterday, when I was face fucking Rosie in my office, and heat stirs in my gut.

I push those memories away, not wanting lust to show on my face, giving the woman in front of me the wrong idea.

"Was that your... girlfriend?" Cindy asks, like the idea itself is absurd.

I let my affection for Rosie fill my smile. "Yeah. She's at home with our sick cat."

I mentally pat myself on the back for the homey picture I painted with that sentence.

"Oh." Cindy shifts on her feet.

"You headed to the speaker in room C?" I change the topic.

Cindy shakes her head. "I'm on a panel in F in about thirty."

"Nice." It really is nice. More women should be speaking at this convention, so awkwardness aside, I'm glad she's here. "You still with the same company?"

She nods. "Yeah, I was promoted to project manager this past spring."

"That's awesome. Congrats."

"Thanks." She pauses. "So, how'd you meet your girlfriend?"

I'm a little surprised Cindy is bringing the topic back up. But the question makes me picture the moment Rosie and I met as adults. Her standing in Maddox's doorway, me thinking she was a fan.

"She runs her own catering company and was hired for my best friend's wedding. It was love at first sight." I grin. "At least for me. She's taken some convincing."

Cindy laughs politely. "Lucky lady."

I shake my head. "Lucky me."

ONE HUNDRED TWENTY-ONE
ROSALYN

I heave out a breath, then answer Nathan's call.

"Morning, Rosie Posie." He's grinning at me. Like he knows I'm still processing his little declaration of love yesterday.

And, of course, I'm still processing.

Who drops the *L* bomb randomly like that?

Did he say it because he really believes he loves me? Or was he just saying it to get that Cindy woman to back off?

And why would he need to say something so drastic to get her to leave him alone?

What sort of history do they have? Because they have to have some sort of history, or else she wouldn't have said *catch up* like she did.

"Show me your feet." Nathan is still smiling.

I roll my eyes and tap the screen to turn on the front-facing camera.

I'm on the couch, with my feet propped up on a pillow on top of the coffee table.

"Following doctor's orders," I tell him dryly. Then I pan to my lap, where Charles is lying on his back, his head between my knees and his feet in the air. "We both are."

Nathan laughs, then coos, "Aw, look at you two."

I flip the camera back so it's facing me.

He's in his hotel room, dressed, but the top buttons of his shirt are still open, and he's lounging on his bed.

"Have you slept with Cindy?" I can't contain the question any longer. I need to know.

"No. Never." His smile dims. "Have you been worried about that all night?"

I lift a shoulder.

"Rosie." He holds a hand against his chest. "I've never so much as kissed that woman. Or anyone else at this conference."

I bite my lip. "Have you ever cheated on anyone?"

He shakes his head, but it's a slow shake. "I have not. But there have been a few women in college who thought we were dating when we weren't, so they might argue otherwise. But I've never cheated on a girlfriend."

I screw up my face. "That's... very honest."

He chuckles, but it's lacking humor. "Price of fame. You can find all sorts of stories, true and false, on the internet. So there's no point in lying."

Something that's not quite pity settles against me. "I hadn't thought of that." My shoulders slump. "Sorry, I just... It's been a long time since I've been in a relationship."

"Me too, Beautiful. But I'm not going to fuck this up. Not with anyone here. Not with anyone anywhere." He sits up straighter. "I know this is new, you and me. But I'll prove myself to you. Prove you can trust me."

His words make my chest hurt as guilt floods me. "I trust you." My voice cracks a little, and I swallow. "I trust you more than I've ever trusted anyone. I just... I just hated the way that woman sounded talking to you. Like she knew you," I admit, giving him some of that trust. "I've never felt jealousy like I did yesterday on the phone with you. And after, well... I just couldn't let it go. I'm sorry."

Nathan shakes his head. "Don't apologize. I promise to never give you a reason to be jealous, but that doesn't mean I don't like it."

"You like me being jealous?" My brows furrow.

"Yeah, Rosie. Call me an asshole, but I like you being heated over another woman trying to talk to me."

"Why?" I ask, not understanding.

"Because it means you care."

My shoulders drop. "I do care. I care about you a lot, Nathan."

"I know you do." His smile is so kind. So forgiving.

Something starts beeping in his room.

"Shit, I gotta go." He glances down at his watch. "Give that cat some belly scratches for me."

I force a smile on my face. "I will."

"Bye, Beautiful. I'll call tonight. And stop worrying. And keep that foot up."

"Promise," I whisper, then he's gone.

I stare at my screen, where Nathan's face used to be, and I think about that word again.

Love.

I think about how much I want to say it to him.

How I want to ask if he really meant it.

But the hope of that...

The hope of love...

The hope of a future. Of happiness.

God, it fucking hurts.

Because that's all it will ever be.

Hope.

Because you can't build a life on a secret.

Because secrets are fragile.

And eventually, they crumble.

Taking everything else with them.

LOVE
LETTERS

I answer Nathan's call, with my camera already pointed at my foot—propped on a pillow—as I lie in bed.

We spoke again last night. It was light but a little subdued since we were both tired and it was late.

But I want to keep the mood upbeat today.

I already feel like I'm failing as a girlfriend, causing Nathan nothing but stress, and I don't want to be that person for him. I want to be his happy place, like he is for me.

"Usually people would have to pay for all these feet pics." I let him hear my smile as I say it.

"Oh, I know. I've been selling these screenshots for big bucks online."

I snort and turn the camera back on myself. "I expect a cut."

"Fifty-fifty?" Nathan offers.

"Hmm." I tap my chin. "I was thinking more like eighty-twenty. Since they're my feet and all."

Nathan narrows his eyes. "Seventy-thirty."

"Seventy-five and you have a deal."

He holds his hand out to the camera, like he's offering to shake my hand. "Deal."

I stick my hand out too, and we pretend to shake on it.

"Give me your info, and I'll transfer you seventy-five cents." He grins.

I laugh. "You've only made a dollar? My feet must be worse than I thought."

"Your feet are adorable."

I scrunch my nose. "Adorable?"

"Uh-huh. I've never really understood the whole foot fetish thing, but now..." He gives a thoughtful look. "If you asked, I'd be willing to put your big toe in my mouth."

"Oh my god!" I recoil against my pillow. "Why would I want you to?"

"You tell me. It's your toe."

I shake my head. "You are unhinged."

"You're the one asking me to suck on your toes."

"I certainly did not ask that," I argue, then I put my hand up to stop the conversation. "How's the convention going?"

Nathan groans. "I'm surrounded by fucking nerds."

I laugh. "Hate to break it to you, Mr. CEO..."

"You wouldn't dare."

I smirk. "Only a couple days left, then you can go hang out with Maddox and talk about football until your chest is covered in so much hair we can sell pics of it for money."

"True, true." He sighs and runs a hand over his sternum.

I shake my head. This man is so weird.

Nathan tilts his head, getting a look in his eyes. "You're still thinking about me sucking on your toes, aren't you?"

"Goodbye, Nathan."

"One sec." I answer Nathan's video call on my laptop, then go back to my Word doc.

He's silent for a few moments as I type before he speaks. "What are you working on?"

I hit save, then minimize the screen, revealing Nathan's

curious face. "Stuff," I say, just to be a pest. "You all done for the night? No fancy dinners?"

I'm lying in bed, back propped against the pillows, already in my pajamas. And Nathan is lying front side down on his bed, bare chest propped up on a pillow, wet hair slicked back, with a few stragglers loose around his temples.

And my god, he's good looking.

He shakes his head. "Told everyone who invited me out that I had other plans already."

"And your plans were to lie naked on your bed, talking to me?"

He smirks. "I've got my undies on." I snort at him calling them undies. "And I grabbed a sandwich from downstairs on my way up. I'm so done with people, I didn't even want to order room service."

"I don't know how you do it. Just one day of those crowds, and I'd be hiding under my blankets."

Nathan props his chin in his hand, and it makes me want to reach out and scratch my fingers through his facial hair. "It's not so bad. I got used to a lot of bullshit and attention during my football days. But I deal with the public a lot less now and definitely have a shorter fuse. And the novelty has kinda worn off. I'd rather be home."

Under the handsomeness, I notice he looks tired. And that makes me want to give him a hug.

But I can't, so I give him the next best thing. The truth.

"I miss you."

His smile is slow. "I miss you too." My heart skips a beat because I know he means it. "Now, tell me what you're working on."

I huff. "You're so nosy."

"I know. Now tell me so I don't have to hack into your computer."

I narrow my gaze at him. "Can you really do that?" Then I remember him getting my grocery list off my laptop and decide he probably already has.

Charles chooses this moment to climb onto my chest, putting himself between me and my laptop.

"Hey, little man. How was your day?" Nathan asks his cat.

Charles turns to face the screen and meows loudly.

"Just one more sleep, bud," Nathan tells him in reply, reminding me that he's coming home tomorrow.

"Is it really okay that you're skipping dinner the last night?" I ask him over Charles's back.

"CEO, remember? I don't need to suck up to anyone."

"True." I run a hand down the cat's back. Then I sigh. "I'm working on that cookbook."

Nathan's brows raise. "Your own cookbook?"

I press my lips together and nod.

The image on-screen tips up to Nathan's ceiling, spins around, then it's back on him as he sits up straight on the bed. "That's amazing! Tell me what you've got so far."

His excitement goes straight to my heart.

So I tell him.

And when he keeps asking questions, I share my screen with him.

And when I do that, he insists on switching from his phone to his laptop so he can see better.

And then we spend the next two hours talking about my cookbook. From chapter titles to the idea of brand deals to the photographers Nathan thinks will be good for still shots...

"This is all still just an idea," I remind him.

He shakes his head. "It's more than an idea, Rosie. You're already doing it."

He's so... excited.

And the warmness of his excitement settles into the center of my chest.

"Thank you." I try to keep my tone light.

"Don't thank me. You're doing all the work."

"Only because of your support." I force myself to keep my eyes on the screen. On Nathan. "No one has ever believed in me like you do."

His throat moves on a swallow. "I'll always be your person."

"I know," I say quietly.

"I think I know what you should title the book."

The side of my mouth pulls up. "And what's that?"

"Rosalyn's Recipes."

It's simple.

It's a mimic of my catering company.

"It's perfect."

ONE HUNDRED TWENTY-TWO
ROSALYN

I'm careful to put my dirty clothes into the hamper, checking that I haven't left anything out of place on the bathroom counter.

Charles circles around on the couch pillow I've placed on the floor for him outside the shower, and I make a mental note to put that back when I'm done showering.

I know Nathan won't care if the condo is clean or messy. But letting him come home to an organized space is the least I can do.

Naked, I reach into the shower stall and turn on the water.

Nathan isn't due home until tonight, but I want to take my time getting ready and pamper myself a little bit. Because if we don't have sex tonight, I'm going to riot.

ONE HUNDRED TWENTY-THREE
NATE

I don't knock before I open the front door, hoping to surprise Rosie with my early arrival.

But it doesn't matter if I knocked or not, because she's not in the living room.

I glance around the great room.

She's not in the kitchen either.

I kick off my shoes and leave my luggage by the door.

As I walk past the kitchen island, I slow.

Glass containers cover the surface, all filled with tiny fish-shaped crackers.

I grin and shake my head.

Rosie told me she made Charles some homemade treats as an apology, but she didn't tell me she made a thousand.

I unbutton my shirt as I walk down the hall.

I throw it to the floor as I enter the bedroom.

I undo my pants as I cross the room.

I kick them off as I stop at the bathroom door.

And when I see Rosie's silhouette behind the frosted glass of the shower, I shove my boxer briefs to the ground.

ONE HUNDRED TWENTY-FOUR
ROSALYN

I hold the razor up under the spray to clean the blades.

Nathan seems to like my... curls, and I'm leaving the patch above my *area* as it is, but I want to shave the rest. I want the rest of it to be silky smooth for his arrival.

One side is done.

I shift my back to the water and put my left foot—brace removed and lying on the floor outside the shower—onto the stool.

With the hand not holding my razor, I pump a healthy amount of my shaving oil into my palm.

When Ruth went to my apartment for my gold dress, I had her grab some more clothes and all my shower items. And as I smooth the oil over my skin, I'm grateful, because I love this stuff.

A waft of cool air fills the shower stall, and I glance over my shoulder.

Then I let out a startled squeak as a completely naked Nathan steps into the shower.

His eyes are hooded, and he has a hand on his already hardening cock as he closes the door behind him.

"What are you doing, Little Rose?"

Frozen, I stare at him. My foot is still up on the stool, knee turned out, giving me room to work and giving him a view of everything.

"Can I help?" His voice is low. Husky.

"Help with what?" Suddenly, my mouth feels so dry.

He reaches down and takes the razor from my hand.

Then he bends so our mouths are just an inch apart. "I want to shave this sweet pussy. And I'm not taking no for an answer."

He closes the distance and presses his lips to mine for the first time in nearly a week.

And he tastes like fucking heaven.

My eyes drift closed, and I reach for him, gripping his naked sides, my one hand still slippery with oil.

He drags his tongue across my lips, and I open for him.

As he invades my mouth, I lower my oil-covered hand and close my fingers around his length.

He groans, and his cock jumps in my hand.

The lubrication makes it easy to slide my hand up and down.

To feel him.

To squeeze him.

The fingers of my other hand dig into his side.

He's here.

He's here, and he's naked, and he's with me.

Something that might be joy bursts inside my chest.

I start to shift closer to him, about to lower my foot, but he grips my hip—holding me in place—as he pulls away.

"Stay." He thrusts his hips forward once into my grip, then

lowers himself to the floor, his dick sliding out of my hand as he does.

Kneeling before me, he's eye level with my pussy.

"I've never done this. But I really want to." He slides his tongue across his lower lip as he looks up at me. "Will you let me?"

Will I let this sex god of a man shave my vagina?

Yes. Yes, I will.

I shift my weight, rotating my hips and opening my stance, revealing more of myself to his gaze.

His mouth pulls into a wicked smile. "Have I told you how fucking perfect you are?"

I reach down and brace one hand on his shoulder. "Not today."

Nathan leans forward and presses a kiss to my inner thigh. "You're fucking perfect." His lips touch my skin with each word.

Then he reaches for the shaving oil I left sitting on the stool next to my foot.

He sets the razor down and uses two hands to dispense oil into his palm.

Steam swirls around us, the water pelting Nathan in the back, but I swear I can still feel his exhale as he leans closer.

"Just this side left," he says to himself as he touches his fingertips to my skin.

I can't help my jolt at the contact, but then he applies a little more pressure as he slides his fingers down the crease where my thigh meets my center, feeling the smoothness of the area I just shaved.

He reaches his fingers between my legs, sliding over until they're aligned with my slit, then he drags them forward.

Even with the residual oil on my skin, there's no mistaking the new wetness gathering there.

Nathan groans. "Just let me do this." His fingers stop against my clit, and he holds them there. "Let me do this first, then I'll make you come as much as you can handle." He drags his fingers off my clit. "Tell me that's okay."

My eyes are nearly rolling out of my head. "Yes. Just hurry up."

He chuckles, and then his other hand is there, smoothing the oil over my skin.

I should be nervous about having someone this close, ready to drag a sharp blade over the sensitive skin of my pussy.

But when he holds me open...

When he drags the razor across my skin the first time...

All I can feel is pleasure.

Pleasure at having his hands on me.

Pleasure at knowing he's hard as stone doing this.

Pleasure at having someone take care of me.

Nathan holds the razor under the shower stream, then starts again.

ONE HUNDRED TWENTY-FIVE
NATE

My cock is fucking dripping onto the shower floor.

I don't know if I've ever been this turned on before.

Which seems to be how I feel every time with Rosie.

The act itself, the glide of the razor over skin, isn't sexual.

But fuck me if it doesn't have me ready to come all over her feet.

My cock twitches, and I put the thought of her cute little toes out of my mind.

There's only time for one new kink today.

I use my fingers to spread Rosie open, checking for any spots I missed.

Her flesh is so soft. So pink and pretty.

If she wasn't covered in this floral-scented oil, I'd devour her. But I know this isn't edible, so I'll settle for fucking her hole instead of eating it.

With one last pass of the razor, I set it down on the floor, out of the way.

Still kneeling, I wrap my fingers around her injured ankle and gently help her lower it back to the floor.

Then I grab the little jar off the stool and look at the label as I stand. "What's this?"

"We don't have to..." Rosie's voice is breathy.

She stayed quiet while I shaved her, but the way she's almost panting is giving her away.

She liked that as much as I did.

"Tell me what to do with it." I change my question to a demand, and I start to unscrew the lid.

Rosie takes it from my hands, holding it farther away from the spray as she takes off the top.

The substance inside is pink, and she scoops out a small amount, maybe the size of a small grape, then replaces the lid.

"It's a scrub. To keep things smooth after shaving." She squashes the scrub between her fingers, then holds it out to me.

I take it from her.

I've used scrubs on my face before, when I had photo shoots, so I'm familiar with the idea.

"I'm going to enjoy this," I tell her with a smirk, then I grip her around the waist with my empty hand and haul her so her back is to my front.

My hard cock nestles against her ass, and she arches into me.

Then I reach around to her front with my other hand and gently rub the scrub over her folds.

I spread my fingers, my pointer finger on one side of her pussy, my ring finger on the other, then I stroke up and down.

The scrub starts to dissolve under my touch, working into her skin, leaving a smooth coating behind.

Against me, I can feel Rosie's chest rising and falling as her heartbeat increases.

That's when I add pressure to my middle finger. Dragging it through her wetness, up to her clit.

"This is the first one," I say against Rosie's ear. "I want at least two."

"First?"

I answer her question by flattening all my fingers over her pearl of nerves and rubbing in a circle.

"Oh. Oh god." She clutches at my arm banded around her waist.

"You can be quick this time, Pretty Rosie." I let my teeth graze the bottom of her ear as I rock my hips against her. "But I'm dragging the next one out."

Her fingers dig into me. "I-I can't stand up."

I tighten my hold on her. "I won't let you fall." I dip my fingers inside her, then focus back on her clit. "Now be my good little girlfriend and come."

ONE HUNDRED TWENTY-SIX
ROSALYN

My core pulses and my knees shake as I come apart on Nathan's fingers.

It's so intense that I close my eyes and let him take my weight, because if it wasn't for his arm around me, I'd collapse to the tile floor.

"That's fucking it." Nathan's groan is loud against my back, and he rocks his hips against me.

He pulls his hand free from my pussy, and a moment later, the water is off.

My eyes fly open when I'm suddenly airborne, in Nathan's arms, bridal style, like when he carried me to his office.

"Can't wait," he grits out, fingers tightening on my damp skin.

We exit the shower, but Nathan doesn't pause for a towel.

Leaving a trail of water, he carries me out of the bathroom and drops me on the bed.

The droplets collecting on my skin soak into the fluffy comforter below me, and my hair is a wet mess around my head, but I can't pretend to care about any of it, because Nathan is crawling over me.

I spread my legs, lifting my knees, and Nathan doesn't stop until he's directly above me.

With his eyes on mine, he reaches between us and lines the tip of his dick up with my entrance.

Love you.

The words are there.

In his eyes.

Stuck in my throat.

Floating between us.

I reach for him, hooking my hands under his arms and gripping his back.

He pushes into me, inch by hard inch.

I pull him closer.

My breath is coming in pants as I stretch around him.

It's been so long.

Too long.

And I need him closer.

"Nathan," I moan, straining my neck up toward him.

"My Rosie," he groans.

Then he shoves his hips forward as he drops his mouth to mine.

Our tongues battle.

My nails dig into his skin.

His cock thickens inside me.

And our breaths are one.

I inhale his exhale.

He fills his lungs with mine.

We move.

My hips lift.

His thrust.

We taste each other.

We memorize each other.

And I cling to this moment between us.

I etch it onto my soul.

I squeeze my eyes shut as tears drip from my lashes.

I love this man so fucking much.

And I want to keep him.

Nathan grunts as he thrusts his hips.

His movements are getting rougher.

He's pushing deeper.

And I know he's close.

A hand moves between us, and his fingers are on my clit again.

"Give me that second one, Rosie. Give it to me now." He keeps slamming inside me. "I'm not pulling out this time. I'm filling your pussy up. I'm stuffing my pretty Little Rose full of my seed."

His filthy words are all it takes.

A sob leaves my throat, and I wrap my arms and legs around him, holding him to me as I come around his length.

Nathan throws his head back and lets out a guttural sound as his cock pulses inside me.

Filling me.

Just like he promised.

ONE HUNDRED TWENTY-SEVEN
NATE

Rosie settles her head on my chest, and I wrap my arm around her back, holding her closer.

Today was... It was everything I want.

I've been on so many trips. Had so many nights away from home. And Charles has made coming home a happy occasion because before him... I was always just coming home to an empty house.

But today...

I press a kiss to the top of Rosie's head.

It wasn't just the sex.

Okay, it's partially the sex because fuck me, that was fucking hot.

I admitted to never shaving anyone, but I didn't admit that I've never come inside a woman bare like that either.

And as much as I want Rosie to know she was the first, I didn't want to say anything that would make her think of the other women I've been with.

I didn't want to think of them either. Because they don't matter.

No one I touched before Rosie matters. And there will be no one after Rosie.

No one else for me, no one else for her.

I stroke my thumb over her shoulder.

The best part of today was coming home to *my person*.

Coming home and having her just be here.

When Rosie yawns, I reach out and turn off the bedside lamp.

After we cleaned up and dressed in pajamas, we ate dinner at the island, with Charles prancing between his piles of treats.

It was the perfect end to a perfect day.

I rub my thumb over her shoulder again as I close my eyes, then remember one last thing. "Almost forgot," I say sleepily. "Tomorrow night, we're having dinner with my parents."

ONE HUNDRED TWENTY-EIGHT
ROSALYN

My knee is bouncing as Nathan parks his SUV in the lot behind the restaurant we're meeting his parents at.

His. Parents.

My knee bounces faster.

Nathan tried to drop me off at the front door—since I decided to leave my crutches at home—but I refused.

I'd rather walk barefoot through a marathon than risk possibly having to make small talk with his parents alone.

Not that I expect Nathan's parents to be anything but pleasant. But for me... this dinner is going to be stressful enough. I don't need it to start any earlier than possible.

Nathan turns the ignition off and places his palm on my knee. "Stop worrying. They know you're coming. They know you're the girl from down the street. They're excited to see you." He tries to comfort me. "It will be totally fine."

I nod faster than I should. "Okay."

"Wait for me," he says and pushes out of his door.

The command is hardly necessary. I'm going to need help unlocking my seat belt because my fingers are shaking so hard.

Because everything Nathan just said, hoping to calm me down, is the exact reason I'm freaking out in the first place.

I don't want them to remember me from that cursed street.

I don't want to talk about them moving away and leaving me behind.

I don't want to answer questions about my past.

My door opens, and Nathan reaches across me to unbuckle me. "You look beautiful, Beautiful. Now, come on, let's eat some food."

ONE HUNDRED TWENTY-NINE
NATE

We walk slowly, Rosie holding my arm for balance since she's walking unaided.

We both know what it means, her not using her crutches anymore. It means she doesn't need to stay with me much longer. And that means I'm running out of time to convince her not to leave.

Maybe dinner with the parents is the wrong call, seeing how nervous she is. But I wasn't coming without her. And my parents are chill. So maybe if she experiences their acceptance, that feeling of family could help convince her I'm hers as much as she's mine.

I hold open the restaurant door and guide her in before me.

I know that her moving back into her own apartment wouldn't mean our relationship is over. She was only meant to stay for three weeks. But there's something... something I can't put my finger on that makes it all feel so huge. Like her leaving would be the worst thing in the world.

Like if I let her walk out my door, I'll never see her again.

ROSALYN

My wide-legged jeans swoosh around my feet, hiding my ankle brace, as I step into the restaurant.

Nathan said it was a nice farm-to-table place but that jeans were perfectly acceptable. He wore a pair too, with a black T-shirt, so I believed him. But I still do a quick visual sweep of the dining room to confirm he was telling the truth.

The place has that vibe that's hard to explain. Like everyone looks rich, but they're all dressed in plain clothes. The kind that cost just as much as the flashy designer brands, only they wouldn't dare put a logo across their purse.

Glad I wore my fancier white shirt with the flowy arms, I press my plain leather clutch to my side.

Nathan leads us to the hostess station. "We're here for the Waller reservation."

The smile the young hostess gives him is nothing short of adoration, and I get it.

I look at him like that too.

"The rest of your party is already seated," she tells him, not even glancing at me. "I'll lead you back."

We follow her through the dimly lit dining room. The Edison bulbs fit the renovated farmhouse aesthetic, and I'm too busy looking around at the decor to notice the table she's leading us to until we're stopping before it.

And the *four* people seated there.

ONE HUNDRED THIRTY-ONE
NATE

Beside me, Rosie tenses, her fingernails digging into my forearm.

I flex my arm, pinning her wrist to my side, trying to give her comfort without making it obvious.

"Mind if we join you?" I smile at my parents.

My mom makes a squeal of excitement, not having noticed our approach. But then she and Dad are pushing their chairs back to stand.

The other couple, a little older than my parents, also rise. And I recognize them but can't quite place them.

Mom grabs my cheeks, and I'm forced to let go of Rosie as she pulls me down to her much shorter height.

"My baby," she coos as I hug her.

"Hi, Mom."

She pats my back, then releases me, only to squeeze my cheeks again. "It's been too long."

"That's enough now. Let the boy go." Dad shoulders in between us, giving me his signature bear hug.

Unlike my mom, Dad is nearly my height, and when he pats my back, it knocks some of the air out of my lungs.

"Hey, Dad." I keep my arm around his shoulder as I angle away, reaching my other hand out to Rosie's shoulder. "This is Rosie. Rosie, my parents."

Rosie looks a little pale, and I wonder if my idea of familial affection is going to have the opposite effect. But it's too late to go back, because Mom is already stepping into Rosie's personal space, pulling her into a hug.

The move dislodges my hand from Rosie's shoulder, and I can see her tense, but she still makes an effort to embrace my mom in return. And it melts even more of my heart.

"So good to finally meet you, honey." Mom steps back just a bit, then grips Rosie's upper arms. "You're so pretty."

A puff of air leaves Rosie, and I know I need to rescue her. "I know, Mom, I've been telling you." I reach out and tuck Rosie into my side.

My dad holds his hand out. "Nice to meet you, young lady."

Rosie puts her palm in his, and Dad gives her one of his wide grins as they shake hands.

"Nate here won't shut up about you," he tells her as he lets go of her hand.

"Yeah, yeah. She already knows I'm obsessed with her." I shake my head. "No point in trying to embarrass me."

Mom gestures to the other woman as she steps around the table. "You remember Mr. and Mrs. Rooney?"

Once Mom says the name, it clicks. "Our old neighbors." I nod to them.

Mrs. Rooney beams up at me, and I once again let go of Rosie and bend down for the hug she clearly wants.

"So nice of you to remember us," the woman says as I embrace her small frame.

Straightening, I hold out my hand to Mr. Rooney. "Nice to see you again."

His handshake is firm. "We had a hell of a time following your career. You made the old street proud."

"Thank you," I tell him, then move so Rosie is back at my side. "You might recall my girlfriend, Rosie Edwards. She lived on the same street, directly across from you, if I'm remembering correctly."

My heart is beating wildly behind my ribs.

He's remembering correctly.

I hold my hand out to Mrs. Rooney. And as she clasps my fingers in hers, her eyes widen, and in that moment, I know she remembers too.

Tears stream down my face as I rush out the front door.

My fingers hurt from where my dad slammed them in a drawer.

I was just looking for tape for a school project. I wasn't looking for fucking money.

Not that there would be money in there anyway. Not in that drawer. Not anywhere.

My bare feet are silent on the cracked pavers, and I slow.

I should've run out the back door into the woods, but the front door was closer. And I needed to get out.

I need to get fucking out.

Pausing when I reach the sidewalk, I tip my head back and stare at the stars above, the light from the streetlamps making them hazy.

Holding my arm across my chest, I flex my fingers.

They hurt like hell, but I don't think they're broken.

Another round of tears spills from my eyes.

I hate him.

I hate him so fucking much.

"Are you okay, dear?" A soft voice startles me, and I stumble back a step.

I lower my gaze from the heavens. There's nothing up there for me anyway.

Standing a few feet away is a woman.

She has a sad smile on her face and a tiny fluffy dog on a leash at her feet.

My heart is still racing from adrenaline and anger and pain. And the buzz of it all in my ears prevented me from hearing their approach.

I blink, trying to dissipate my tears.

But I don't answer her.

I can't.

Because I'm not okay.

"I can call the police if you'd like," she whispers.

Embarrassment and shame flood me as I realize this is our neighbor from across the street. The house with The Rooneys on the front door.

More tears fall. Wishing I could tell her yes.

But I shake my head.

I'm only seventeen. If she calls the cops, there are only two outcomes.

One, they don't do anything, and I keep living with a monster. Only now, that monster will become even meaner because I'd gone to the authorities. The one thing he always warned me never to do. And him being worse than he is now... I don't know if I can survive that.

Or two, they believe me and take him away. And then I go

into the system, taking my chances with strangers, with nothing and no one to look out for me. It could possibly be better, or it could be worse in ways that I don't even want to imagine.

The woman is silent for a moment.

I know she wants to do something. Ask questions. But I can see it when she accepts the truth of the situation.

That there is no good outcome for me.

Not today. Not tomorrow.

Mrs. Rooney tips her head to the hand clutched to my chest. "Would you like some ice for that?"

Pain throbs across all my fingers, and I know I shouldn't accept... but I nod.

"Here." She holds out the leash. "You hold on to Snowball for me, and I'll be right back. We just stepped outside, so she might have to do her business," she adds, making it seem like I'm doing her a favor rather than her using the dog as a ploy to keep me in place.

But I like dogs, so I reach out with my uninjured hand and grip the leash.

I hold it as tightly as I can so the dog can't run away.

Mrs. Rooney nods, then turns and hurries across the street to her house.

The dog watches her owner walk away but doesn't attempt to follow.

When the woman enters her house, I look down at the dog. "Hi, Snowball."

The dog opens its tiny mouth, and her little tongue pops out. It makes me smile.

Like really smile.

And it feels... foreign.

I don't remember the last time I smiled like this.

I crouch down and reach out to pet Snowball, forgetting all about my injured hand until my fingers connect with her long white fur.

I wince, but I stroke her coat again.

"If life was different," I tell her, "I'd have a pet like you."

The door across the street opens, and I look up, watching Mrs. Rooney as she crosses back to us.

When she steps onto the sidewalk, I stand and hold the leash back out for her.

She takes it, then hands me a Ziplock bag filled with ice and wrapped in a thin hand towel embroidered with little pink hearts around the edge.

I try to hand her the towel back.

She shakes her head. "You can keep the towel. It's nothing. But use it between your hand and the ice. You shouldn't put ice directly on your skin."

"Thank you," I tell her, but I won't keep the towel. I'll return it to her mailbox before I go to bed.

Her fingers twist in Snowball's leash. "Would you like me to stay with you for a little while?"

I don't have to look back at my house to know that's a bad idea.

My dad is probably back in his chair, but there's always a chance he'll push aside the curtains and look out the front window.

I shake my head and take a step away.

She nods once, accepting my answer. "If you need anything..." She glances at my house, then back to me. "You can always knock on our door."

I won't do that either.

My problems are mine. Not hers.

I set the towel-wrapped ice on the back of my hand. "Thank you," I tell her again. My voice is quiet but loud enough in the silent night. I lower my gaze to the little dog. "Bye, Snowball."

Then I turn and walk through the grass with my bare feet, circling around to the back of my house so I can go into the woods.

Later, before I go back inside, I cross the street and set the folded towel in the Rooneys' mailbox.

Her kindness was nice, but there's no room for pity from strangers in my miserable existence.

I can't let anyone else get tangled in my father's web.

And I promise myself, from this day on, I'll always run out the back door.

Mrs. Rooney clasps my trembling hand in both of hers.

"It's nice to see you again," I say quietly, hoping she can hear my sincerity and my plea that she won't bring up that night.

She nods. Once. Then twice.

"It is so very good to see you." Her eyes shine, but she swallows and nods again. "So very good."

ROSALYN

I let Nathan help me into his SUV, and once I'm in my seat, I wave goodbye to the Wallers and Rooneys for the hundredth time.

When Nathan shuts my door and the overhead light in the car turns off, I slump.

The darkness outside, combined with the tinted windows, means no one can see me. And as Nathan's parents hug him, again, I take the moment alone to breathe.

To just fucking breathe.

I don't know why I was stressed about meeting Nathan's parents. If it had just been them, tonight would've been a breeze. But no, their old friends had to surprise them.

Apparently, Nathan's parents are just in town for two nights, tonight and tomorrow, for a concert, then they're heading back to Ohio, where they still live. But the Rooneys like the same band, so the husbands coordinated tickets, surprising the wives.

It's sweet. For them.

But a total nightmare for me.

I take a deep breath and tip my head back against the headrest.

Nathan already knows my dad was awful. But seeing Mrs. Rooney, remembering that night... It's a stark reminder of my history.

A reminder of why I can't stay with Nathan.

The driver's door opens, and I take in the happy expression on his face.

His family is so wonderful.

So loving.

It's no wonder he looks like that after seeing them.

Nathan reaches over and squeezes my thigh before buckling himself in.

I'll wait until tomorrow to tell him I'm moving out.

ONE HUNDRED THIRTY-FOUR
NATE

I hold Rosie's hand on the drive home, and I note the moment she falls asleep, her grip going lax on my fingers.

I want to squeeze my hand around hers. Want to make her grip me back.

Something happened tonight when we walked up to the table.

Something passed between her and our old neighbor.

At first, I put it down to Rosie's overall nervousness. She was stressed before we even arrived. But as dinner went on, as the questions loomed but never got asked, I thought about it. Really thought about.

The stories Rosie has told me.

The violence inside her home.

The piece of shit she lived with...

The Rooneys were across the street. *Directly* across the street.

They had to know.

I didn't know.

But I was a kid. And Rosie's dad didn't start hurting her until years after I left.

But the Rooneys still live there.

They had to fucking know.

But they didn't help her.

No one helped her.

As I slow for a red light, I glance at Rosie's sleeping profile and can't help but feel like I'm still missing something.

She knows I know about the abuse she suffered.

But I just have this... *feeling* that there's more.

That there's something else she's keeping from me.

Because even with her asleep beside me, I can feel the walls she's starting to rebuild.

Last night, we connected in a way I never have with anyone before.

And tonight, she's slipping away.

I swallow and take my foot off the brake.

Tomorrow.

We'll talk tomorrow.

ONE HUNDRED THIRTY-FIVE
NATE

After staring at the ceiling for forty-five minutes, I carefully slide out of bed.

Rosie makes a small sound of protest, but when I tuck my pillow against her front, she settles back into sleep.

That bad feeling in the center of my gut just won't go away.

Rosie is kind and caring and the love of my life. And I don't know why, but it feels like my whole future is riding on tomorrow.

I can't let her go.

Can't let her move out.

I move quietly into the closet and tug on sweatpants and a T-shirt.

My plan is thin at best, but maybe if I can bring more of her things here, she'll feel at home. And she'll see how serious I am.

Society might think it's too soon, but I don't care what anyone but Rosie thinks.

Charles is standing in the closet doorway when I turn around, watching me.

I scoop him up and carry him over to the bed, gently setting him on the mattress. "Keep an eye on her."

He sits, heeding my command and not rising as I walk out of the bedroom.

I pause in the kitchen and pull a small notebook out of a drawer.

I write a short note, letting her know I'll be right back, in case she wakes up while I'm gone. Then I find her keys and leave.

I feel like an absolute creep entering her apartment in the middle of the night, but no one sees me, and no one stops me.

Locking the door, I start walking through, wondering what I should take with me.

There's hardly anything on the walls.

Not much for decoration on the counters.

I pause in the kitchen and pull open the freezer door. She mentioned freezing homemade soups, and I spot the stack of containers. I let my fingers bump over the lids and decide to take as many as I can fit in my freezer back home.

Food is obviously Rosie's love language, and maybe bringing her food to her will help with that at-home feeling.

After closing the freezer, I move on to the bathroom.

Ruth brought most of Rosie's toiletries over already, and when I find nothing but cleaning products under the sink, I decide I can skip this room.

Then I step into her bedroom.

I grab both the pillows and pile them at the foot of the bed.

There's a throw blanket crumpled up on the floor that I shake out and fold, then set next to the pillows.

I move to the nightstands and find random things—hair clips, charging cords, and nail files in the first. But in the second, I find a small velvet bag.

I smile when I pull it open, finding a slender vibrator inside.

She might get mad at me for going through her private drawer, but she'll forgive me when I use it on her.

I toss the pouch onto the pile of bedding.

I lower myself to the ground and look under her bed but find nothing except a single sock.

I grab the sock, then turn on my knees to her closet.

Pulling the doors open, I find it much emptier than the last time I was here. Ruth cleared out most of the clothes that were still hanging, exposing more of the bottom of the closet.

I plant my hand on one of the plastic storage containers stacked along the floor and push myself up.

And as I stand, my eyes catch on something I didn't see before.

Behind the plastic containers is a slender olive-green metal box.

A lockbox.

I stare at it. Knowing it's private.

But the longer I stare, the harder my heart beats.

This feels like last time. But it feels worse.

And I know it's not my place.

But I'm past doing what's right.

I close my fingers around the cold metal and pull it free.

It has weight to it, but I think that's just from the box itself because when I shake it, I don't hear any noise.

Setting it on the bed, I drop the sock on the mattress, and I try to open the box.

Locked.

My eyes bounce around the room, but I have no idea where

to look for the key. And for all I know, she doesn't even keep the key here.

But I won't let that stop me.

I pull my phone out of my pocket and hit Tony's contact, selecting a video call.

It only rings twice before he answers. "You know, I could be sleeping."

I take note of the bright lights around him. "Could be, but you aren't."

He rolls his eyes. "What do you need?"

I pick up the lockbox and hold it so he can see it. "I need to open this."

"Where are you?" He narrows his eyes at the screen. "You back at your girl's place?"

I nod. "Can you walk me through breaking it open?"

He lifts a brow. "Not any quicker than I could do it myself."

"Yeah, well, I don't have time to wait for..." I pause when he stands, and I take in more of the space around him. "Are you in a fucking airplane hangar?"

He nods. "I'll be there in ten." Then he hangs up.

"What the fuck?" I shake my head as I carry the box to the kitchen and set it on Rosie's small island.

Then I pace.

Until ten minutes later, as promised, Rosie's *locked* door opens, and Tony Stoleman steps into her apartment.

I take in his head-to-toe black. "Did you just get into town, or are you just leaving?"

He tips his head at me. "You want me to open that? Or you want to ask your girl to do it?"

I run my tongue along my teeth. "New deal, I won't ask you what the fuck you're doing hanging out in a private hangar." I sniff the air. "Or why you smell like gasoline. And you won't lecture me about women."

Tony flashes me a grin. "I agree to your terms."

Without another question, Tony picks up the box and has it open in a matter of seconds.

He sets it on the counter.

"You find something that needs taking care of, let me know." Tony backs toward the door.

"You offer that to all your friends?" I remember the last time we were in this apartment together and the offer he gave me then.

"Just my favorites." He smirks.

"I appreciate that. Truly."

His nod tells me he understands, then he pulls the front door open. "Gotta go catch that flight."

The door shuts behind him, and I turn to the box.

Inhaling slowly, I lift the lid.

And then I hold my breath as I take out the single sheet of lined paper, folded into thirds.

It's just like the others.

Until I open it.

Because this one isn't written to me.

> *Dear _____*
>
> *I don't actually know who I'm writing this to.*
> *There's no one left. No one to care.*
> *Hasn't been anyone for a long time.*
> *Honestly, I thought writing this would be harder.*
> *Maybe I'm just too numb.*
> *And maybe that's the point. That there's nothing left to fight for.*

But if you're reading this, then I'm sorry you had to find my body.

I step back.

Feeling like someone just hit my chest with a baseball bat as I reread that last line.

Her body.

Find her fucking body.

Is this...

I tug on the collar of my shirt, feeling like I can't breathe.

I didn't want to be anyone's problem, but I can't go to prison. I just can't.

And if you're here, looking for me, then you already know I murdered my dad tonight.

I had to.

It was him or me. And I only had enough pills for one of us.

I assume I'll get caught.

I didn't do anything to cover it up.

I can't. I'm too tired.

And I just don't want to be tired anymore.

ONE HUNDRED THIRTY-SIX
ROSIE
(AGE 19)

I hunch my shoulders as Dad shouts my name, but I keep my hands steady.

I can't drop this. If I drop this...

My throat tightens.

I won't drop this.

Keeping my eyes down, I move into the living room and set the meal on the small TV tray next to my dad's chair. "Here's dinner."

"About fucking time. And bring me another beer," Dad snaps before noticing I already have one on the tray for him. "What's that?" He points to the bowl.

I'm already stepping away, getting out of reach, before I reply. "French onion soup."

He grunts.

It's one of his favorites, but he'll never say thank you.

Not hitting me is the closest thing to a compliment he's capable of.

Sticking with my usual routine, I back out of the living

room. But instead of retreating to my bedroom, I silently step into the kitchen.

From this far corner, I can see the back of his chair and the back of his head.

It would take effort for him to turn all the way around to see me, so I stay where I am, ready to crouch down behind the U-shaped counter, out of sight.

It's a risk, staying down here. But even with the bruise around my eye finally faded from our last encounter, tonight is worth the risk.

I need to see.

Need to watch.

Need him to eat his fucking poison.

He shifts, reaching for the bowl.

My heart races.

Eat it.

Just fucking eat it.

The TV volume is loud, but I still hear the clink of his spoon against the ceramic dish.

My research was done at the library, and only when I had spare moments between my jobs, but I double-checked everything.

The pills I've saved from my hospital visits.

The extra blood pressure medication I've been adding to his morning coffee all week.

The extra time I spent on this particular batch of soup, making sure the flavor was intense enough to cover the taste of my special additions.

It should work.

It has to fucking work.

My throat is dry, but I don't dare lift my cup of water off the counter.

I can't let him know I'm here. Watching.

I need this to work.

I don't know if I'll survive this life after he's gone, but I need to outlive him.

Even if it's just by hours.

Dad tips his head back, and I lean over the counter, trying to get a better view of him gulping down the last of the soup.

Excitement and nervousness swirl inside me.

This *has to* work.

Nothing happens.

Dad sets his bowl down.

Long minutes go by.

What if this doesn't work?

The amount I gave him is supposed to act quickly.

He picks up his beer.

I grip the counter, thinking back over everything I researched.

Where did I go wrong?

He tips his head back, chugging down the bottle.

Until he's not.

His body lurches.

Liquid sprays from his mouth.

Then he's convulsing.

He's making sounds.

Maybe trying to call for help.

But I don't move.

I grip the counter harder and stay where I am.

He thrashes.

Tries to get up.

Gurgles.

And then... stillness.

My heartbeat thunders in my ears.

But he doesn't make another sound.

I watch the clock above the microwave and stay there, silent, for another ten minutes.

Then, when I'm sure he hasn't moved, I look away from my dad and his chair, and I walk upstairs.

I keep my eyes forward.

And when I reach my room, I step inside and close the door behind me.

I've imagined this moment for so long.

For years.

And now that it's here... I don't feel anything.

There's too much uncertainty for me to feel relief.

But maybe there's room for peace.

I sit at my desk, overlooking the woods.

I open my desk drawer and pull my bag of marshmallows out.

Eating one slowly, I stare into the forest.

I have another. And another. Savoring all of them, just in case...

And when the bag is done, I reach back into my drawer.

I move aside the box cutter that I stole from the restaurant I work at and pull out a piece of paper.

I get through the word *Dear* and have to pause, because who am I even writing this to?

Thirty minutes later, I tuck the letter under my mattress, then head back downstairs to call 911.

I tell the paramedics I was upstairs while Dad was eating and that I didn't hear anything out of the ordinary.

They seem to believe me.

The doctors at the hospital seem to think it was natural heart failure.

And I seem to be getting away with murder.

That's when I see Nathan on TV. In that cold antiseptic waiting room.

My old friend.

My confidant.

And I know... I know I can never drag the real Nathan into my life.

Not when I'm a murderer.

Not when there's no statute of limitation on homicide.

Not when my decisions could ruin his life.

So when everything is done and I go back home, I sit at my desk and write my second letter of the night, letting Nathan go.

ONE HUNDRED THIRTY-SEVEN
NATE

"Rosie, Rosie, Rosie." My vision blurs as I bump into the wall. "Why didn't you tell me?"

Agony radiates through my body as I slide down the wall until I'm sitting on the floor.

I clutch Rosie's fucking suicide letter in one hand and press the other hand to my chest.

And then I cry.

I've never cried so much in my life.

I've never felt *so much* in my life.

Not until Rosie.

Not until this beautiful woman.

This lonely girl.

This child version of *my person* who went through so much hell.

I curl forward.

And I remember the last letter in the box.

The last one she wrote me.

The one where she said she saw me on the TV in the hospital.

I think of the way my heart broke reading that.

How I read it... but how I didn't fucking understand.

A sound crawls out of my throat. And it's anguish.

This is the secret.

This is the barbed wire Rosie keeps wrapped around her soul.

And she called it murder.

It wasn't fucking murder.

It was self-defense.

I press my hand harder against my chest, like I can push my heart back in time.

Like I can help her.

She was just a kid.

At fucking nineteen, Rosie was still a child who had to kill her father in self-defense.

It was him or me. And I only had enough pills for one of us.

I squeeze my eyes shut and focus on trying to breathe.

I was so close to losing Rosie.

A sob seizes my lungs.

I was so close to never having her.

Behind my eyelids, I picture the life I want us to have together.

I picture her happy.

I picture her safe.

I picture the children we'll have.

And I cry even more for the future we almost lost.

And then I think about Rosie, right now, all alone in my bed.

I shove up to my feet and stumble toward the door.

She'll never feel alone again.

Not ever.

Not for a moment.

With the letter in hand, I forget about everything else I was going to take with me, and I leave Rosie's apartment.

She's not coming back here.

She's not leaving me.

I won't let her go.

I won't let her go.

I repeat those words in my head as I drive back.

As I enter my condo.

As I walk straight to my bedroom.

And when I see her.

When I see my Rosie.

I drop the letter and strip my shirt and sweatpants off.

I need to be close to her.

I need to feel her heat against my skin.

Instead of going to my side of the bed, I climb in behind her, and I wrap her in my arms.

I hold her as close as possible.

I hold her as my tears soak into the pillow.

I hold her even after I fall asleep.

ONE HUNDRED THIRTY-EIGHT
ROSALYN

Warmth surrounds me.

I inhale the scent of laundry and cologne, reminding me exactly where I am.

In Nathan's bed.

The weight against my back and across my side throws me off for a moment, and I crack my eyes open.

The bed before me is empty.

I stretch my arm out, unable to reach the other side.

Nathan was in his spot when I fell asleep, but now he's behind me, spooning me with his heat.

I close my eyes and soak in the feel of him.

Maybe he got up to use the bathroom and decided to climb onto my side because it's closer.

My lips pull up in a small smile as I picture his butt hanging over the edge of the bed.

Then my eyes open again.

Thinking about going to the bathroom makes me realize how badly I have to go.

I nervously drank about five ginger ales during dinner, and now I'm paying the price.

Craning my neck, I look at the clock.

Four a.m.

If I don't go now, I'll wake up again in an hour, having to pee so bad my stomach will ache.

Trying to stay sleepy so I can go right back to bed, I keep my eyes half closed as I shimmy out of Nathan's hold and crawl across his side of the mattress.

I hear the thump of Charles jumping off the bed, then he follows me into the bathroom.

I don't turn any lights on, having learned my way around, and I scratch the top of Charles's head as he bumps into my shins while I sit on the toilet.

The cat continues to follow me as I wash my hands, then head back into the bedroom. And I soak in his companionship.

Out of habit, I walk toward my side of the bed, forgetting it's occupied.

I'm yawning when something crinkles under my foot.

Instinct of stepping on something foreign has me jerking my foot away.

And I almost keep moving.

Almost ignore it and go back to bed.

But Nathan never has anything on his floor.

I blink in the darkness, my eyes adjusting enough to see the pile of clothes also around my feet.

What...

My attention goes back to the paper.

And the longer I stare at it, the harder my heart beats.

Bending, I reach down and pick it up.

The paper is folded in thirds. Like a letter.

With Nathan's back to me, I angle the paper toward the

window, where small amounts of city lights are sneaking through.

The paper is lined, with one frayed edge, like it was torn out of a notebook.

A desk that overlooked the woods behind the house.

My lungs struggle to pull in breaths.

Please, no.

My hands start to shake.

Please. To anyone that might be out there. Please don't let this be what I think it is.

My throat is so tight it's hard to swallow.

Please.

I unfold the paper.

And everything stops.

It's my letter.

The letter.

The one with my biggest secret. My deepest shame.

Why?

Why did you have to find this?

Despair, thick and toxic, fills my soul.

I don't read the words on the page.

I don't have to.

My hand drops to my side, and I look at Nathan sleeping soundly. Feet away.

My Nathan.

The man who stepped back into my life and changed everything.

The grown-up version of the boy who befriended me when no one else did.

I don't know how he found this. Or why he went to my apartment.

But he did find it. And nothing else matters.

I take a step away from the bed.

There's no way I can stay now.

I don't know how he could come back here and crawl into bed with me after reading this.

I don't know what he had to tell himself to make it okay to sleep next to a killer.

But whatever it is, I won't let him live with it.

I take another step.

I want to touch him.

Just once more.

One last time.

But I can't risk waking him.

If he wakes up, he might try to tell me it's okay.

But it's not.

It will never be okay.

Or he might tell me to go.

He might not forgive what I've done. What I've kept from him. And him spooning me in bed... It could've been his goodbye.

Heat builds in my eyes.

Not yet.

Turning away from the man I love, I move through the bathroom into the closet and quietly fill one of my duffel bags with clothes, stuffing the letter into the side pocket.

I can't break down yet.

With my bag over my shoulder, I pause for a moment, just one, to watch Nathan's back rise and fall with breath.

Telling myself this is for the best—that he deserves better than what I can offer—I turn to leave.

I take one step, then something tugs on my pants.

Looking down, I find Charles. His teeth are in the hem of my sleep pants, like he's trying to make me stay.

The last bit of control inside me snaps, and my tears start to fall.

I bend down and lift him into my arms, hugging him tightly.

His body vibrates with a purr, and I press my face into his side.

"I'm going to miss you most of all," I whisper.

Charles nuzzles his face against my shoulder.

I pull back and press a kiss to his forehead. "Keep an eye on him, okay?"

I kiss him once more, then set him on the foot of the bed.

When I reach the bedroom door, I lock the handle before pulling it closed behind me.

I don't want Nathan to wake up alone.

ONE HUNDRED THIRTY-NINE
NATE

Something hard hits the bridge of my nose.

"Shit," I groan and roll onto my back.

Charles leans over my face and meows.

It's so loud I wince.

"Fuck, man, give me a moment."

I look at the ceiling, early morning light filling the room.

And then it all comes crashing back.

The night before.

The letter.

The fucking heartbreak.

Charles meows again.

I reach for him, not wanting him to wake up Rosie.

I turn my head to the side.

Where's Rosie?

I sit up.

Charles bumps his head into my elbow.

The bathroom lights are off.

The bedroom door is shut.

Where...?

My eyes move to my clothes on the floor.

Just my clothes.

I scramble out of bed.

Where's the letter?

I toss my pants and shirt aside, but the letter isn't under them.

I stride into the bathroom, double-checking.

Why didn't I burn that fucking letter?

My heart starts to pound.

I was going to talk to her about it this morning.

I was going to hold her in bed and tell her it would all be okay.

I was going to make her understand that we would be okay.

I race to the bedroom door.

The handle clicks when I turn it.

She locked it?

I rip the door open.

And immediately I know...

She's gone.

The walls press in on me as I jog down the hall.

"Rosie!"

But she doesn't answer, because she's not here.

Charles jumps onto the island, and I glance at him, then turn my attention to the counter.

The notebook I used last night is still out, but it's turned to a different page. A new one, filled with words.

I don't think I can survive another one of Rosie's letters.

But I also can't do anything *but* read it.

With anxiety clinging to every cell in my body, I pick up the notebook.

Dear Nathan,

I'm sorry I never told you.

I don't know how or why, but I'm sorry you found out this way. And I hope you'll understand why I couldn't tell you.

I wanted to.

I wanted to tell you everything, but I knew that once I did, it would be over.

And even though I knew it was coming, I didn't want it to be over.

If you feel like you have to call the police, I won't blame you. But I won't be at my apartment.

I was ready to die back then. But I'm not ready for that anymore.

You've given me so much. And I will never be able to thank you enough.

But you told me not to pretend.

And that's all this ever was.

You were always a pretend comfort for me, and I never should have crossed that line into reality.

We were only meant to be letters in a box.

I won't let my life ruin yours.

Love,

Rosalyn

Rosalyn.

She signed it fucking *Rosalyn*.

Putting distance between us with every word.

I tear the page out of the notebook and crumple it in my fist.

She thinks I'd call the fucking cops on her.

How could she believe that?

How could she even think that?

Because she's had a lifetime of disappointment and isolation.

I spin around and stride toward my office.

If she thinks I'll let her go, she's out of her damn mind.

I drop into my chair and fire up my computer.

I'm not letting her go.

Not today.

Not ever.

As my equipment wakes up, I initiate a call.

Tony answers. "For real, do you ever fucking sleep?"

"What do you know about medical records?"

"Now, that's an interesting question." I've caught his attention. "And lucky for you, I know quite a bit."

"I can handle the digital, but I need the physical copies destroyed."

He hums. "That can be done. Where?"

My fingers tighten around the phone. "My hometown."

"Name?"

I tell him.

Hanging up, I pull up the software that shows me Rosie's location.

The glowing dot is steady on the map.

I zoom in.

Two towns away, at a chain hotel.

She didn't believe me when I said I could find her. But I wasn't lying.

And I was never pretending.

She'll understand that soon.

I just need to do a few things first.

I switch tabs on my laptop, looking between my bank account, a list of rental apartments outside of Chicago, and another list of places in northern Minnesota.

If I stay in Minnesota, I'll be able to keep my business licensing stuff the same. But if I stay in Minnesota, I'm easy to find.

Different state. Different business name. That's the smarter choice.

I click on the other tab I have open for Hawaii.

Maybe I should put an ocean between Nathan and me. If he decides to look for me, he would never look there.

I glance at the Wi-Fi symbol at the top of my screen and wonder if Nathan can track my laptop somehow.

I turned my phone off yesterday.

I should've done it the second I left his condo, but I needed the GPS to get to this hotel. And after I checked in, I cried myself to sleep and didn't wake up until noon, which is when I turned my phone off.

I need to email Presley.

Need to figure out what to do with the rest of the events I've booked this year.

I put my elbows on the little desk and drop my head into my hands.

I worked so hard to have independence. But it was just that. Hard.

And I don't really want life to be hard anymore.

Maybe I should just let Rosalyn's Restaurant go.

I can get a job at someone else's restaurant. I can work to survive until this heartbreak passes. Then I can—

The sound of something sliding across the rough carpet has my head jerking up.

I look at the door.

It's still closed.

But my breath catches.

Because lying on the floor, two feet from the door, is a folded piece of paper.

A letter.

I stare at it.

Then at the door.

He found me.

He came for me.

Fear and hope collide inside my chest.

I brace my hands on the desk and push myself up to stand.

My legs tremble with each step.

He wrote me a letter.

I pick it up.

The fear that he's on the other side of the door with an officer and an arrest warrant is outweighed by the hope that he isn't.

I open the letter.

Dear Rosie,

It took me longer than it should have, but I got your letters.

I wish I'd gotten them sooner.

I wish I'd found you sooner.

And more than anything, I wish it was me who killed him.

I would have done it for you.

Over and over, I'd have done that for you.

You deserve so much more than you've been given. And you did what you had to do.

I'm so proud of you.

You're not broken or bad or any of the other things you might think.

You're the someone special I've always wanted.

You're my person.

And your secrets are mine to keep and protect.

Just like you, my Pretty Rosie. Because I'm going to keep and protect you too.

And my feelings have never been pretend.

My love for you is real.

Now open the door.

Letting hope win, I open the door.

ONE HUNDRED FORTY-ONE
NATE

The door swings in, and I step forward.

My body slams into Rosie's.

I hoist her into the air, her arms and legs wrapping around me.

The feel of her.

The weight of her.

She's mine.

Everything she is... is mine.

"You're not alone anymore." I hug her tightly. "You'll never be alone again."

She presses her face into my neck, and I can feel her choppy breaths as I hold her even closer.

"I'm sorry." Her voice breaks on the words.

"No." I move into her room. "No more apologies." I press my face into her hair. "But no more secrets, Rosie. Even if you think you're saving me, no more secrets."

She nods against me.

I sit on the edge of the bed, Rosie in my lap.

I rub a hand up her spine. "Please stop crying. It breaks my heart to hear you cry. Everything will be okay."

She sniffs. "But what about..." She lifts her head. "What about what I did?"

"No one will ever know." I brush a strand of hair off her face. "He's gone. His ashes can't be tested. His records are gone. He never fucking existed." I run a hand over her hair. "I would've come for you yesterday, but I needed to get that handled first. I'm sorry I took so long."

Her bright blue eyes are still filled with tears as she blinks at me. "You—You did that?"

I nod. "He can't hurt you anymore, Rosie."

She throws her arms around me, and the sobs that come out of her are filled with relief.

And as I hold her, I can feel the shift.

I can feel the weight lift off her shoulders.

I can feel her exhale her pain.

I move my hand up and down her back, soothing her, promising her I'm here.

"Thank you," she whispers.

Over and over, she whispers it.

Together, we inhale.

This woman of mine.

I finally loosen my hold so she can meet my gaze. "No more secrets," I repeat.

Her eyes search mine. "I only have one left."

I cup her cheek. "Tell me."

She flattens her hands against my chest, her palm over my heart.

"Whatever it is, Beautiful. We'll handle it." I coax her.

She nods. "It's just that I never told you... how much I love you."

I swallow.

Then I swallow again.

Rosie presses her hand more firmly over my heart. "I love you, Nathan. You're... You're everything I want. But you're more than that. You're everything I need."

I slam my mouth to hers.

Salty tears flavor our kiss. I don't know if they're mine or hers, but it doesn't matter. We're one now.

One heart.

One soul.

One future.

My fingers tangle in her beautiful red hair, and I pull our mouths apart.

"You're not leaving."

She shakes her head. "I'm not leaving."

I press our foreheads together. "I don't just mean the state, Rosie. I mean my place. My home. You're not leaving. I'm not spending another night of my life without you beside me. There's no such thing as too fast. Not with you. Not for us. Tell me you understand."

Her exhale dances across my lips. "I'm never leaving."

"Good." My mouth pulls up into a smile. "Now tell me you don't have to check out anytime soon."

Rosie bites her lip, and I use my thumb to pull it free.

I trace her lip. "Tell me."

"I don't have to check out."

"Good," I repeat, then roll her onto her back.

ONE HUNDRED FORTY-TWO
ROSIE

His clothing disappears.
  Mine falls away next.
  Our limbs tangle.
  Our mouths open.
  He moves between my thighs.
  I spread for him.
  And when he presses into me, he tells me he loves me.
  When he covers me, he tells me *how much* he loves me.
  When he touches me...
  When he follows me over...
  I feel the truth of his words.
  I feel the forever.
  And I hold on to it.
  I hold on to him.
  And I promise to never let go.

ONE HUNDRED FORTY-THREE
NATHAN

The sun is almost set by the time we climb out of the hotel bed.

I had planned to whisk her away the second I got my hands on her, but then she told me she loved me, and all my plans went to hell.

I tighten my fingers around hers, and she looks up at me with such a happy expression that I have no choice but to kiss her. Again.

"Okay," I say authoritatively. "We are leaving now, and your van is staying here."

She smiles at me. "That's fine."

"And you're coming home with me." I narrow my eyes, daring her to argue.

Rosie nods. "I'm coming home with you."

"But we're making a stop first."

ONE HUNDRED FORTY-FOUR
ROSIE

Nathan pulls into an empty parking lot for an empty park.

"All that just for you to dump me in a park," I joke.

Nathan puts his SUV in park and gives me a flat look. "Har, har, funny girl. Now get out."

I'm grinning when I open my door.

I honestly have no idea what we're doing here, but Nathan could be taking me to a snake petting zoo, and I'd go with him.

I love him. And I trust him. And I feel...

I take a deep breath of the fresh air.

I feel like a whole new person.

The trauma is still there. The pain. The hurt.

But it feels like it's been put inside a box. And that box has been sealed, so the stuff inside can't crawl out anymore. It can't consume me anymore.

Nathan opens and closes the rear door of his vehicle, then comes around to my side, carrying a large backpack.

This new peace I have, it's all because of him.

He found me.

Saw me.

And falling in love with him is healing me.

Nathan holds his elbow out for me, and I take it.

We walk across the grass, the deep orange of the sunset lighting our way but telling us we don't have too much time before it gets dark.

I half expect Nathan to stop in the middle of the open field and lay out a picnic. Even though we had food delivered to the hotel room.

But he turns us toward one of the pavilions, stopping at one of the freestanding grills.

Grill is a generous term, since it's little more than half an iron box topped with a grill grate on top of a pole in the ground.

"You have me intrigued," I tell him when he sets his bag on the picnic table nearby.

He smirks at me over his shoulder and pulls out items to start a fire.

Nathan works quietly and quickly, setting the fire starter brick in the bottom of the little grill, topping it with small pieces of wood. He uses a lighter to get the brick going, and while the fire slowly crawls across the wood, he turns back to the bag.

"If you pull a bag of hot dogs out of there, I'm going to be impressed."

Nathan laughs and turns around with his arms full of *not* hot dogs.

My smile falters as another wave of affection for this man crashes over me.

In his hands is a box of graham crackers, two chocolate bars, and a bag of plain white marshmallows.

"Nathan..."

"Rosie Edwards, will you make s'mores with me?"

I nod, and together we skewer the marshmallows onto the end of roasting sticks that Nathan also pulled out of his bag.

I control the roasting.

Nathan holds the crackers.

And we lean against each other as we eat them while the sun disappears behind the horizon.

"Thank you." I look up at Nathan's handsome features. "For everything. For this."

His smile is soft. "We're not done here."

He takes the rest of the wood pieces piled on the table and puts them on the fire.

The flames grow, the glow getting brighter around us.

Nathan moves back to the bag, and the next thing he pulls out is a hoodie.

"Here, it's getting cool."

I take the sweatshirt from him, because he's right; with the sun down, the temperature has dropped.

I pull it on, then look down at the front.

It has the HOP University logo on it. The school where he played college football.

"I love it." I run my hands down the front.

The expression on Nathan's face is so serious as he looks at me.

"This is how it should've been." His words are thick. "We should've been together then. You should've worn this in the stands while I played." He shakes his head. "I have so much to make up for."

"No. You don't." I step forward and place my hand on his chest. "You don't."

"I do. And I want to start over. From the beginning." Nathan reaches into the backpack and pulls out the last item.

A shoe box.

He opens the lid, revealing the row of letters. "I think we should burn them. Together."

The ones I wrote to him but never sent.

The ones I pretended he read.

The ones he found.

My vision blurs as I look up at him. "I think that's a good idea."

He pulls out the last letter first, the one I wrote him the night my dad died.

The night I killed him.

He hands it to me.

My fingers tremble as I take it.

Then I reach into my pocket and pull out the other letter I wrote that night.

I folded it a few times to fit it in my pocket.

I meant to destroy it. Wanted to be rid of it. But I wasn't sure how.

I hold it out to Nathan. "I think you should do this one."

His throat works as he takes it, and he clenches his jaw.

I can see it on his face. See the way that letter hurt him.

I step into him, hugging him to me.

"When I wrote that," I whisper, "I thought there was no one left to care. No one to notice if I was suddenly gone." His body hitches against mine as he hugs me back just as tightly. "Thank you for caring, Nathan."

"Always," he whispers back. "Always, my Little Rose."

Nathan kisses the top of my head, then releases me.

He unfolds the letter and holds the corner of the page to the flame.

It catches, and I watch as the words of my confession turn to ash.

My guilt crumbling into nothing.

Decades of fear floating into the night sky.

When only a piece is left, Nathan drops it into the fire, and we watch it disappear.

And then, one by one, we burn them all.

The small bursts of light as each one catches cleanse the past.

Until only the envelope is left.

The envelope that contains the letter Nathan left me in the woods.

The envelope with the wrong address on the front and the letter I tried to send him.

The pair of letters that started it all.

Nathan picks it up, then sets the box on the table.

He holds it out. "I don't think we should burn this one."

I take it from him, nostalgia shimmering around us.

"I—" I turn the envelope over in my hand and...

And it's different.

The address is different.

There's no UNDELIVERABLE across the front.

I open it.

The two letters are there.

But there's also another smaller envelope.

I pull it out.

It's addressed to me. At my address on *that* street.

My fingers trace over the return address, handwritten in the corner.

Nathan's corrected Ohio address.

My eyes meet his.

Nathan dips his head to the envelope in my hand. "It's twenty-five years late. But it's yours."

With shaking hands, I tear open the envelope. And I pull out the letter.

It's the reply to the first letter I ever wrote him.

As though it was delivered.

As though he got it.

DEAR ROSIE,

I'M SO GLAD YOU WROTE TO ME.

I MISS YOU TOO. AND IF YOU'D ASKED, I WOULD HAVE HUGGED YOU.

I WOULD DO ANYTHING FOR YOU.

YOU'RE MY BEST FRIEND. MY SOUL MATE. AND I HOPE WE CAN WRITE EACH OTHER LOVE LETTERS FOR THE REST OF OUR LIVES.

AND WHEN WE'RE ALL GROWN UP, I HOPE YOU'LL MARRY ME.

YOURS FOREVER,

THE BOY FROM THE WOODS

Tears roll down my cheeks.

For younger me. For current me. For all the versions in between.

Nathan lowers before me, one knee against the grass. "I'll never stop loving you." He holds up a ring. A giant square diamond on a gold band. "And I'll never stop needing you. Say you'll be mine."

I close the distance between us, reaching past the ring to hold his face, making sure he understands. "I've always been yours, Nathan Waller. And I always will be."

EPILOGUE 1 – NATHAN
(3 WEEKS LATER)

The oven timer goes off.

I look around, but there's no sign of Rosie.

Not wanting to be responsible for anything burning, I turn the timer off, and using hot pads, I take the tray of mini meatballs out.

I'm tempted to pop one into my mouth, but I can see the steam rolling off them, so I resist.

People are coming over in a couple of hours. My parents, Maddox and family, Tony...

They're coming to watch Max's game on TV. But we're also using the opportunity to announce our engagement.

Hence the meatballs.

And the sliders.

And the kebabs.

And tarts.

And confetti marshmallows.

To say Rosie is nervous is an understatement.

I keep telling her not to be, but if she's not in the kitchen, watching her food, she must be off doing another project.

Maybe I should do something to take her mind off everything…

I smirk as I stride through the condo looking for Rosie.

Then I stop dead in my tracks. Because I've found her.

She's in our little laundry room, kneeling on the floor, with her front half in the dryer.

My cock throbs as it hardens inside my pants.

"Jesus Christ," I growl, stepping closer.

"What was that?" Rosie starts to pull out.

"Stop."

She pauses.

"Stay right there."

"Seriously?" she asks, but I'm already rushing away.

"Don't move!" I shout over my shoulder as I sprint to the bathroom.

I rip open the bottom drawer, pull out two items, then sprint back.

"Nathan. What on earth?"

"Stay there," I pant.

"The hoodie string is caught in the stupid dryer hole." She explains why her shoulders are inside the dryer.

Using one hand, I undo my belt buckle and yank it free, dropping it to the ground.

She starts to pull herself out of the dryer again, and I drop to my knees behind her, gripping her hips. "Please. Pretty fucking please. Pretend to be stuck."

Rosie pauses. "Are you for real?"

I grip the waistband of her leggings and start to drag them down her hips, pulling her panties down at the same time.

"Nathan!"

"You were planning to change anyway, so it's okay if we ruin these."

"Wh-what are you doing?" She's already breathing heavily, so I know I've got her.

"I'm going to fuck you, Rosie. Right here."

"In the dryer? Why?"

I grin. "Because you look like a porn star."

Then I slap her bare ass.

She squeaks, but her back arches. And I know she likes it.

"My dirty Rose."

I shove my pants down to my knees and shuffle forward between hers.

"This is going to be quick," I warn her as I pick up one of the two items.

"Why, what time is it?"

I chuckle. "It's not going to be quick because I'm in a hurry. It's going to be quick because I'm putting my dick in your ass." I reach forward and use one hand to spread Rosie's cheeks so I can pour lube directly onto her hole. "And I'm not going to last."

"But..." She gasps. "People are coming over."

I set down the bottle and massage the slippery liquid over her rear entrance. "Yeah, and while we make our little announcement to everyone"—I push one fingertip in—"you're going to be leaking cum from your ass."

"Nathan." She moans my name as I move my fingertip in and out.

"Just an inch." I add a second finger. "Maybe two inches." I twist my fingers. "But by the end of the year, you're going to take all of me. Remember?"

I pull my fingers free and grab the bottle to apply a little more lube to her tight hole.

"Can you do that for me, Rosie?"

Setting the lube back down, I reach underneath her and groan when I find her dripping.

I rub one circle around her clit, then pull my hand away.

"Ready?" I ask as I line my dick up with her slicked-up asshole.

Rosie tilts her hips. "What are you doing back there, Mr. Waller?"

"Fuck," I groan.

My dick pulses, and I have to squeeze it hard to keep from coming on the spot.

This little minx pretended like she didn't know what sort of porn I was talking about.

What a liar.

I grip her hip with one hand, holding her still.

"I need to inspect your work, Miss Edwards." I press against her entrance. "Need to make sure you're doing your job correctly."

"But that... that doesn't go there." Her words are breathy. And I know she's trying to sound concerned, but there's too much heat in her voice for me to believe her.

I push harder, and she starts to spread around me. "This will be our little secret. No one needs to know."

She moans. "It's too big."

I don't think she's acting.

I've had my fingers in her ass, but this is the first time with my cock.

The first time she's been stretched this far.

"Relax, Miss Edwards." My breathing is coming out jagged. "Relax and let me in."

Rosie relaxes, and I push the head of my cock past her resistance.

"Oh, Mr. Waller." She whimpers, and her body slumps into the dryer.

"Breathe through it," I say to both of us.

Then I reach down for the second item.

The one I found in Rosie's apartment.

The item I made sure to pack when we moved her stuff out of that place and into mine.

I hold down the button, turning it on.

"Mr. Waller?" Rosie lifts her head, still inside the dryer.

"Shh." I jack my length, keeping the head of my dick in her ass. "I just need you to hold still a little bit longer, Miss Edwards."

Rosie inhales, like she might say more, but then I reach under her and press the vibrator between her thighs.

There's no easing into it. No teasing. I hold it directly over her clit.

The sound she makes is guttural, and her muscles clench around me.

"Fuck." I push in another half inch. "Fuck." I pull back out until the ridge around my tip meets her resistance.

Then I hold still.

I keep my dick just inside her.

I hold the vibrator on her clit.

And I tighten my grip as I stroke the exposed length of my cock, letting my knuckles bump into her flesh on each pass.

"Oh fuck, oh fuck." Rosie starts to pant. "M-Mr. Waller, I'm going to come."

"If you come, I'm going to fill this ass. It will be your fault."

"I can't—" Her words cut off with a cry as the orgasm takes over.

Rosie's body tenses, then shakes.

Her muscles seize around me.

And I hold the vibrator there for another second before I drop it and grip her hips with both hands.

The vibrator bounces noisily across the floor, but the sound is drowned out by the blood roaring through my ears.

My cock starts to pulse, and I pull Rosie back and jerk my

hips forward, sinking a few more inches inside her as I fill her with my release.

My vision flickers, and I have to catch myself on the dryer when my body buckles forward.

"Holy shit." I press my forehead to Rosie's back.

Rosie snickers. "That was hot."

I shake my head, thinking how fucking lucky I am. "Rosie?"

"Yeah?"

"I fucking love you."

EPILOGUE 2

HANNAH UTLEY-LOVELACE

I set my spoon on my plate and lean back in my seat.

Maddox moves his arm from the back of my chair to over my shoulders. "Full?"

"I don't know why I never learn." I moan.

My husband chuckles. "We don't learn because the food is so damn good."

I sigh. "That's true. And that dessert." I stare at the empty plate before me. "Chelsea outdid herself on that one."

"She's really in her element here," Maddox agrees.

Rosie smiles at us from across the table. "When I told that food critic last week that a sixteen-year-old made our dessert menu, he demanded to meet her."

I raise a brow. "Chelsea never told us that."

Rosie laughs. "Because I told him no. I said he could meet her when she's eighteen."

"I knew I loved you," I tell her as my mother reaches across to pat Rosie on the arm.

I look over to the open kitchen and catch Chelsea looking over at our table.

Are you talking about me? she mouths.

I nod with a grin and wave her over.

I know she has some cleanup to do still, but the kitchen of Rosalyn's Restaurant is closed for the night, and we're here celebrating.

MADDOX LOVELACE

I can't help but grin at my best friend. He's so fucking smitten. It'd be embarrassing, except I know exactly how he feels.

Ruth laughs at something, then she waves her hands in a wild gesture at Chelsea.

Chelsea rolls her eyes, then changes course toward the hostess stand. Her girlfriend is working tonight, and since she practically lives at our house when the girls aren't working or in school, it's only fitting that she sits with us too.

"We need two chairs." Ruth looks around.

"Here's one," Waller says as he hauls Rosie out of her chair and onto his lap.

"Aww." Ruth beams.

I roll my eyes.

"You'll have to help me out, Honey, but you can sit in my lap," Willard, the birthday boy, says to my mother-in-law.

She blushes but stands from her chair and settles herself in his lap.

Hannah groans good-naturedly, and I chuckle.

Willard retired from my company last year, and at 5:01 on his last day, he asked permission to ask Ruth out on a date.

I always thought he was married, but turns out he was a widower, much like Ruth, and just kept his ring on.

It took some getting used to, just like it took some getting used to calling him Willard and not Donut Guy. But they're happy, and he's a fun guy to have around.

And according to Ruth, if they're still an item when Chelsea moves away to college, she'll move in with him.

I'm not sure what it'll be like suddenly having half of the household gone, but I know I won't be bored.

Not with Hannah at my side.

NATE WALLER

"Night, Rosie," Hannah calls out as they walk the other way down the sidewalk. And I can't help but love that everyone calls her Rosie now.

I tug my wife into my side and press a kiss to her head. "I'm so proud of you."

She sighs. "I'm proud of all of us."

I hum in agreement.

Rosalyn's Restaurant, the actual restaurant, has been open for one year. And it hasn't just survived, it's thrived.

Presley is the head chef. Chelsea is on track to have whatever job she wants—if she wants it. And Rosie has found a reliable staff for the catering side of the business.

She did it all.

I was just here to stand at her side. Supporting her. Showing her she mattered. Showing her she was loved.

And loving Rosie is the easiest thing I've ever done.

Our steps slow as we reach our vehicle.

My wife tips her head back to look up at me. "Take me home, Husband."

ROSIE WALLER

Nathan hands me my cup of peppermint tea, then picks up his bottle of beer, and together, we walk through the house.

The kitchen has two islands and a pantry twice as big as the one in Hannah and Maddox's house. And even though I don't do much of the catering prep anymore, we still make good use of the space.

We pass through the living room and turn into the den.

Nathan steps past me to open the door to the back deck, and I pause to look at the bookshelves along the side wall.

Next to the framed postcard-sized rose painting is one of my proudest achievements.

The first copy of *Rosalyn's Recipes*.

Nathan holds the door open, and I step through.

I plan to do a second book.

Possibly more. But there's no hurry.

I set my tea down, then lower myself into the chair facing the backyard.

Nathan sits in his chair next to mine.

It's our ritual.

Coming out here at night.

Sitting on the patio of the house we built together.

Nathan reaches across and rests his hand on my belly.

I place my hand on top of his.

Everything is going to change again.

In three months, our family will grow by one.

And as I sit here, looking at the forest behind our home, I can't help but hope that our children will want to play in the woods.

The end of the Love Letters Series.

ACKNOWLEDGMENTS

I'd like to thank Kimberly-Clark, who Google says is the inventor of facial tissues. Because goddamn, I cried A LOT writing this book.

Rosie and Nathan, I love you. And I'm glad you're happily in love with each other. Because y'all took it out of me.

Thank you to Mr. Tilly for always being there. As my support, my sounding board, my chef, and for taking care of literally everything when I bury myself under crazy deadlines. Love you.

Thank you to my mom for being my alpha reader and for keeping up with my chaotic schedule.

Thank you, Kerissa, for being fucking awesome—as a friend, a PA, a beta reader, and an overall glorious human. Your encouragement always gets me through those late-ass nights.

Thank you to Nikki for giving me your tears. And thank you, Gabby and Elaine and Sam, for the constant love.

Thank you, Liz, for putting up with my eight-minute voice messages just to ask a single plot question that could be explained in three sentences. You get it, and I love you for it.

Thank you, Ali, for reading everything early and for being so damn excited about it every time. Your support is so special to me.

Thank you to Jeanine and Beth for being world-class editors. You make me look so smart even though I couldn't teach a second-grade punctuation lesson to save my fucking life.

Thank you, Wander Photography, for taking such amazing hot guy photos. And thank you, Lori Jackson, for turning them into such great covers. And for making such stunning discreet covers.

Thank you to all my ARC readers. I know how valuable your time is, and I appreciate you so much.

Thank you to my reader group. (BeanBag Book Club on Facebook) Your excitement brings me life.

And thank you to all my readers. You make my life possible. I never imagined I'd be here, making a living off writing stories. But here I am. And I love it.

And there is so much more to come.

ABOUT THE AUTHOR

S.J. Tilly was born and raised in Minnesota, which is why so many of her books are based there. But she now resides in the beautiful mountains of Colorado with her husband and misfit herd of rescue boxers.

When she's not busy writing a new book, she can be found plotting her next book...

To stay up to date on all things Tilly, make sure to follow her on her socials, join her newsletter, and interact whenever you feel like it! Links to everything on her website www.sjtilly.com

ALSO BY S. J. TILLY

The Alliance Series

(Dark Mafia Romance)

NERO

KING

DOM

HANS

The Sin Series

(Romantic Suspense)

MR. SIN

SIN TOO

MISS SIN

The Darling Series

(Small Town Age Gap)

SMOKY DARLING

LATTE DARLING

The Sleet Series

(Hockey Rom Com)

SLEET KITTEN

SLEET SUGAR

SLEET BANSHEE

SLEET PRINCESS

The Bite Series

(Holiday Novellas - Baking Competition)

SECOND BITE

SNOWED IN BITE

NEW YEAR'S BITE

Printed in Great Britain
by Amazon

49555372R00269